THE CANE CREEK REGULATORS

OTHER FIVE STAR WESTERNS BY JOHNNY D. BOGGS:

The Lonesome Chisholm Trail (2000); *Once They Wore the Gray* (2001); *Lonely Trumpet* (2002); *The Despoilers* (2002); *The Big Fifty* (2003); *Purgatoire* (2003); *Dark Voyage of the* Mittie Stephens (2004); *East of the Border* (2004); *Camp Ford* (2005); *Ghost Legion* (2005); *Walk Proud, Stand Tall* (2006); *The Hart Brand* (2006); *Northfield* (2007); *Doubtful Cañon* (2007); *Killstraight* (2008); *Soldier's Farewell* (2008); *Rio Chama* (2009); *Hard Winter* (2009); *Whiskey Kills* (2010); *South by Southwest* (2011); *Legacy of a Lawman* (2011); *Kill the Indian* (2012); *And There I'll Be a Soldier* (2012); *Summer of the Star* (2013); *Wreaths of Glory* (2013); *Greasy Grass* (2013); *Poison Spring* (2014); *The Killing Trail* (2014)

THE CANE CREEK REGULATORS

A FRONTIER STORY

JOHNNY D. BOGGS

FIVE STAR
A part of Gale, Cengage Learning

GALE
CENGAGE Learning·

Farmington Hills, Mich • San Francisco • New York • Waterville, Maine
Meriden, Conn • Mason, Ohio • Chicago

LIBRARY OF CONGRESS CATALOGING-IN-PUBLICATION DATA

Boggs, Johnny D.
    The Cane Creek regulators : a frontier story / Johnny D. Boggs. — First edition.
        pages ; cm
    ISBN 978-1-4328-2852-3 (hardcover) — ISBN 1-4328-2852-5 (hardcover)
    1. Teenage girls—Fiction. 2. Vigilantes—Fiction. 3. Frontier and pioneer life—South Carolina—Fiction. 4. South Carolina—History—Colonial period, ca. 1600–1775—Fiction. I. Title.
PS3552.O4375C365 2014
813'.54—dc23   2014027421

First Edition. First Printing: December 2014
Published in conjunction with Golden West Literary Agency.
Find us on Facebook– https://www.facebook.com/FiveStarCengage
Visit our website– http://www.gale.cengage.com/fivestar/
Contact Five Star™ Publishing at FiveStar@cengage.com

Printed in the United States of America
1 2 3 4 5 6 7 18 17 16 15 14

For Walter Edgar

★ ★ ★ ★ ★

1766

★ ★ ★ ★ ★

CHAPTER ONE

Emily ran.

She wanted to scream, but didn't think she had enough breath. Besides, what was the use? Hours earlier, she had crossed Spring Branch and traveled so far down the Cherokee Path that, when the renegades surprised her, no one back in Ninety Six could have heard her. Even the warblers and grasshopper sparrows that had been singing that morning had flown away.

The three men had startled her, silently appearing from behind a giant Oglethorpe oak on the other side of the trail. Two wore beards and greasy buckskins, while the other was clean-shaven, all dangerous. All carried hatchets and knives in their belts, and each held a rifle.

"She's a devilish good piece," the one with the leather eye patch had said.

When they surprised her, Emily had been on her knees beside a ditch, filling a tin pail with blueberries. She had almost screamed, but the fat man with the blubbery cheeks had brought a finger to his lips, smiling, telling her: "Keep your breath to cool your porridge." That had stopped her from crying out. That and the fact that the third man, the tall, dark one donning a ribbon shirt and calico turban of the Cherokees, had tossed his long rifle to Eye Patch, and slowly, noiselessly moved toward her, his eyes as hypnotic as a rattlesnake's.

They could be long hunters, merely on their way to the tavern at Ninety Six, she tried to tell herself, but Emily knew better.

"Ain't you the moon-eyed hen?" The Cherokee had broken the silence, flashed her a black-toothed grin while unbuckling the belt that held his knife and hatchet. Eye Patch and Blubber Cheeks had laughed.

Which is when she overcame her paralysis, grabbed the pail, and flung it, blueberries and all, into the Cherokee's face. As soon as the pail left her hands, before she even heard the pail strike and the Indian cuss, she had gathered her legs, leaped across the ditch, and fled into the woods. Into the timbers, dodging hardwood trees, crushing saplings under her feet, feeling the briars and brambles rip at her dress, her skin. A branch knocked off her bonnet, and she felt a trickle of blood run through her blonde hair. Her lungs burned. She bent over, kept moving, turning, and spinning, deeper into the forest, leaping over rotting trees, over a sinkhole. Dashing. . . .

To nowhere.

Emily knew her mistake. She should have stayed on the Cherokee Path, headed back to Spring Branch, north and west to Ninety Six, where she would have been certain to run into some trader or settler. Or even south on the path until it merged with the trail to Keowee. Yet for all she knew, other blackhearts might have been posted down the trail to intercept her if she fled. Heading into the woods had been a foolish notion, a decision fueled by panic. She could hear the men's feet crushing the leaves and twigs behind her. Gaining on her.

She couldn't hide. The marauders were too close. Darkness would not come for hours, so she wouldn't live long enough to see this day's sun set. Her decision had cost Emily her life, and she hated herself for being so careless, so foolish, for acting like a frightened child.

On that warm summer morning, sixteen-year-old Emily Stewart was living in the Back Country, having settled there with her family barely six years after Robert Gouedy had opened the trading post in the district. Many Charlestown traders thought Gouedy's post lay ninety-six miles south of Keowee, a major Cherokee town, hence the settlement's name: Ninety Six. No hyphen. Emily's father often joked that the hyphen had been the first thing Gouedy had traded for a sizeable profit.

In 1754, her father had left Georgetown to build a tavern near Gouedy's post. Three years later, Breck Stewart had returned to fetch Emily, her mother, and brother to the frontier. Another brother and a sister had been born since they had settled in the hilly forests of South Carolina.

With the exception of several months during a war with the Cherokees a few years back, Emily had been living on the frontier for nine years. She knew what life was like in the Back Country. She was no fool. During that time, she had seen just how far away Ninety Six was from the landed gentry of the Carolina coast, where women dressed in fine silk, carried parasols and fans to protect their features from the heat and men donned white wigs, fancy waistcoats, and cocked hats. Ninety Six and the Back Country were peopled with women in homespun and men in buckskins, often a rough lot. How often had she heard her father complain to Gouedy about the scoundrels and wastrels who raided the settlers, the traders, who robbed, plundered, killed.

And, sometimes, they committed the most unholy of sins.

As she ran, Emily kept telling herself that she was a Stewart, and not just any Stewart, but a Stewart of Appin, as her father so often reminded her. Breck Stewart could tell stories of his ancestors that dated to the 14th Century in the Gælic West. Stewarts had fought at Halidon Hill, at Inverlochy, at Sheriffmuir. Emily's family traced its heritage and bloodline to Duncan, the Second Stewart of Appin, who had built Castle Stalker on the Cormorant's Rock at Loch Linnhe. In 1726, her grandfather and grandmother had sailed from Glasgow to America with two young sons merely for the adventure of settling in a New World. That same blood with its love of adventure coursed through Breck Stewart's veins, and had brought him and his family from the safety and wealth of Winyah Bay to the wilderness of Ninety Six District.

Emily Stewart's heart pumped the same blood, which now dried in her hair and appeared on her arms and hands from the scratches left by sharp briars.

Imbecile! She ground her teeth, loathing herself, and lowered her head while raising an arm, the sleeve of her dress ripped and ragged, to slap away another branch. She circled an oak, moved in another direction, but which way she ran, she didn't know. Here the forest grew so thick, the trees so high, she couldn't see the sun. She wasn't only being chased by three vermin, she was totally lost.

She opened her mouth, sucked in air and gnats. She tried to spit, but couldn't do anything but swallow, and keep moving, dodging, sweating. But this deep in the forest, the trees and brush thickened, and it became harder to run. She felt herself slowing, then saw the clearing, stepped into it, and felt the breath knocked out of her.

Landing on her back, she opened her eyes, lungs screaming for air. At first, she saw only streams of light, orange, red, white, flashing across the blackness. When her vision cleared so that she could see the green canopy of trees above, the tall Cherokee stepped into her line of sight.

Beads of sweat peppered his forehead. His turban was gone, and, like her dress, his ribbon shirt had been torn. The Indian must have left his belt behind, along with the knife, but he had managed to pick up his hatchet.

Her eyes studied the weapon's deadly iron blade.

Chest still heaving, the Cherokee wiped the sweat off his

brow, and stepped over her, his moccasins pressing against the sides of her blouse. The sound of dead leaves being crushed grew nearer, and the Indian lifted his head, but only for a moment, before he looked down at Emily. Slowly he kneeled, lowering himself onto her stomach.

A man bolted out of the woods, but Emily couldn't see him. Didn't have to see him, for when he spoke, she recognized the voice.

"She runs . . ."—Eye Patch had to catch his breath—"like a . . . damned . . . deer."

The Cherokee ignored him. He set his hatchet on the ground, then leaned over, his hands gripping the collar of her dress. "Let's see your wares, child," he said, his mouth just inches from her face.

Behind her, the hard-breathing man croaked out a laugh.

She had expected the Cherokee's breath to reek, considering his rotten teeth, but to her surprise it smelled of the mead her father often served in the tavern. Sweet. Of honey. Although frozen in fear, Emily bit her bottom lip. She wanted to close her eyes. She wanted to die right then and there. But then the Cherokee looked up. Emily felt his fingers tighten on the folds of her dress. Her fists clenched.

He seemed about to say something to his friend, but abruptly he straightened, his hands releasing Emily's dress. His hands went up, reaching behind his back at something that he couldn't quite grasp. He still sat atop her, but his body began trembling, the dark face paling.

"Ashwin . . . !" Eye Patch called out from the edge of the timber. Then louder, in a voice filled with terror: "Great God!"

Not until that moment did Emily notice the bloody obsidian point of a spear protruding from the Indian's chest. He was trying to stand, somehow coming off Emily's stomach as blood began seeping from the corners of his mouth. He moved his lips as if her were attempting to speak, but then his eyes rolled into the back of his head, and he fell hard to the side, death rattling in his final breaths.

A war whoop followed. Emily rolled over, came up to her knees as a new figure, a young man in deerskins, rushed from the woods. Behind her, Eye Patch screamed, cursed, and Emily heard the metallic click as the blackheart tried to cock the long rifle. A savage grunt sounded as the young man slammed into Eye Patch. Emily whirled around.

The newcomer straddled Eye Patch, who was reaching up with his free hands, clawing for the young man's eyes. One hand gripped the throat. Emily's young savior turned his head, reached for the knife.

Recognition came dully, and her lips parted. Emily knew this boy, a Cherokee about her own age. He brought many animal pelts in to Robert Gouedy's trading post.

"Go-la-nv." Her mouth moved, but she doubted if anyone had heard her. Yet she had no doubt. This was Go-la-nv Pinetree. Of the Deer Clan Cherokees.

She recalled something else. She remembered that she was Emily Stewart of the Stewarts of Appin, and she was not helpless. She looked to her side, saw the dead Indian, his blood pooling among the dead leaves. Her right hand found the hatchet, and she gripped it, took a step toward Go-la-nv Pinetree and Eye Patch, and stopped. Pinetree had found his own stone tomahawk, which he brought down on Eye Patch's head.

Immediately Pinetree leaped off the body of the man whose skull he had just crushed. He turned, spotted Emily, said: "Are you . . . all right?" The voice was guttural, urgent, but the words perfect English.

The hatchet slipped from her grip, dropped onto the soft ground. She blinked, trying to think, her head bobbing slightly. Suddenly her eyes widened, and her lips parted. She tried to scream a warning, but Go-la-nv Pinetree was already turning at the sound behind him.

Too late, Blubber Cheeks stormed out of the woods, panting, breathless, dripping with sweat. His huge body slammed into the thin shape of the young Cherokee.

Emily blinked. The big man straddled Pinetree, who turned his head, screaming at Emily: "Run! Run!"

Blubber Cheeks's fat hands cut off anything else the Cherokee could say.

"You . . . unclicked . . . cub!" Blubber Cheeks spit into Pinetree's face. "I'll . . . kill you . . . you stinking . . . bastard."

Emily turned. She leaped over the dead Cherokee's legs, and was ready to start back into the thick forest, out of this clearing that already smelled of blood and excrement and death. She would follow Pinetree's advice. Get out of there.

Run! Run!

Yet she had not gone more than ten steps before she made herself stop. She was still lost. She didn't even know if she could make it back to Ninety Six. But something else made her turn back to the two men scuffling in the clearing. Go-la-nv Pinetree had saved her life. She could not, would not, leave him to be strangled by a fat lout like Blubber Cheeks. By Jehovah, she was Breck Stewart's daughter. She was Emily Stewart.

No longer breathing heavily, no longer stunned, Emily turned back, again stepped over the dead Cherokee. Moving with intense purpose, she paused only long enough to scoop up the Indian's hatchet.

"Puny . . . little . . . cur." The fat man's thumbs pushed into Pinetree's throat. "I'll gut you . . . like a . . . fish. Take . . . your . . . scalp."

She stood behind him, the hatchet raised over her head. *No, she told herself, not like this.* It was not fitting for a warrior of Appin. Go-la-nv Pinetree looked into her eyes, and she could

15

see that he was still telling her to run. She ignored him.

"Hey!" she yelled. "You fat piece of dung!"

The fat man whirled, keeping one hand on Pinetree's throat but with the other reaching for the pistol stuck in his belt behind his back. He looked at Emily, and yelled: "You young tatterdemalion!" He almost laughed, until his eyes settled on the sharp-bladed trade hatchet. Quickly he released his left hand, bringing it up in a defensive move, his right hand still fumbling for the pistol.

He screamed something, but Emily refused to listen, hearing only her own voice: *"Creag an Sgairbh!"* Emily's grandfather had taught her that Gælic battle cry. The rallying cry of Scottish warriors. The name her father had given his tavern. Cormorant's Rock. The homeland of the Stewarts of Appin since James IV, King of Scotland, had appointed Duncan, Second Stewart of Appin, as the chamberlain of the Isles.

The hatchet came down savagely, striking Blubber Cheeks in his forehead so hard she had to let go of the hickory handle. The blow silenced the fat man's yells. His eyes seemed to cross and focus on the handle, as blood poured down his face.

Emily stepped back, heart pounding, and watched the fat man topple onto his side. She swallowed down the bile rising in her throat, refused to look at the scavenger she had just killed, and took a tentative step forward, then extended her hand to help Go-la-nv Pinetree to his feet.

CHAPTER TWO

"We are descendants of free-born Britons," Breck Stewart said, "loyal to the Crown, yet we find ourselves in a state of barbarism and degeneracy and often at the mercy of the profligate, impudent, and audacious horse thieves, cattle stealers, hog stealers, and such bold and dangerous scoundrels who hold all order and decency in contempt."

Donnan Stewart, Emily's older brother, leaned over, giving her a nudge and whispered: "When shall Da' pin up the basket? He has been talking for an hour already."

Emily shoved him away. "Don't be such a noodle," she said softly but sharply.

Donnan often acted silly, though he more often came across as surly. She tried to remind herself that her brother meant well, was not complaining, but rather was merely trying to make Emily relax, maybe even smile, hoping to get her mind off what had happened in the woods that morning.

Or maybe he was just bored. She wasn't sure she could hold that against him. For months, probably for better than a year now, they had been listening to their father state this same case, over and over. Nothing more than words. It was only just a month ago that he had gathered the settlers at the tavern after Alroy O'Fionnagáin's barn had been burned to make his same argument.

But today seemed different. Breck Stewart sounded different, and Emily had never seen him so angry—his face a heated red, his ears even darker. His eyes flamed with a hatred that frightened her almost as much as had those three blackhearts in the woods.

The two dozen men and women who were crowded tonight inside the tavern did not look bored. Practically everyone within shouting distance of Ninety Six had converged on Cormorant's Rock. Emily spotted Virgil Hickox and his wife standing beside Thomas Taylor, who had risen from bed with a sick stomach to attend the meeting. Even Ninety Six's sole freedman, Benjamin Cooper, stood beside the doorway.

Breck Stewart may have enticed many men to the tavern with the promise of free bumbo—Stewart's special drink of rum, water, and sugar—or persico, his cordial blended with mashed peaches. Yet few of those gathered today had even lifted their noggins once Stewart had begun to speak.

Emily watched as her father sat down on a keg, but kept on talking. His black, buckle shoes must have begun pinching his feet. Robert Gouedy had told him many times he should wear moccasins, but Stewart refused to give up his shoes, probably the last tie he had to Georgetown, the Atlantic coast, and civilization. His shirt was osnaburg, dyed brown, his forest green waistcoat was missing most of its buttons, and his tan breeches were patched and tied up just below the knees, revealing a pair of unmatched plaid stockings.

He looked around the room, settling his gaze on Alroy O'Fionnagáin, whose head bobbed in agreement with everything Stewart said. Then he singled out Robert Gouedy, who sat still, elbows on the table and hands clasped. And when he looked at the red-headed Ferguson—Emily could never remember the man's Christian name—the burly hog farmer frowned, closing his eyes at the memory of the attack on his place last winter.

Finally Breck Stewart's speech ended, and he made his way back behind his bar where he filled a stein with the mead he brewed himself.

Robert Gouedy rose from his seat. "Thank you, Breck."

Almost immediately, in the back of the tavern, a string bean of a man in buckskins with greasy hair stood up.

"Aye, James Middleton, what say you?" said Gouedy.

"I say it's the damned Cherokees," Middleton said in a loud lisp. "We should clean those red devils out."

Emily sucked in her breath, watching her father make a beeline out from behind the bar, but Robert Gouedy had seen this, too, and moved quickly to block Stewart from committing the day's fourth killing.

"James Middleton," Robert Gouedy said, "you are wrong, sir. Wrong and blind."

"Because you trade with those thievin' devils?" Middleton said, and lifted his wooden cup as if that made his point.

"Aye, I do," responded Gouedy. "We all do in some form or the other."

Although Breck Stewart stood still, his fists shook in tight balls at his sides.

"But was not one of them vermin a Cherokee?" Everyone could detect the challenge in Middleton's voice. He hated all Indians, and Cherokees in particular. His family had been killed during the Cherokee war back in 1760.

Now Stewart pushed his way past Robert Gouedy. "Now see here, Middleton!" Stewart wagged his long finger at the greasy hunter. "If not for another Cherokee . . . that boy right over there . . . well, I'd hate to think. . . ." He couldn't finish, and Emily was thankful for that.

She looked at young Go-la-nv Pinetree, who sat cross-legged on the floor near the open door to the tavern. Impassive. Maybe disinterested. For a moment, she even thought Go-la-nv might be asleep, but that would have been next to impossible with the shouts echoing through the tavern. Slowly the young Cherokee raised his head, looked from one face to another before he saw Emily. He gave a little shrug. Emily had to smile at that, which was a good thing. After this morning, she wasn't sure if she could ever smile again. Go-la-nv Pinetree dropped his attention back to the floor and picked up a large onion-skin marble, probably one her younger brother Alan had dropped.

"Yes, yes, yes," Middleton was saying. "Everybody this side of Cane Creek knows how commodious young Emily is. But tell me this, Breck Stewart, what was your daughter doing so far out in the woods . . . alone?"

This time it was Emily who leaped up, knocking the stool over onto Rachel Rowe's knees. Blood rushed to her head, and she could feel her ears reddening with rage. Above the myriad shouts inside the tavern, Emily's voice rose.

"I am no doxy, Mister Middleton, and I resent your insinuations . . . but not as much as I despise your bigotry." She pointed back toward the Go-la-nv Pinetree. "Yes, he is Cherokee, but he saved my life, sir. And two men among that nefarious trio . . . they were white men. Who looked a hell of a lot like you!"

Behind her, Rachel Rowe gasped at the use of profanity. Even in the Cane Creek country, teen-age girls did not swear, at least not in public, and not in front of their fathers. On the other hand, had she been sitting inside a tavern in Georgetown or Charlestown or even Pine Tree, she figured the local citizens would already have branded her a harlot and excommunicated her from the Presbyterian Church. Yet another thing that separated the Back Country from the rest of the colony.

She had spoken her mind. Back along the Carolina coast, or across the Atlantic in England, women were encouraged to avoid engaging in conversation such as this. This was a man's country. But the people who thought like that did not live in the Back Country. With an attitude like that, they wouldn't survive in a place like this.

"Box his ears, girl!" someone cried from the far corner.

"Aren't you the dog whipper." Donnan had stopped cleaning his fingernails with his knife to whisper into her ear.

She slapped at him, but saw James Middleton grinning, being nudged and goaded by the other men in buckskins beside him. He raised his hat, and bowed at Emily.

"No offense, Miss Emily," he said, and turned to her father. "All I mean, Mister Stewart, is that it is not safe for young women . . . or any women . . . to be alone that far from our settlement."

Many men and women voiced their agreement with that statement, and Emily knew she would be reprimanded later by her mother and father, and probably everyone in the district.

" 'Tis not safe, these days, I fear, for men to be alone, either," Alroy O'Fionnagáin said, his voice soft, the brogue heavy, but everyone in the tavern had heard, and those thirteen words brought a momentary silence inside the cabin.

"The problem," Stewart bellowed, "is that there are no courts and no law here! The Crown even refuses to allow us to raise a militia!"

Emily turned, picked up the stool, apologizing to Rachel Rowe, and sat down. She sighed. The arguments that followed she had heard countless times over the past year or two.

One might find a magistrate down in the settlement south of here called Pine Tree, but his honor would wield almost no power, at least not enough power to thwart the blackhearts terrorizing the Back Country. The only criminal courts, and the only jails, could be found in Charlestown.

"We are more than one hundred and twenty miles from Pine Tree," someone said. "And then it's almost one hundred more to Charlestown."

"Pray tell, what good is a court or jury in Charlestown?" Ferguson said. "To us, they are foreigners, and our affairs are foreign to them, as well."

A woman yelled: "They know not of our troubles in Charles-town!"

A man sang out: "And the governor cares not a fig for what we must endure!"

"Aye, but the merchants in Charlestown love the peltry we bring them." Even James Middleton had joined the cause.

"And the peace we have forged with the Cherokees," a burly man said, pointing at Go-la-nv Pinetree.

Even a few years before Emily's grandparents had settled in Georgetown, the Assembly in Charlestown had created five precinct courts to ease the burden—and silence the com-plaints—of those who had chosen to settle deeper inside the colony, away from the coast. The problem, of course, was that no attorney, no solicitor, no judge agreed to attend these new courts—even to try small debt cases—and, by 1741, the Crown had ruled such courts, such precincts, illegal.

Down along the confluence of the Peedee River and Lynches Creek, settlers had petitioned again for a county court back in 1752, and within two years other such requests had reached Governor James Glen.

"The Assembly, the governor, the entire populace of the Low Country are deaf to our cries!" Her father was at it again, only this time he had climbed atop the bar. "Here we live with a conflux of the most undisciplined sort of mankind, ignorant evil-doers who espouse the meanest principles. Horse stealers, murderers, fornicators, and other felons." He was walking up and down the bar, and now even Go-la-nv Pinetree had forgot-ten the small marble and seemed captivated by Breck Stewart.

"We have pleaded our case countless times with the Assembly. We have threatened those scalawags who torment us. This morn-ing, three of those wretched individuals were slain. But our fight, our call for justice, has not ended. No, friends, neighbors,

I daresay it has not even begun. To hell with Charlestown! That is what I say."

·The room fell into silence. No one muttered agreement or dissent. Men and women sat or stood, staring, barely even breathing. Beside her, Emily's big brother seemed struck dumb.

"I say this, and to this I swear," Stewart continued. "If I cannot answer these fiends by ballarag, I will by dirk and blunderbuss." He stopped, sucked in a deep breath, and slowly exhaled, looking at the faces of his neighbors.

After a long pause, Robert Gouedy cleared his throat. "Be careful, Breck," he said. "For what you suggest could be called treason."

"It is treason!" Joseph Robinson shot up from his seat, whipping off his cocked hat. "I will not listen to such talk."

Robinson was a newcomer to South Carolina, a Virginian by birth, and always loyal to King George. Emily was surprised even to see Robinson here. Most of the people in Ninety Six disliked Robinson almost as much as they disliked Birmingham Long, a farmer on the Long Canes. Long was not here, because he lived too far away to have been summoned on such short notice.

"Treason," Stewart said, his voice calm now, "is betraying one's own government. Here in the Cane Creek region, we have no government."

"Except ourselves!" someone shouted.

No echoes of affirmation joined that lone voice.

Robinson remained standing, shaking with rage.

"You suggest," said Ferguson, the hog farmer, "that we form a militia?"

"To fight the wastrels and killers, aye." Breck Stewart nodded. "That is exactly what I suggest."

"It is treason, my friend!" a woman's voice called out. "No matter how you say it, no matter how necessary and just, it remains treason."

"They might put you in stocks, Stewart, for such sentiments," Robinson said, but at least he had stopped shaking. "Or brand you for sedition."

"We are men!" Stewart barked.

A new fear gripped Emily. Her father was just stubborn enough to write a post to the governor or the Assembly, and she knew that would be enough to land him not in the stocks, but in the Charlestown jail for a long, long time.

"How much longer must we watch our friends toil all year to build a home . . . only then to have it wiped out by vermin, by the scum of this great continent?" Slowly Breck Stewart climbed off the bar, assisted by Robert Gouedy and another man, but he continued to talk. "If this colony is to endure or even survive, we must have justice." He swung his arm toward Emily, who now blushed with embarrassment. "If it were your daughter out there. . . ." He could not finish.

For the first time in her life, Emily heard her father's voice crack with emotion, and she watched as tears welled in his hard eyes. He had to turn, find the mead, which he gulped down.

Robert Gouedy put an arm around Stewart's shoulders, and whispered something. His head bobbed, and Gouedy turned back to face the throng, while Stewart leaned against the bar, his body trembling.

"There is a new governor in Charlestown," Robert Gouedy said. "Perhaps he will listen to reason."

" 'Tis true, 'tis true," said Alroy O'Fionnagáin as he bobbed his head in agreement. "And Chief Justice Shinner has spoken on our behalf in the past."

"To deaf ears," Ferguson put in.

"Yes," Mrs. Cochrane said. "Before I see my sons and my husband in balls and chains and condemned to the squalor of a Charlestown prison . . . or, God forbid . . . bound for the cord and the gallows for treason . . . I would rather send someone to talk to this new governor, and to speak to the Assembly."

"I agree with Missus Cochrane," Robinson said. "Let us not do something rash that may land all of us before a Charlestown magistrate . . . or, worse yet, before bayonets of the King's army."

Heads nodded in affirmation, but James Middleton snorted. "Would not cutting off the heads of the three rascals killed this morning by the young button of a Cherokee, and then sticking them on three pikes, and placing them on the Charlestown Road just a few rods outside our settlement . . . would not that deter the cowardly lot of killers?"

A few women gasped. Emily frowned. Pinetree had killed only two of those louts. She had killed Blubber Cheeks.

"We are not scoundrels," Robert Gouedy said. "We are decent, God-fearing men and women. Loyal to His Majesty. What you suggest. . . ."

"Would get the attention of those blackhearts," Middleton interrupted.

"Perhaps, but I would have a difficult time sleeping at night."

"I would not," said Donnan Stewart.

Emily turned, mouth agape, staring with incredulity at her brother. He wasn't being flippant. He was dead serious.

Donnan felt her eyes on him, and turned toward her. He did not blink, did not look away, did not back down. The frontier had hardened him. Well, what had happened this morning, what had almost happened to his sister—that had changed Donnan Stewart. Changed his sister, too.

"Those unfortunate souls were brought back this afternoon," Robert Gouedy said. "They were buried. As Christian as possible. If you would like to dig them up. . . ."

Disgusted, Middleton waved his hand and muttered an oath.

"As Christian as possible," Mrs. Cochrane offered, and

pointed at Gouedy. "Which brings us to something else entirely. When you speak to the new governor, would it be possible . . . could we perhaps get a clergyman to Cane Creek and the Long Canes?"

"Yeah!" a man in the back of the tavern called out. "That way me and Betsy could be legal in the eyes of God and the King. And that son of our'n would never know he was a bastard."

"Just like his old man," another commented.

The men laughed, but a blushing Mrs. Cochrane stormed through the open door.

"I propose that we petition the governor," Breck Stewart said, "and the Assembly." His voice had softened, maybe from all the orating he had been doing, or maybe because he already knew what the result would be after another trip to Charlestown, another meeting with the colony's leaders. "Again, we shall list our grievances. . . ."

"Our *requests*," Joseph Robinson interjected.

"Our requests," Gouedy agreed, staring hard at Stewart, warning him with a hard glare to curb his tongue.

"Let us take a vote," Ferguson said.

But Emily knew such formality was unnecessary. The settlers of Ninety Six would vote to send a delegation to Charlestown to see Chief Justice Shinner and the new governor, to ask for help. For justice. To get rid of the vermin terrorizing the Back Country. Robert Gouedy would go. So would her father, and Emily prayed that he'd let Gouedy do all of the talking.

CHAPTER THREE

With Donnan Stewart and Go-la-nv Pinetree, Emily walked away from the settlement—if one could call Ninety Six a settlement—and Cormorant's Rock Tavern down the Charlestown Road. They passed the fields of tobacco and hemp where Gouedy's slaves worked in the heat, and the rows of peach trees. They did not speak until they came to the intersection with the Cherokee Path.

The Cherokee grunted and started off for Keowee, but Donnan called out his name. When Pinetree turned, Emily watched her brother shuffle his feet, and study the acorns littering the ground. She understood he couldn't do it, so she spoke up herself.

"Thank you, Go-la-nv. For what you did. We both thank you. My father thanks you."

The Cherokee nodded, but said nothing. Donnan kept staring at the acorns. He didn't even look at Pinetree as he retreated down the trail.

"Are you that proud?" she asked Donnan, shaking her head in disgust but feeling the heat rise in her face when Donnan had the audacity to laugh.

"It is right you should thank him, Sister." He spit to his side. "He saved your life, not mine."

She pointed a finger under her brother's chin. "I paid my debt, Donnan. I cleaved the head of one of those blackhearts. I saved Go-la-nv's life."

"Just do not tell Mum," Donnan said. "She would never find a husband for you if word got out about what a savage you are."

As he started to chuckle, Emily whirled around and stormed down the Charlestown Road, walking away from Ninety Six.

Her brother had to run to catch up. "Did not you hear that warning that you should not travel alone?"

"I shall do as I please," Emily declared.

They had come to the stockade built during the Cherokee troubles of 1760. She stopped walking to study the wooden structure, now covered with weeds and ivy, many of the pine logs turning to rot. Immediately forgetting all about her feud with Donnan, she heard herself asking: "What was it like?"

"Inside?" Again Donnan spit to his side. "Just be glad Da' sent you back to Georgetown during the uprising." Self-consciously he brought the fingers of his right hand to his face, which still bore the scars left by the pox. After a heavy sigh, he pointed to the graveyard next to the ruins of the small fort. "I forget their names," he said, his voice distant. "I remember the water. How bad it smelled. I remember Mum crying, bathing my face with damp towels. Or maybe I just remember Mum telling me that's what it was like."

"If and when she talks about it," Emily said.

"Aye. Machara Stewart is not one to resuscitate memories such as those," Donnan agreed.

Emily turned. "What do you think will happen? To the . . ."—she tried to remember the word—"the . . . petition?"

" 'Tis not the first such petition we have sent to Charlestown," he said.

"Then . . . you think the Assembly . . . ?"

Donnan cut her off. "When was the last time you were in Charlestown?"

It had been during the Cherokee uprising. Her grandparents had brought her from Georgetown to Charlestown to the slave

28

market so that Grandmother Elizabeth could buy a servant for Emily. Emily couldn't have been more relieved when her grandparents could not find chattel they deemed worthy of the price or worthy of their granddaughter. She shrugged.

"I was there last fall with Da'. Remember?" Donnan said. "Da' met with Governor Glen, with Lieutenant Governor Bull, with other members of Charlestown's aristocracy. Do you know what I remember most about that trip?" He didn't wait for a response. "It was what someone . . . whose name I have purged from my memory . . . said at a dinner. He told Da' . . . to his face . . . and with me right there . . . 'It is impossible to raise a gentleman away from the tidewater.' "

She cocked her head, grinned, unable to resist the impulse to say: "Well, Brother, in your case I would say that man was correct."

He shook his head as he began to laugh, and Emily laughed with him. Their annoyances at one another forgotten, Donnan said: "Nothing will happen. Da' will not be put in the stocks, nor flogged. Our committee will make their pleas, and return with rum and silk and trade beads for Go-la-nv and his people. And when the fiends burn another barn or steal another horse, Da' will pass out more kill-devil and mead. And we shall listen to our friends and neighbors bandying words about what we need to do."

"You have become such a cynic."

"Aye. That I am. Do you wish to journey on to Mister Gouedy's trading post?"

Emily shook her head. "That I have seen. I. . . ." Emily froze. When she looked down the road toward Gouedy's post, she saw two men in buckskins walking toward them. She blinked. Caught her breath. She was certain it was the Cherokee and Blubber Cheeks, even though she knew it couldn't be. She stepped back, tripping over Donnan's foot, falling to the ground.

Donnan was at her side instantly, pulling a Queen Anne flintlock from his belt that she hadn't even noticed. He thumbed back the hammer, aiming at the approaching men, while Emily tried to climb to her feet, to run.

" 'Tis all right, Emily," Donnan assured her softly once he could clearly see the faces of the two men. He lowered the hammer of the pistol.

Heart pounding, Emily rolled over, still unable to stand, thinking she might wet herself. She closed her eyes tightly, shook her head as she heard Donnan call out: "Hello, you two old Huguenots!"

"Bonjour, mon ami."

When Emily heard the greeting, she opened her eyes as she reprimanded herself: *Idiot.* She cursed herself, pushed up off the ground, brushing off the pine needles and dead leaves from her dress. She no longer imagined seeing the Cherokee or Blubber Cheeks—or their ghosts. In front of her stood Dr. François Bayard and his friend, the farmer Pierre Maupin, both of whom lived on Cane Creek about six miles from Ninety Six. She blushed from embarrassment, but the two Huguenots were unaware of her blunder, or her fear. They were embracing Donnan as she walked up the road, attempting a grin.

The doctor stepped forward, sweeping off his hat, bowing, speaking in rapid French that she couldn't understand. Although she had known several Huguenots down in Georgetown, Emily knew little about them, except for what she had heard at the tavern. They were Protestants who had left France years earlier, and there were many living in the colonies, especially in South Carolina.

"We missed you at the meeting," Donnan told Maupin, who cocked his head curiously, then looked in question at his companion.

Dr. François Bayard was older than the farmer by ten years

or so, a heavy-set man with an almost feminine face and penetrating blue eyes. He butted the long rifle he carried on the ground and asked: "What meeting?"

"Da' sent word earlier this afternoon," Donnan said.

"Not to me," Dr. Bayard said.

"Nor I," the farmer added. The buckskins worn by Pierre Maupin fit him a lot better than they did Dr. Bayard. Maupin was rail thin, bearded, with a furrowed brow, brooding brown eyes, and a long-stemmed pipe that Emily had never seen out of his mouth or hand. Nor was it ever lit.

"Was Joseph Robinson there?" Maupin asked.

Dr. Bayard was already shaking his head before Donnan replied in the affirmative.

"*Merde*," Maupin said.

"Mind your manners," the doctor said, lifting his rifle into the crook of his arm, indicating Emily with a nod of his head. "I am sure Mister Robinson merely forgot to tell us of the meeting. Just as last time."

"The arrogant swine," Maupin said. "I wish he would return to Virginia."

"He cannot," said Dr. Bayard. "I understand he left after some sort of scandal."

"I apologize," Donnan interrupted the two. "I shall tell Da' the next time he sends word to Cane Creek that he should tell the courier to deliver the word personally to one or the other of you."

"No apology is needed, my good man," Dr. Bayard said. "What was this meeting about?"

Emily slipped beside her brother. "Just more of the same," she said. "Talk about sending another group to petition the governor and Assembly for some help."

They didn't respond for several moments. Maybe Huguenots were like the gentry in Charlestown and Georgetown or any other settlement along the tidewater. They weren't used to having women, or young girls still in their teens, interrupting a conversation among men.

"Has there been another incident involving some *scélérat*?" the doctor asked.

Donnan turned to his sister, then looked back at the two neighbors.

"Scoundrel," Maupin translated.

Emily drew in a deep breath. "Three red scoundrels," her brother answered. "Raising havoc on the Cherokee Path past Spring Branch."

"Only one," Emily said curtly, "was an Indian, Donnan. The other two were white."

"Men of that ilk paid Pierre a visit yesterday," the doctor said.

"Smashed my tomatoes and stole a bovine," Maupin said glumly. "Did you catch and flog the prodigals?"

"Da' and Mister Gouedy and the others might still be meeting at Da's tavern," Emily sang out. "If you want to report what happened to Mister Maupin. . . ." She stopped herself from saying anything further, fearing she might break into tears.

"Aye," Donnan said. "Let us walk back with you, if you are bound for Ninety Six."

The doctor laughed. "We are not bound for Ninety Six, Donnan Stewart."

Maupin cut in: "We are bound for Cormorant's Rock!"

"For rum, the nectar of the gods!" sang out the Dr. Bayard.

"For kill-devil," Donnan agreed, laughing. Emily smiled, relieved they were walking back to Ninety Six. On the way, the doctor told of the giant fish he had caught in Cane Creek the previous day.

★ ★ ★ ★ ★

The tavern had grown silent. It stood two stories high with a pitched roof of wooden shingles. It was not made of rough-hewn logs like most of the homes in the region, but of squared cedar timbers, eighteen inches high and nine inches deep, dovetailed at the corners, and thoroughly chinked. At the tavern, Emily had heard many men say that Gouedy's fort was a stockade but that Cormorant's Rock was safe.

Inside, a giant fireplace dominated the north side; outside, a commodious covered porch stretched out along the east wall and was always crowded on warm summer evenings. A split-rail fence surrounded the property, which included an outdoor oven for baking bread, a smaller summer cook shack, the privies, and Machara Stewart's garden. The bottom story was one giant room, where Breck Stewart served his liquor, and a smaller winter kitchen, where Machara cooked her stews, breads, and pies. The upper story held four rooms, one bedroom for the two Stewart adults, one for the four children, and two rooms for any guests who might need to spend the night.

That evening, the cabin smelled of bacon and rum. Donnan swept the floor in silence, while Emily's mother washed the dishes out back with Emily's younger sister Elizabeth, named after her grandmother in Georgetown, and her younger brother Alan.

Although most of the district had been here that afternoon, it was a quiet night. The Huguenots had been the last to leave, full of lamb stew, corn pone, and ale.

Emily sat at a table by an open window, a candle flickering from the breeze, making it hard for her to read her Bible. Not that she was trying too hard. Her mind kept going back to what had happened that morning. She kept seeing Blubber Cheeks, kept telling herself that she had actually killed a man.

"So . . . Emily."

She almost leaped out of the chair before realizing it was her father standing next to her.

"Easy, child," Breck Stewart said. "I did not mean to give you a fright."

"I am sorry, Da'." Her heart was pounding. She settled back into the chair, and looked past her father. Donnan, it seemed, had swept dirt, trash, and himself right out of the tavern.

Breck Stewart pulled out a chair across from Emily and slid into it. "Are you all right, Daughter?"

She nodded. Then added honestly: "As well as could be expected."

"A bad morning."

"It could have been worse."

Breck Stewart's head bobbed. He brought his massive hands onto the table, and seemed to stare at his fingers as he flexed them. That went on for a full minute. Emily closed the Bible and waited.

"We have a petition to deliver to the Assembly," Breck said at last. "A good one, I think."

Another long silence.

"Goudey, myself, and two others will depart on the morrow for Charlestown."

"We shall miss you, Da'."

"Six days there," her father said. "Six back. Probably four days in Charlestown."

"Sixteen days." She wanted to fill the silence, but she doubted if her father had heard.

The last time Breck Stewart had left for Charlestown, he had asked Emily if she wanted him to bring her back a gift "from civilization." She waited for him to ask the question again, and when he did not, she knew what was coming, and dread knotted her stomach. She drew in a deep breath, held it briefly, and silently exhaled while her father stared at his fingernails.

After another intolerable silence, Breck Stewart looked across the table at Emily. "You shall come with us, Daughter."

Her heart sank, for she knew what her father would say next.

"We will go to Georgetown. You will spend at least the summer and fall visiting with your grandparents."

What had happened today must have scared him something fierce. Summer was the sick time along the Carolina coast. Many people fled Charlestown, Georgetown, and other settlements for fear of those deadly summer diseases—malaria, yellow fever.

"Da'," she said softly, "Ninety Six, Cormorant's Rock . . . this is my home. Cane Creek. The Saluda. The Broad. Long Cane Creek. This is. . . ."

"No place for a girl," her father finished the sentence for her.

"Is Rachel Rowe going? Or Mister Gouedy's daughters? Or Jemima Cochrane? They. . . ." She stopped, knowing that while she might be sixteen years old, her father could still send her to the woods to fetch a switch and then hide her for impudence and disrespect. She wasn't so old she could not remember her last whipping. Hell, she seemed to get them more than Elizabeth or Alan.

"They are not my daughters. You will go."

"What about Elizabeth?" Emily asked.

"She is too young."

Feeling that anger rising again, Emily almost said something she knew she would have regretted. She had to bite her lip as Breck Stewart spoke to her about the harshness of the frontier and that he was beginning to regret ever bringing her to Ninety Six.

"You should be a lady. You deserve pretty things. You should meet a fine gentleman in Charlestown. Or Georgetown. 'Tis where your mum met me."

"You forget, Da'," she said, "who I am."

He cocked his head. "And just who are you?"

"A Stewart of Appin."

He leaned back, grinning widely, shaking his head. "Aye, that you are, Daughter, that you are. But the Atlantic Ocean will do you a world of good. There are days that I miss the salt on the breeze, hearing the waves crash, seeing the sails in the harbor. I should have left you with my mum and da' during the last bit of unpleasantness."

She had one last argument, and fired it. "Da', I think that this morning I proved that I know what it takes to live in the Back Country, what it takes to survive here. With all due respect, Da', I am not your mother. I am . . ."—she grinned, hoping to win him over—"your daughter. A Stewart of Appin."

Breck Stewart's face remained granite. "I know you are, Daughter. I know what you have said is the truth. You are a Stewart, and you know how to handle yourself in this lawless country . . . which is exactly why I must send you to the coast, to civilization."

CHAPTER FOUR

The man at the market swept off his hat, bowing at Emily, and saying: "Welcome to the prettiest flower and the most flourishing city of all His Majesty's colonies."

Emily didn't see it that way. She hated Charlestown.

It dwarfed the coastal town she had known, and she found little here to remind her of Georgetown, where her grandparents operated an indigo plantation.

In Georgetown, an island sheltered them from the harsh Atlantic, and the Sampit, Waccamaw, and Black Rivers flowed gently toward the ocean. In Georgetown, all she had to worry about were alligators, snakes, and mosquitoes. In Charlestown, everything frightened her.

Her father had told her that only Philadelphia, New York, and Boston had a larger population in the colonies than Charlestown. Walking along the streets, she found it hard to believe that any place had more people than this overwhelming city.

They passed churches and market places, theaters and coffee houses, and taverns—Dillon's and the City Tavern on Broad Street, Sign of the Bacchus, Henry Gignilliant's—so many that she could not count. Men wore white wigs, and fine coats, and spoke the King's English, not the coarse Back Country talk of Ninety Six. Women wore embroidered dresses of the finest silk, and carried fans. Emily had even spotted a couple of women showing off their beaded satin shoes.

Merchants and planters. Soldiers and sailors, the latter speaking myriad languages that Emily could not make sense of. His Majesty's officials, indentured servants, and another class of people Emily had never seen. Beggars in filthy clothes, on their knees, pleading for a shilling. Her father and Robert Gouedy walked on without glancing at the poor creatures, and Emily, head down, hurried past.

She also saw slaves—men, women, children. These she had seen many times on the Stewart plantation in Georgetown, at the Gouedy place, and other farms around Ninety Six. Yet she didn't think she had ever seen this many slaves. They seemed to make up half the city.

They even passed whipping posts and stocks. The posts were empty, but some of the stocks held men—two actually held women—looking pathetic, helpless with their hands and heads sticking out from the heavy wooden yokes. A young Negro, merely a boy, had to stand on his tiptoes to keep from choking to death. Gouedy and Stewart merely walked past them, as did everyone else in Charlestown, scarcely even noticing the poor men and women. Everyone but Emily. She would never forget the images of these poor people.

Earlier that day, with the bells at St. Michael's tolling ten times, they had arrived in Charlestown and parked the wagons in the lot. A merchant, a man with a French accent and wooden leg, inspected the deerskins, flour, and hemp they had transported from Ninety Six.

"Fix us a glorious price, Henri," her father had told the Frenchman, "the best you can offer. And do not insult me or you shall rue this morning. We shall return tomorrow."

"He means what he says, *monsieur*," Gouedy had said, to which the trader had grinned and nodded, muttering something in French that caused Gouedy to laugh heartily.

All around her, Emily saw hogsheads, tierces, and barrels of rum, gin, ale, wine, and what must have been thousands of empty bottles waiting to be filled. Flour, hemp, cured brown tobacco wrapped in giant sheets of canvas, hogsheads of indigo, barrels of rice.

Yet it was not just a massive city of strange people and products, of shouts, of the smells of salt-water and the warm breeze from the ocean. Cows and horses grazed on the grass that clawed its way up from underneath the cobblestone streets. Emily had to step over dead rats, and she encountered packs of mangy dogs, and groups of fat cats huddling in the alleys.

They registered at an inn along the Cooper River, depositing their grips in their rooms, and then headed toward Broad Street. Emily stopped frequently to gape at the fortified wall built decades earlier to protect the city from the Spaniards, the pirates, the French.

Her father pointed at a two-story building on the battery. "The ground floor," he said over the shouts of men and women and the snorts of horses and mules, "used to be the guard house. The top floor was the council chamber, which is where the Assembly and governor met!" He winked. "Ask me, and the Assembly and governor should have been confined to the bottom floor."

Shaking his head, Gouedy laughed, but his grin faded quickly and he shook his head. " 'Tis one of the problems we face trying to get the Assembly's attention. Charlestown's jails cannot hold the city's criminals, let alone those to be found in our district."

Breck pointed to a clear path. They hurried before the people filled it in.

At the corner of Meeting and Broad Streets, they stopped, and Emily stared at the new structure. "I shall arrange an appointment in the State House," Gouedy said, "but it might be a good idea if you were to pay a friendly visit to William Bull."

"Indeed," Breck said, and, turning, he said to Emily: "Follow me, Daughter." Which she did, not daring to let her father get more than two steps ahead of her.

At the corner of Meeting and Ladson Streets, Breck Stewart knocked on the fine door of a stuccoed brick building that, to Emily, resembled a castle. She thought her grandparents were wealthy, but they certainly did not call a place like this home. It was three and a half stories, with windows on each side of the door, three windows on the second and third floors, all with shutters closed.

An immaculately dressed Negro opened the door, and Stewart whispered something to him, then turned and motioned for Emily to follow. She climbed the steps, and stepped inside paradise, albeit a dark paradise.

They waited inside the parlor, Emily afraid to sit down on the furniture, as dirty as she felt, as filthy as she surely must have become on the long trip from Ninety Six. She could not understand why Robert Gouedy and her father had insisted on visiting the colony's lieutenant governor now. They should have freshened up at the inn, rested, then paid a visit in the morning, when it might be a tad cooler.

Outside, the bells from some church began announcing the noon hour.

Several minutes later, the black man opened the door, and in walked a woman in a sacque-back gown of pink and cream stripes, with a satin skirt and sleeve ruffles, satin embroidery, all in all the most dazzling dress Emily had ever seen.

Stewart, who had no reservations about sitting down, rose, bowed, and, taking the woman's proffered hand, kissed it before straightening his back. "Missus Bull," he said, "allow me to present my daughter, Emily Stewart of Ninety Six."

The woman's smile seemed both pleasant and genuine as she curtsied and stepped toward Emily. She looked to be in her late thirties, maybe early forties, still slender, still with exquisite features. Emily found it hard to believe that this beautiful woman had married William Bull, a man who, she had heard her father once say, "had a face that could sink ten thousand ships."

"Why," Mrs. Bull said, "she is so lovely. You do me a great honor by bringing her to my house, sir. But you are here to see the Lieutenant Governor, I presume."

"Missus Bull." Emily tried to return the bow without tripping over her feet.

"Child, you shall call me Mary Hannah, and I shall call you Emily, if that suits you." Without waiting for a response, Mrs. Bull turned to Breck. "Mister Stewart, you should find William at the Corner Tavern. I will summon Charles and he will take you there by carriage."

"I can walk. . . ."

"In this dreadful heat. I think not, sir. And you will leave this darling child of yours with me. We will have strawberries and cream with my . . . ahem . . . other guest." She was already ringing a silver bell. Almost immediately another Negro servant appeared at the entrance to the parlor. Before Emily could say a word, the slave and her father had left her inside this palace with Mrs. Bull and a second woman who had appeared as her father headed out the door. The woman looked Emily up and down, and, unable to hide her distaste, she perched herself in a parlor chair and began immediately to fan herself.

"Is it always this hot, Mary Hannah?" the woman asked Mrs. Bull.

"Hot?" The lieutenant governor's wife laughed. "Wait until August." She rang the bell again, ordered food, and presented Emily to Lady Charles Montagu.

"Charmed," said the governor's wife, and then began to fan herself furiously. She wore a purple periwinkle silk crepe gown embroidered with silver leaves and silver filigree buttons forming a square around the blouse.

"Please, Emily, sit down. Tell us all about Ninety Six," urged Mrs. Bull.

Emily sat on her hands, hoping they might keep her clothes from dirtying the brocade chair. It was dark in the parlor, too dark with the shutters closed—to keep out the heat, she presumed—for her to get a decent look at the governor's young wife. She was much younger than Mrs. Bull, bigger, and, Emily quickly decided, repulsive and obnoxious.

"I cannot wait until we leave for New York on vacation," Lady Montagu said. "This place is oppressive. How is the heat where you hail from, child?"

This place, Emily thought, *might not feel so hot if her highness did not exert herself so in flapping her damned fan with that flabby arm. That alone produces more heat than the pendulum pumps of an indigo machine.*

"Hot now," Emily said, "but most in the district expect a hard winter."

"How so?"

"Ma'am?"

"How . . . can . . . you . . . predict . . . a . . . hard . . . winter?" She enunciated each word as if she were speaking to a small child.

Mrs. Bull rolled her eyes and, making sure the governor's wife could not see, gave Emily a sly wink.

"Bark," Emily said. "And hides."

That got Lady Charles Montagu to stop with the fan. She even lowered it to her lap, eyes suddenly curious, and asked: "How is that?"

"Tree bark, Lady Charles," she said. "It is thicker than normal. Thicker, actually, than anyone in the district has seen in years. Even the Cherokees say so."

The large woman leaned forward. "Cherokees? Do you mean

that your men actually speak to such heathen savages?"

"We all do, Lady Charles," she said. "And they are not what I would call heathen . . . at least compared to some of the white. . . ."

Mrs. Bull cleared her throat, and rang the bell, and Emily understood she had best watch her tongue around a gentrified lady like the governor's wife. Maybe around Mrs. Bull, too.

The slave who had answered the door reappeared, and Mrs. Bull asked that tea and slices of watermelon be served before the strawberries and cream.

With a nod, the man disappeared once more.

"And the . . . hides?" Lady Charles asked, obviously finding the word repulsive.

"Fur skins are thick, too. Animals have an instinct, Lady Charles. They know when bad weather is coming."

She sniffed in disgust, and picked up her fan.

"And what, child, do you do for culture in . . . what is it that you call your town?"

"I would not call it a town, Lady Charles, but it's called Ninety Six."

"A peculiar name, is it not, Lady Charles?" Mrs. Bull said.

"I find it idiotic," Lady Charles said. "Who on earth names a town a number? As I was saying, child, are there concerts in your . . . ?" She waved her hand.

"There is music," Emily said. She hoped Lady Charles did not ask for more information, because if she had to mention bagpipes, fiddles, and Jew's harps, she feared the governor's wife would suffer an apoplexy.

"Are there books?"

Before Emily could answer that her mother had a Bible, Mrs. Bull said: "Oh, Elizabeth, how could I have forgotten to mention the Charlestown Library Society."

Emily let out a silent sigh of relief as the woman turned her attention to the lieutenant governor's wife.

"Goodness, why it is almost twenty years old," said Mrs. Bull. "Many of our city's fine young gentlemen . . . William is now the president . . . established this fine society merely to benefit from the latest books and periodicals from London. It has grown quite substantially and the materials have been moved from the homes of our librarians to. . . ." She paused to take a sip of tea.

"And where is your fine library now?" Lady Charles asked.

Mrs. Bull sniffed. "Well, it was at the Free School, but, until we have funds for a new library, it is on the upper story of Gabriel Manigault's liquor warehouse."

Emily blushed, and, seeing the look on Lady Charles's face, she felt Mrs. Bull's embarrassment.

"I suppose your library resides in a groggery, too, my child?" she asked.

"Da' keeps the Bible there," Emily said. "And we live upstairs."

She had had enough of Elizabeth Montagu's attitude.

"And what do young *ladies* do in Ninety Six?" the fat woman said.

Well, less than two weeks ago, I split a murderer's skull open with a hatchet.

Emily didn't say it, but she wished she had.

Charlestown, Emily discovered, did have one thing in common with Ninety Six. Everything that got done here got done in a tavern. Charlestown just had a lot more than Ninety Six's sole inn. And while you never found a *lady* inside one of Charlestown's "groggeries", as Lady Charles Montagu would call them, her father told her that half of the tavern licenses in the city had been issued to women.

"How can that be?" she asked.

Her father smiled, and straightened the collar of his coat. Breck Stewart had rescued his daughter from the boredom of the Bull house on Meeting Street, after paying his respects to Mrs. Bull and Lady Charles. They had taken a hack to their inn.

"Artisans are forbidden to run a tavern," he said. "To get around that bit of legality, they marry someone. She pays for the license, and he drinks for free."

Emily grinned. "Does Mum own the license for Cormorant's Rock Tavern?"

Laughing, he walked over to the chair where she sat, and tousled her hair.

"Is that what you desire for me?" she asked. "That I should own a tavern?"

His laughter stopped, and he leaned over, eyes serious, and said quietly: "I should hope that your goals are much loftier than following in your old da's footsteps."

She changed the subject quickly. "When am I bound for Georgetown?"

After more than three hours with Lady Charles, she thought Georgetown and her grandparents might be a reprieve. She even had convinced herself that quilting bees, spelling bees, songs, and games of hopscotch, jump rope, rolling hoops, and "London Bridge" might be fun. On the other hand, her grandfather, after a bit too much rum, had been known to take her to see a cockfight. She didn't much care for the sport, but it certainly beat playing blind man's bluff.

"Are you that sick of Charlestown?" he asked.

"Indeed I am."

His laughter filled the room. "As am I, too, Emily. I do not know how a man survives in this city. Certainly it is not Georgetown."

"It is not Ninety Six," she said quietly.

He did not hear. "There are certainly few shillings to be made running a tavern in this city. One tavern for every five free-born men." He shook his head, but Emily decided that would explain all of those containers of rum she had seen at the mercantile—and even more on the wharves. "Besides, they also fine a person five shillings for drinking or serving drinks on Sunday. Perhaps we need no law in Ninety Six if they will be fining us for drinking on Sundays." He had moved away to pull on his buckle shoes, then doffed a wig and turned, cocking his head and grinning at Emily. "Do I look like a gentleman?" he asked.

"Another meeting?" She sighed.

"After we take our supper."

"In another 'ordinary'?" Emily pulled a fake smile to show her father she was joking. But, of course, she wasn't.

"No, not at a tavern, but here at this inn," he said, shaking his head. "Then I shall meet Bull, Gouedy, and Shinner at Shepheard's Tavern. We had to adjourn our meeting this afternoon so that Bull could fetch the chief justice and governor." His head shook. "The governor is not much older than you."

His wife, Emily thought, *will turn him into Methuselah.*

It all made sense, of course. Solomon's Lodge No. 1, Free and Accepted Masons had been organized at the tavern on Broad Street almost thirty years ago. The first theatrical troupe to perform in the city had done so at Charles Shepheard's place. They called the tavern's long room "the courtroom", and for good reason—before the floor above the guardhouse on the battery and before the State House had been finished, the governor, lieutenant governor, and the Assembly met in Shepheard's Tavern. Apparently government officials still met there.

Yes, just like Ninety Six, Emily though to herself.

"But to answer your question . . . ," her father said.

She looked at her father, resplendent in his coat, if a bit

frayed, and wig. Question? Emily had forgotten what she had asked.

"Georgetown will wait another day until your grandfather arrives. I thought you might care to accompany us to New Market Course."

"What is that?"

"It is how the gentlemen and ladies of Charlestown entertain themselves, usually in the winter and spring, but a special event has been scheduled for the morrow . . . even in the heat of July."

She waited.

"It is a racecourse, Emily. Horse racing."

"Can I ride?" she said.

He rolled his eyes. "You are a wonder, Daughter. Let us eat our supper now. Then to bed with you."

CHAPTER FIVE

She did not care what ladies were wearing in Paris, or what Lady Charles Montagu thought of *Love in a Village* by some Irishman named Bickerstaff, or even Mrs. Bull's opinion on Bishop Thomas Percy's *Reliques of Ancient English Poetry*. So Emily tried to ignore the chatter around her and focus on the conversation of the men seated below. Although she was surprised to see that most of the jockeys were slaves, it was the horses being saddled for the race that interested her most. Especially the dun.

Located on a pasture east of the Broad Path, Charlestown's New Market Course had opened in 1760, forcing another racetrack, The York Course, which had been built on Charlestown Neck much farther from the city, to close. New Market was much fancier than any course found in the Long Canes, but then any such racecourse in the Ninety Six District was usually decided ten to fifteen minutes before the race was run.

It was always something like: "You shall ride underneath that big limb hanging from the elm, straight down the pike to Spring Branch, fetch the flags in the clearing, then ride as hard as you can, leaping over the fence in front of Breck's tavern, and . . . careful not to trample Missus Stewart's garden . . . right betwixt the well and Ol' Benji Cooper's work shed. Mister Gouedy and Mister Thomas shall be official judges. Do not flog the other jockeys with your quirts, if possible."

"I do not understand how you live in this furnace." Mopping

his brow, the governor sounded just like Lady Charles.

"Well, sir," Justice Shinner said, "as they say of South Carolina . . . in the spring, it is paradise. In summer, it is hell. In autumn, it is a hospital."

"When I have need to find a new court jester, I shall know upon whom to call," said Lord Charles Montagu, who appeared to be a young man, not much older than Donnan. "This is simply unbearable," he added.

Even Emily found the heat and humidity oppressive, but she knew that Chief Justice Shinner had not been joking entirely. Spring in South Carolina, especially along the coast, could be considered paradise indeed, but during the summers, temperatures often topped one hundred degrees. The rivers, swamps, and marshes bred mosquitoes, and many, many people—those who could afford to, anyway—often left South Carolina around May, not to return until autumn. By then, many of those who had stayed were recovering, if they were lucky, from malaria or yellow fever. Some settlers in Ninety Six had fled from Charlestown after the terrible yellow fever outbreak of 1748. She had thought of trying to use that fear as an excuse to return to Ninety Six, but she knew it would never work with her father.

In forty years in the New World, her grandparents insisted that they had never fled Georgetown out of fear in the summer. Of course, they usually went to their summer home in the High Hills of the Santee, but occasionally they stayed on the coast. They had never been sick a day in their lives, and both were in their mid-sixties and as spry as their only surviving son.

"There are different kinds of heat," Emily's father said. "We face our own version of hell in Ninety Six."

Emily almost laughed. Breck Stewart knew how to turn a conversation to the subject that interested him.

Lord Montagu asked: "And in what level of hell do you find yourself?"

"Our plague is not malaria, but freebooters."

"I was warned of this in Huntingdonshire," Montagu said. "The western portion of our province seems to be something of a penal colony. Perhaps it should be annexed by the colony of Georgia." He laughed at his own joke.

Emily whispered to herself: "And when I have need to find a new court jester, I shall know upon whom not to call."

"What is that, my dear?"

Emily sucked in a breath, and turned to Lady Charles Montagu, still fanning herself, still sweating like a pig.

"Nothing, my lady. I was just talking to myself."

"No." The fat woman folded her fan and used it as a pointer. "What is *that*?"

Emily leaned forward, squinting, trying to figure out what on earth the governor's wife was pointing at down along the course. She couldn't be asking that, could she?

"The . . . horse?" Emily said.

"That, dear child, is no horse."

"It is a marsh tacky," Emily explained. "This is a race of local marsh tacky horses."

"Tacky, indeed," Lady Charles Montague said.

Emily muttered an oath, caring not a farthing if Lady Charles heard. Her father had bought a marsh tacky years ago, and she had found the chestnut mare to be one tough horse. Small, sure, no more than fourteen hands, with a short back, long shoulders, and a deep, narrow chest. She turned her attention back to the dun, wondering how much the owner would want for him—in Charlestown, probably a small fortune.

"What should I expect from such a blight on good culture? Marsh tacky," the governor's wife muttered as her fan went back to work. "I suppose one has never heard of a thoroughbred or Andalusian in this colony."

Emily forgot about the dun stallion and the sweating Lady
Charles, and leaned forward again, straining her ears. She had
missed part of the conversation, but now sharp-faced William
Bull was talking to the governor, and his voice sounded ani-
mated.

"Governor, you speak of the men who settled in the Back
Country as the dregs of society, and, in doing so, you insult our
visitors . . . Squires Stewart and Gouedy."

Montagu sighed and waved his own fan faster.

"Men like these are what this colony needs, Governor,"
continued Bull. "They have already driven back the Cherokees
and opened up parts of this colony for more settlement. They
are not vagabonds, Lord."

"They are canaille," declared the governor.

Emily cringed as her father's hands balled into fists as William Bull kept talking.

"No, Lord Montagu, these are His Majesty's tenants,
landholders all. They are free white Christian men, over twenty-
one years of age, who have lived in South Carolina for more
than a year, own fifty acres . . . in Mister Gouedy's case, much,
much more . . . and pay at least twenty shillings a year in taxes."

"Then they should serve in the Commons House of Assembly," the governor said.

" 'Twas the point I am making," Bull said. "They. . . ."

It wasn't Stewart, but Gouedy who made the interruption.
"And do you know how many assemblymen are from the entire
Back Country, Governor? Four. Four men to represent the vast
majority of people and land. Charlestown has six alone. And
Georgetown has. . . ."

"Yes, yes, yes." Montagu rose, his back soaked through with
sweat, and ripped off his wig. "I cannot abide such heat any
longer. Write your petition, gentlemen, and present it to my

secretary. Elizabeth, let us retire to our residence. I doubt if it will be cooler, but at least these infernal biting bugs will be fewer."

They sat inside the George Coffee House. Emily had to give Charlestown credit—never had she tasted coffee this good. It even seemed to cool her off. Although she had been rescued from spending another unbearable afternoon with Lady Charles Montagu, she really wanted to know how the dun marsh tacky had fared in that race.

"We need a man to speak on our behalf," Gouedy was saying. "Someone who carries much more influence than you, Breck, or I."

"I know of no one in the Back Country more respected than you, Robert," her father said. "And William Bull and Justice Shinner have pleaded our case for two years now. Montagu is a damned fool, who belongs in England."

"It's not just the governor, Breck." Gouedy shook his head. "We have a provost marshal. . . ."

"One." Breck laughed. "One man. With a jurisdiction that covers the entire colony. A provost marshal, with no deputies, who lives . . ."—he couldn't help laughing even harder—"in England! And who draws most of his annual wages . . . as a damned playwright."

"There is talk of Marshal Cumberland hiring a deputy," Gouedy offered.

"Aye. That I shall believe when I see him in Ninety Six with a writ, a pistol, and sheriff's bracelets for prisoners," said Stewart.

"There is more talk."

Stewart set his mug down, waiting, as Gouedy shot a quick glance at Emily before returning his gaze to her father.

"She has heard everything and more, Robert," Breck assured him.

Emily loved her father even more for that.

"Bull said that the governor feels more pressure," Goudey said, "not from us, but from Parliament and London." He waited until a young couple had passed well out of earshot. "The Stamp Act passed last year created such an uproar in Charlestown. . . ."

"What of it? There was a Sugar Act. So now. . . ."

"Now, people in this colony and colonies elsewhere protested. They claimed it was unfair to be taxed without representation. This Stamp Act. . . ."

"Hurt Charlestown," Stewart interrupted. "Not us in Ninety Six. And, by Jehovah, Parliament repealed that act last year. Bah . . . protesting a silly act. How about protesting for what we need in the Ninety Six District? Bridges and law and order. A jail, for God's sake. And maybe a church. Or at least a clergyman."

Later Emily realized that the newcomer could not have timed his entrance more perfectly. This tall, lean man, with brilliant green eyes and fine dark hair, stepped up to the table at that very moment, holding out a slender hand, and smiling. "I believe, sirs, that I might be able to help you in that regard."

Emily, Goudey, and Breck Stewart stared in silence at the tall, neatly attired man. The stranger smiled. Slowly Goudey shook the man's hand, but when the stranger turned to Stewart, the big innkeeper took the offered hand and turned it over, running his coarse finger over the palm.

"Not one bloody callous do I see," he said. "And what be it that a tall man like yourself can do to help us out . . . in regards to law and order? For I do not suspect you are a bridge builder."

When his hand was released, the young man smiled. "You misunderstand me, sirs. Do I have the honor of speaking to Squire Robert Goudey?"

"Nay." Stewart flipped a finger at Goudey. "That's Goudey. I am Breck Stewart."

The man's eyes lighted on Emily.

"My daughter, Emily," Stewart said. "Who is bound for Georgetown on the morrow," he added quickly.

"An honor." The man bowed, and then turned to Robert Gouedy. "Sir, Lord Montagu, our governor, has asked me to seek you out, for if you are bound for the Back Country, I would like to travel with you. I am a minister of the cloth, sirs, fresh out of the seminary. I am the Reverend Douglas Monteith."

"Monteith." He had Breck Stewart's attention. "A fine Scottish name. Yes, by all means, you must travel with us. At least taking you home will get Jemima Cochrane off my arse. You are Presbyterian, are you not?"

With a sheepish smile, the Reverend Douglas Monteith shook his head. "I am Anglican, sir, and an itinerant. I shall travel across the Back Country, beginning in the Peedee, for such is my desire, and then I plan to move across north and west, but eventually I should bring the Word to Ninety Six."

"Anglican." Stewart snorted and sipped his coffee. "That damned Church of England. Such is my bloody luck."

When the tapping began on her door the next morning, Emily sighed. She had recognized her father's footsteps, and knew she could put off her banishment to Georgetown no longer. She was already dressed, and packed, and had been for more than three hours. Sleep had not come easily, and so she had finally given up.

Georgetown, and a summer—and who knew how much longer afterward—awaited her. Boredom. No hardwood forests. No horse races. No Sundays in the tavern. No bandits, on the other hand, but then no Go-la-nv Pinetree, either.

Cursing her luck, she rose from the chair, crossed the room, and opened the door. Immediately she regretted having had those thoughts.

"Father!" she blurted, an appellation she never used. "What has happened?"

Breck Stewart's face was pale, and he seemed distant as his hand, holding an envelope and sheet of paper, dropped to his side. His voice was hollow as he said: "Are you ready, Emily?"

"Yes." Tears of fear welled in her eyes.

"Come along. We must find some breakfast. Then we are to meet Robert and the parson at the stables." He blinked, and then seemed to bring himself back to the present. He even laughed, waving the letter at her. "Your prayers have been answered, Daughter, for you sha'n't be going to Georgetown this summer, after all."

She wanted to ask why, but was afraid to ask.

"A note from your grandmother. Yellow fever is rampant in Georgetown," he said. "We are going home. To Ninety Six."

CHAPTER SIX

The itinerant minister, Reverend Douglas Monteith, writhed on the ground, clutching his private parts and spewing sobs and gasps. As Robert Gouedy and Breck Stewart ran to attend the poor soul, Emily walked past the preacher, took the reins to the marsh tacky that had just laid the Anglican low, and led the dun a few rods away.

"I am . . . dying," Monteith moaned.

"No," said Gouedy, "but it is possible that Breck's new horse has rendered you unfit for nuptial rites."

"Watch your tongue, sir," Stewart said sharply. "You forget my daughter is in our company."

Emily shook her head. Her father kept forgetting just how old she was. Hell's fire, she thought, she felt practically like an old maid. Rebecca Rowe was to be wed, possibly as soon as Preacher Monteith arrived in Ninety Six, and Darlene Courtney, two years younger than Emily, already had an infant son.

"I apologize for my course language, Miss Emily." Gouedy swept off his cap of animal skin, and bowed.

You might consider looking after the parson, and not worrying about my delicate ears, Emily almost said, but then the reverend rolled over and vomited.

She rubbed the dun's neck. Emily did not know how much money her father had spent on the horse, but figured he was worth it—no matter the price—even if it had finished third in that race at the New Market Course. He could breed with the chestnut mare, and while a marsh tacky might be better suited for the swamps of the Low Country, such a horse would do just fine in the hills and forests of Ninety Six.

A few minutes later, once the preacher could stand, Gouedy and Stewart helped Douglas Monteith to a stump on the side of the trail.

"I told you . . . it was . . . a sin"—the preacher sucked in a deep breath, turned his head, moaned again—"traveling on the Sabbath. It is a sin. This is punishment from God."

"Nay, it is punishment from him." Stewart pointed to the dun. "I warned you about walking behind any horse or mule, Parson." Stewart turned, jutted his jaw toward one of the wagons, and Emily understood. She tethered Ezekiel to a spoke, scurried onto the wagon, and found the stoneware jug procured from Dillon's Tavern in Charlestown.

"We will not ride today," Monteith said sternly. "I forbid it. God forbids it."

Emily hurried to her father, and handed him the rum.

"Well. . . ." Gouedy grinned. "It is certain that you sha'n't sit in the saddle for a day or two. At least, not without much discomfort."

"He can ride in the wagon," Emily said. "I shall ride the marsh tacky."

"Not today," the preacher said.

"Yes, today," Stewart said as he withdrew the cork from the keg, took a swig, and then passed it to Gouedy. "When we get you to the settlements on the Peedee," Breck said softly, "you can return to your calendar and rest on Sunday. But there is no Sunday when we are on the trail." He looked down the wood-lined trail. "Not in the Back Country, Reverend."

"But staying here is. . . ."

"Dangerous," Gouedy said. "We are few. Two men. A preacher. A girl."

"And this is no likely camping spot," Stewart put in. "We are miles from Pine Tree and two days from the Welsh Neck. If we stay here, we risk attack from the rogues who scavenge this country for fools that tarry."

"But. . . ." Monteith sighed. "We are not that far from Charlestown."

"We are far enough," Stewart insisted.

Monteith shook his head. "To what kind of country hath my church sent me?"

"You are not in England, sir." Gouedy returned the jug to Stewart, who brought it to the preacher's lips.

"Drink this," Stewart said softly. "Kill-devil will dull your pain."

The preacher drank, and Gouedy said: "The temptation in the wilderness."

"Don't be sacrilegious, sir," Stewart said, taking the jug away from Monteith, and passing it back to the trader. "As the parson says, today is the Sabbath."

"Since when?" Gouedy laughed, and drank.

For the life of her, Emily could never understand why anyone settled in the Peedee.

Well, actually she did know. Years ago, her father had told her how the provincial government had offered bounties—bribes Gouedy had called them—to anyone twelve years or older who would settle there.

She just didn't think that any amount of money was worth it. This region lacked the hills of Ninety Six, and the forests weren't full of hardwoods. Instead, pines grew so thick and so tall that crossing through the country seemed like traveling inside a tunnel. Even at noon, the sunlight appeared to be fading, and the trees trapped in all the heat and humidity that could lay travelers low. Besides the forests, there were the swamps, foul-smelling stagnant water filled with croaking toads, snapping turtles, alligators and, worst of all, mosquitoes.

She swatted one of the latter.

"Last year," Stewart joked, flicking the reins as the four horses pulled the wagon toward the Welsh Neck, "I saw a mosquito swallow a crow. Whole."

Having recovered from his incident with the horse's hoof, the Reverend Monteith laughed, then slapped his neck. His hand came away bloody, and he said: "Thunderation, sir, I fear that was no joke."

Gouedy was leading the way in his wagon, with Emily on Ezekiel behind him, and Stewart and the preacher in the second wagon, laden with their haul from Charlestown.

The men in the wagons laughed as Emily brushed at the gnats hovering in front of her face. She didn't know which she disliked more, those annoying gnats or the bloodsuckers. She could not wait until they had left behind this swampy, dark country and returned to Cane Creek and Ninety Six.

Ten mosquito bites and an hour later, they used the ferry to cross the Peedee River at Long Bluff. The river had risen from recent rains, carrying logs and driftwood that moved like battering rams, but the Dutch men running the ferry knew their trade, and knew the river.

A short while later, they were pulling up in front of Devonald's Tavern at the Welsh Neck.

Owen Devonald sat on the porch, a slave girl standing at his side, her only apparent task to fan her master. The young girl said nothing, did not even look toward the newcomers, just kept waving the homemade contraption of sticks and parchment over the innkeeper, who alternately sipped tea and smoked his pipe.

"Prynhawn da," Devonald said, snapping his fingers to dismiss the thin mulatto. *"Croeso."*

"Speak English, old man!" Gouedy shouted while reining in his wagon. "You no longer reside in Wales, Devonald, but America."

Devonald's hair, once black, had begun to show streaks of gray. He sported high cheek bones and a firm jaw, and his olive skin was shiny with sweat. He wore deerskin pants, a dirty linen smock that came almost to his knees, shoes of soft leather with ties instead of buckles, and a wide-brimmed straw hat, pinned up in the front.

"And a fine America it is, too," Devonald commented, setting his pipe on a tray. In defiance of Gouedy, he repeated his Welsh greeting, then translated. "Good afternoon. Welcome." He pushed himself to his feet as the slave disappeared inside the inn. "You have some people nay I have seen, Breck."

Emily turned in the dun's saddle to watch as her father set the brake before dropping from the driver's box to the ground. The Reverend Monteith climbed down, still moving gingerly from his run-in with Ezekiel two days earlier. He seemed to be hurrying toward her, perhaps to help her dismount, but she surprised him by swinging down easily, almost bumping into him, which caused the Anglican to back away quickly from the animal.

"My daughter, Emily," Stewart told Devonald. "You've met her before, years ago."

"Aye, when she was but a button," he said. "But this is a woman full grown. Who . . . thank the Almighty . . . looks nothing like you."

Emily smiled and curtsied. No matter what her father said, she could act like a lady.

Ignoring Devonald's jibe, Stewart gestured at the pastor. "This is the Reverend Douglas Monteith."

"Monteith, eh?" Devonald said, stepping off the porch. "Presbyterian?"

The minister replied: "Anglican."

"Well, damn my soul to hell." The trader grinned. "I mean, condemn my soul to Hades." He swept off his hat, and bowed at Monteith. "It is a blessing to have a man of your faith in a place like the Welsh Neck."

"I think we have a fair trade, Owen," Gouedy declared, chuckling, "an Anglican itinerant for some Cheraw bacon?"

"How about tossing in that little marsh tacky?" the trader asked.

"You do not have enough sterling to buy that dun, my friend," said Stewart.

Now she knew why her father and Gouedy had agreed to escort the Reverend Monteith to an out-of-the-way place such as the Welsh Neck. It had nothing to do with Christian charity or to protect a newcomer to the American colonies. It was all about trade.

Primarily her father wanted to be able to serve the tasty bacon shipped down from the settlement of Cheraw, almost in North Carolina. No one from the Waxhaws to Charlestown knew how they did it in Cheraw, but, throughout most of the colony, everyone considered Cheraw bacon a delicacy. So after a rum-fueled negotiation, two slaves loaded the heavily salted pig meat, as Emily's father referred to it, onto the wagon, along with flax and two hogsheads of indigo, in exchange for cash and some newspapers Stewart had collected in Charlestown. Bartering completed, they retired inside the Welshman's tavern for catfish stew, corn pone, coffee, or a more potent drink, and conversation.

"Has there been trouble with bandits here along the Peedee?" Gouedy asked.

Devonald spat out what Emily guessed was a Welsh curse. He lifted his mug and downed the grog, slammed the mug on the table, and shook his head. "Squire Wilds was raided a fortnight ago. Says he has only six hogs left. The infernal villains shall reduce the entire Back Country settlers to poverty."

"We met with the new governor in Charlestown," Gouedy said.

"And?"

Gouedy shook his head.

"Emily,"—Stewart cleared his throat—"you have finished your dinner, so why not enjoy the afternoon . . . outside. We shall be along shortly."

Dismissed. Kicked out. Sometimes she was still treated like a kid. Like a girl. But she dared not argue. The Welsh Neck was not that far from Georgetown, and, yellow fever or not, she did not want to risk igniting her father's wrath and finding herself being shipped off to her grandparents.

They left the Reverend Douglas Monteith with Owen Devonald. The minister would preach in the Peedee, make his way to Cheraw, the Waxhaws, into North Carolina and briefly along the Great Wagon Road before journeying back into South Carolina, to the Cowpens, Ninety Six, then down to Pine Tree and perhaps back to Charlestown.

Wishing him luck, and warning him to keep his eye out for stray hoofs, Emily, her father, and Gouedy left the Welsh Neck and turned back toward Pine Tree, and eventually north for home. They would camp that night at the farm of Dogmael Jones just a few miles away. Staying on a Welsh Baptist's farm was a lot cheaper than with Owen Devonald.

Or, at least, that had been their plan.

Dusk approached quickly as they eased the horses and mules into the Joneses clearing. The first thing Emily noticed was the quiet. Then she saw the dog lying on the porch, not moving, appearing dead.

Breck Stewart set the brake, and checked his rifle. Robert Gouedy had already jumped from his wagon, his rifle cocked.

"Dogmael?" he called out. "Dogmael Jones!" No answer. The cabin's lone door was open a crack. "Bethan? Wil!" Gouedy even tried calling to the youngest of the daughters. "Seren?"

Emily bit her lip as she looked around. The door to the chicken coop, now empty except for feathers, had been ripped from its fastenings. Horses had trampled several rows of corn.

"It is Sunday," Stewart said as he climbed off the wagon, "and they are Welsh Baptists. They could have gone to meeting. They. . . ." He stopped. He knew better. "Stay here, Daughter," he said. Then, putting a slight distance between themselves, he and Gouedy began to approach the cabin, their rifles aimed at the open door.

Emily had no intention of going anywhere. She dismounted Ezekiel, and stood, her heart pounding. She found herself praying that the Jones family be at a Baptist meeting, be far, far, far from this place.

Stewart stepped onto the porch, and over the dead dog. Gouedy stood at the steps, his rifle remaining aimed at the door as Stewart pushed it open with the muzzle of his long rifle. He moved to the side, rifle at the ready, turned around, and leaned against the rough-hewn logs, color draining from his face.

By that time, Gouedy had come up the steps and moved inside the cabin.

Emily heard his choked cry.

"Dear God . . . !"

Stepping inside, Stewart lowered his rifle, wiped the sweat from his brow, and called out to his daughter: "Do not come in, Emily! Do not come in here. . . ." And he pulled the door shut behind him.

She moved away from the marsh tacky and toward the span of mules, trying to remember the members of the Jones family

63

alive and happy. She had not visited since returning from her banishment to Georgetown after the Cherokee War. Her father had called Dogmael Jones—"A hard-shell Baptist, as hard as they come."—and he had certainly seemed strict. More so, Emily thought, than the Reverend Monteith. Once, Mr. Jones had told Emily that she could never be baptized because she was not a believer.

"I believe in God," she had snapped back. "And in Jesus."

"You are Presbyterian," he had countered. "Thus saith the Lord."

Bethan Jones was a couple of years younger than Emily, quiet, hardly ever making eye contact with anyone, especially her father. Seren would be maybe ten years old now, Emily wasn't sure. The child had said scarcely a word when Emily and her father had visited here the last time on their way back to Ninety Six. The whole visit she had clutched her older sister's neck. Wil? He was Emily's age, maybe a year or two older, with black hair and dark eyes that always seemed locked on Emily, until she spotted his gaze—then he would quickly turn away, smiling. Their mother had died when Seren was barely a year old. Emily had never known her.

Emily looked back at the cabin, the door still shut, but candlelight now flickering through the cracks in the window's shutter. The sun had settled behind the tops of the pines, and although the heat was still intense, she shivered. Again, she studied the ruined rows of corn, the raided chicken coop, and then her gaze settled on the pigpen. The rails to the pen had been kicked down, and nothing seemed to be left inside but mud, straw, manure, and footprints.

It was then that a snort caught her attention, and she looked past the fields. Two hogs had survived the attack and they were nudging at the ground at the edge of the woods, grunting, pawing, eating. Suddenly snarling, the bigger one charged the other pig, and that animal—which certainly wasn't small—dis-appeared, squealing, into the forest. Satisfied and alone, the hog returned to its meal.

She didn't even realize that she had started walking toward it until she began crossing the furrows of the rows of carrots and potatoes. Stopping, she glanced at the side of the cabin. The hog snarled, and she looked back at the animal. It had stepped away from its supper, baring its teeth, trying to intimidate the intruder. Emily glanced at her hands, realizing that she held the club Mr. Gouedy always carried in the driver's box of his wagon. She didn't remember picking it up.

Armed with a heavy, spiked stick, she found her resolve and moved toward the pig, holding the club with both hands. The hog came toward her, but Emily didn't retreat. By the time she had crossed the last row, she could see the linen petticoat at the side of a felled tree. Next to it was a shoe. The hog had returned to the other side of the downed timber, snorting furiously.

Which is when Emily knew what the pig was eating, what lay on the other side of the timber. Cursing, she charged, sending the big hog scurrying into the woods.

Emily stopped, looked down. The club slipped from her hands, and she spun, falling to her knees, the tears cascading down her face. Turning toward the cabin, she screamed.

CHAPTER SEVEN

They had gathered inside the Jones cabin, these men from the Welsh Neck, including Owen Devonald and Reverend Monteith.

From the loft, Emily couldn't see them. In fact, it took a few minutes before she remembered what had happened. Then a sob caught in her throat, and she turned her head on the soft pillow that already was soaked through with tears. Seren Jones's face came back to her, and she pulled the pillow over her face, wishing it would suffocate her.

Down below, she heard voices.

"What kind of man deflowers a child? And then . . . ?"

"No man." Her father's voice. "But a beast."

"Any sign of the older one . . . what was her name?"

"Bethan." That sounded like Owen Devonald.

"No sign."

"I fear that these vermin have taken her with them." Again Emily recognized her father's voice, but he sounded older and tired.

Another voice. Someone just entering the cabin. "Mister Stewart, what in heaven's name did they do to young Wil?"

Silence.

Emily squeezed her eyes shut, shaking her head. She had prayed, but God had denied her solace. Now she knew what her father and Mr. Gouedy had found inside the cabin.

"They heated a poker in the fire," her father finally answered, "and held it at the poor lad's feet."

"In the Lord Jehovah's name . . . for what reason?"

A few curses followed before her father responded. "My guess would be that they were torturing young Wil so that he would reveal information about any hidden money, jewelry . . . anything of value."

"Dogmael Jones had nothing of value," Owen Devonald said. "He was poorer than William McGee's slaves."

"He had his life." This from the Reverend Douglas Monteith, who no longer sounded like an outsider. His words were firm, harsh, bitter. He had been welcomed to the Back Country. His first service as an Anglican itinerant preacher would be to conduct a funeral.

A funeral for three.

Four, if they found Bethan's body.

The sound of men's shoes clomped up the steps, across the porch and into the cabin. "Curse this new moon." The accent was Irish. "We shall never find the trail. By my reckoning, they have disappeared into the swamps."

"How many men do you guess?" Gouedy asked.

"Ten," a guttural voice grunted. "Twelve."

"Ten or twelve of the basest of all men."

"As Stewart said . . . they are not men."

"Perhaps now the governor will hear our pleas. When a ten-year-old girl is. . . ."

"Silence!" the reverend thundered. "A boy in his teens and a girl even younger lay dead in this home, next to their father. Have you men no decency, no respect for the lives that have been snuffed out by the most wretched lot? Do not speak politics . . . of talking to Governor Montagu. Take off your hat, sir."

Yes, the Back Country had baptized Douglas Monteith.

That's when Emily realized where she was exactly—in the

loft of the Jones cabin, in the bed once shared by Bethan and Seren. Again, she screamed.

Downstairs, sipping rum from a mug held in Owen Devonald's shaking hand, Emily looked up into the faces of the long-haired, bearded Back Country men. Anger replaced embarrassment. She could feel the blood rushing to her head, her ears heating up, and she slammed the tin cup on the table, and snapped: "I am all right. You do not have to stare. Have you not ever seen a girl cry before?"

"Easy, sister." Devonald drank the remainder of the rum himself.

"There is nothing for us to do till dawn," a red-headed Scotsman said. "The bandits have gone, there is no trail, there is nothing. . . ."

"No." A short, swarthy Indian entered the cabin. Long-haired, he wore a hat decorated with glass beads and three feathers, deerskin breechcloth, and moccasins. Tattoos covered his face, his body, and large triangular earrings made from shells hung from his ears. He was Ye Iswa, one of the River People.

Emily had seen Catawba Indians as far north as Ninety Six. They usually brought woven mats or pottery to trade, but this one carried only a bow in his long, muscular arm.

"Did you find them, Blue?" the redhead asked.

Emily saw where the Catawba had gotten his name, for when he turned to face the Scotsman, she saw two blue tattoos of snakes—their heads copper—rising from the back of his breechcloth up to his shoulder blades.

The Indian nodded.

"Where?" Breck Stewart demanded.

She had no idea what the Catawba said, but Devonald understood.

"I think he means Miles Anderson's farm," Devonald said.

The Indian grunted, apparently recognizing the name.

"Where's that?" Stewart asked.

"Just down the river," the innkeeper replied with a vague gesture, "at the confluence with Swift Creek."

"How many men?" the redhead asked the Indian.

The Catawba flashed the fingers of one hand three times. Fifteen.

Someone swore, but Stewart was already heading toward the door. "I shall unhitch our mules. If anyone needs a mount, they can borrow one of my animals. Throw a blanket over its back, if you do not mind riding bareback. Anyone who wishes to stay here . . ."—he stopped to glare at the man who had cursed at the number of bandits—"so be it."

"Wait," Reverend Monteith said.

Stewart turned, looked at the Anglican.

"What of this Anderson? Does he have family?" the preacher asked.

Stewart nodded, and looked at Devonald for the answer.

"Anderson gave up six months ago," he said. "The cursed lot had beaten him. Took his family back to Pennsylvania."

Turning back, Stewart swept out the door, the reverend right behind him. Emily followed, but she paused when she saw the bodies laid out on the porch. They were wrapped in coarse woolen blankets. It was too soon to have built coffins. She hurried past.

"Where are you going, child?" the Scot asked, as he followed Emily to the wagon

"I am not staying here," she said as she began to help her father unhitch the team.

"Stewart," the redhead said, "we are riding after fifteen hardened criminals. I shall not put this child in harm's way."

Stewart stopped working with the harness. Several of the men held torches, and the flickering light shifted Stewart's face from light to shadow, so Emily had trouble seeing him, when he said: "He is right. . . . You should stay here."

"With them?" Her voice cracked. She could not even look back at the porch.

"They cannot bother you," the redhead said, and grinned.

"We cannot spare any man to take her back to the inn," Devonald said. "Nor will I leave one here as a nursemaid."

"I need no nursemaid," Emily snapped. "I live in the Ninety Six District. I live near Cane Creek and the Long Canes. I have already killed. . . ."

"Hush," said her father as he put a hand on her shoulder. She obeyed.

"She is stronger than many men I have seen," the preacher put in, and Breck Stewart concurred.

"She can reload our rifles if such be the need. She rides with us," Stewart announced.

"Breck . . . ," one of the men started to say, but as the torches illuminated the look on Stewart's face, any argument died away.

Two miles from Swift Creek and the Anderson farm, the torches were doused. A mile from the cabin, the riders dismounted their horses, and led them down the marshy trail, ready to stifle any whinny. When they reached the clearing, they stopped.

"They are still there," Devonald whispered.

"Damned fools," someone said.

"They will pay dearly for such cockiness."

Emily could see candlelight through the shutters of the cabin, maybe fifty yards from the trail. Around her came the sounds of flintlocks being primed and cocked. She could smell the sweat of the men, almost taste their fear.

The red-headed Scot, who had introduced himself as Allaway Skeates on the ride over, assumed command.

"Owen, you and the Catawba move to the back of the cabin.

The woods should give you much needed cover. Clarke, pick five men and take on the barn. That is where they will have left their horses. But be careful. These men may be arrogant, but fools they are not. They will have a guard in or near that barn."

"One is posted by the north wall," said a bald man in blue woolen britches and a red linen coat. "He was lighting a pipe, I presume, before he moved out of our view."

"Blue," Skeates told the fierce Catawba, "kill him."

Somewhere in the darkness, the Indian grunted.

"The rest of you men will follow me. We will find cover near the well and the woodpile. Parson, you and Miss Stewart, should stay with the horses and mules. Keep them silent until the shooting begins."

Emily started to protest, but her father had moved beside her, handing her the hackamore to the horse he had ridden.

"You said I would reload," she whispered to him.

"I lied."

"But. . . ."

His voice turned firm when he said: "Have not you seen enough death, Daughter? Stay with the preacher."

The minister said quietly: "Let us gather to pray before we begin our battle."

"No," said Skeates. "Save your breath and your prayers until these swine have paid for their sins."

Emily could hear the men moving through the darkness. Soon, however, the only sounds that she could make out were the swishing of the tails of the horses and mules, and the whispered prayers of Douglas Monteith.

She slid her hand over the marsh tacky's nose, just to do something, and chewed on her lower lip. She heard something else, too—her own voice, barely audible, echoing the Anglican's prayer.

O God, whose name is excellent in all the Earth,
and thy glory above the heavens . . .
. . . give us a mighty deliverance from the open tyranny and
oppression from the cruel and blood-thirsty enemies . . .
. . . We bless and. . . .

A gunshot ended the prayer.

Emily started to move toward the shot, but the minister's hand gripped her shoulder, stopping her, pulling her back. This time, Emily did not resist. More shots followed.

The cabin's door opened, and she thought she saw the shadow of a man—nothing more than a silhouette framed by the doorway—start out onto the porch, stagger, and fall back inside. At that point, someone inside must have blown out the candle, because then there was nothing but darkness, except for the flashes from muskets, rifles, and pistols.

Between the echoes of the shots came curses from both inside and outside the cabin. An Indian whooped once. A man screamed. The mules and horses began pulling hard on their tethers.

"Reverend," Emily said, turning to try and see through the dark, "get a good hold of the mules. It's a long walk back to the tavern." Then she turned back, still holding the hackamores to four horses, including Ezekiel. Sucking in a deep breath, she dropped to her knees, and watched.

Five minutes passed, the shooting ceased, its echoes trailing off in the woods. Emily rose, stroking the nearest horse, glancing behind her to make sure the preacher was still there. She couldn't see him, but she could hear him saying something to calm one of the mules.

Then came a loud voice from inside the cabin: "What is the meaning of this outrageous act? What sort of ruffians are you to ambush . . . mere wayfarers bound for Georgetown?"

"Ask Dogmael Jones and his family!" Skeates called back.

"You damned fiends from hell!"

"We know nothing of what you speak."

"The hell you don't! We followed your tracks. Surrender or die!"

"We know no man named Jones. We are strangers. Our home is Wilmington in His Majesty's colony of North Carolina."

"You are a liar and a scoundrel!"

Several minutes of silence passed.

Then: "We are thirsty. That is why we stopped here."

"If you do not toss down your firearms and come out of that cabin, we will give you much to drink. Coal oil . . . poured down the chimney."

"Barbarians!"

"We left our mercy at Dogmael Jones's home, and we are not barbarians. We are . . ."—Skeates paused to think of a proper response—"we are . . . regulators."

"Balderdash!"

"Come out or take your medicine, which shall prepare you for the fires of hell."

During the next block of silence, Emily moved away from the horses and over to the edge of the trail, where she tried to see up ahead through the blackness and into the cabin. She thought she knew what was going on inside, though. The men would be dousing the fire in the fireplace, moving the ashes or anything hot as far away from the opening as possible. Well, at least that's what she would be doing if someone had threatened to pour coal oil down her chimney.

Footfalls came from behind her, but she didn't turn, knowing it was the reverend.

"Miss Stewart," he said, "I do not recall seeing any buckets of coal oil with us."

She answered grimly: "That's because nobody brought any."

Several seconds ticked past before the Reverend Monteith

chuckled. "Ah . . . I see. . . ."

Emily shook her head in disgust.

"What will happen next?" the preacher asked.

"I doubt if anything will happen before dawn," she said with a shrug.

So they waited. Emily spent the rest of the night staring at the cabin, the shadows, looking for her father, praying that he was and would remain unharmed.

Shortly after sunrise, the outlaws surrendered after Skeates assured them they would be transported to Charlestown where they would be turned over to the colonial authorities.

Five of the outlaws had been killed—three of them sentries caught outside the cabin, and two on the inside, who were carried out and dropped without ceremony onto the dirt. Two of the prisoners had suffered minor musket wounds. None of the regulators, as the Scot had named them, had been injured, although two of the horses had bolted away during the fight.

"A sorry lot," Breck Stewart told Owen Devonald as the guards bound the prisoners' hands with rawhide cords.

"Aye," Devonald agreed as he put his pipe between his lips, studying the murderers.

Rags passed as clothing on these men. Two were Indians and three were Negros. Runaway slaves, most likely, although the three men refused to say anything, refused even to lift their gaze from the ground. The leader of the group wore an eye patch and an earring. A man with a pirate's beard laughed, but Emily knew this performance was nothing but a façade. He looked petrified.

"Where is the girl?" Devonald demanded.

Tilting his head, the bearded man jutted a firm jaw toward Emily, who had joined her father, Monteith, and Devonald. "Why there she is, sir. And a right fetching creature she is."

The innkeeper slapped him hard across the check. "Damn your insolence, swine. I mean Bethan Jones."

"I do not know that name."

Another slap, but the man merely shrugged.

She could be anywhere, Emily thought to herself. *Dumped into the swamps. Buried beneath pine straw. Sunk into the creek or Peedee River. Or, the men could be telling the truth. They could be innocent travelers.* But Emily doubted that. She sighed. *Poor Bethan Jones. Likely she's dead, to be denied a Christian burial, denied the chance to rest for eternity with her family.*

Allaway Skeates came over toward Emily, her father, the reverend, and Devonald.

"I thank you for your help, sir," he said, and held out his hand toward Stewart.

"It was my duty, sir."

"Mayhap this will convince the Assembly and the governor that what we claim is happening away from the tidewater is not the mere delusions of frightened settlers."

"Mayhap it will."

Emily detected little certitude in her father's voice.

Skeates picked up on Stewart's doubt. "Well, sir, we cannot just string them up from the highest limbs."

"Can't we?" Devonald said.

Monteith cleared his throat.

"Preacher," the innkeeper said, "do not tax yourself, sir. We gave these scoundrels our word that we would take them to Charlestown and that is Allaway's task."

Stewart shook the Scot's hand. "Fare thee well, sir."

"Thank you, Mister Stewart," Skeates said, then turned and bowed at Emily. "And thank you, girl." Then to the parson: "Thank you, sir. Both of you showed grit."

An hour later, Skeates led his guards and the prisoners down the trail, bound for Charlestown. For those that remained behind was left the job of burying the dead here before returning to Dogmael Jones's cabin.

For a proper funeral.

Chapter Eight

Summer passed with a welcomed monotony for Emily. She spent most of her days helping her mother with chores, picking vegetables in the garden, cooking, cleaning, and grooming the two marsh tacky horses. Rarely did she walk down the Cherokee Path, and never alone. She found herself spending more time with Elizabeth, doting on her younger sister, even playing dolls with her—and Emily loathed playing dolls. After a few months, Emily stopped seeing the pale, dead face of Seren Jones whenever she looked at Elizabeth, and those nightmares that jerked her wide awake and in a cold sweat became rarer as the days shortened and the nights turned chillier.

Autumn also seemed to cool the temperatures of the men, including her father's and her brother Donnan's. The fall arrived early, as both the long hunters and Cherokees had predicted. The bandits terrorizing the countryside lessened their raids, so eventually life returned to normal around Ninety Six.

She sat at a table outside the tavern with her mother, cleaning the last of the carrots from the garden, while Elizabeth and Alan played together nearby.

"Joseph Robinson is visiting today," her mother said absently.

Emily scraped dirt off a crooked carrot, and shook her head. "If Da' will let him in. . . ." She stopped herself from slicing off the tip of a forefinger, realization almost knocking her off the bench. "What for?"

Without looking up from her bowl, Machara Stewart

shrugged, but Emily saw the smile on her mother's face.

"Da' hates that cur," Emily said.

This time her mother looked up. "Your father hates no one. They might not agree on everything, your father and Joseph, but. . . ."

"Joseph! When did you become so familiar with that pompous Virginian?"

Her mother removed the bowl from her lap, and set it on the table. "He brings business," she said sharply, "to this tavern."

"Too much business."

"Now . . . Emily."

"Joseph Robinson is such a gilly-gaupus." Actually he was more of a king-loving son-of-a-bitch than just an awkward jerk. Emily, however, refrained from telling her mother all of that. She stood, the heat rising in her face, and turned. Alan and Elizabeth looked up from the ground, a lead soldier in Alan's hand and Elizabeth's mouth hanging open. Their eyes locked on Emily, and she quickly looked back at her mother.

"I do not like Joseph Robinson," she said.

Machara grinned. "Truth be told, Emily, I did not think much of your father when he first called on me."

Whirling, Emily looked for some way to escape. The fishing poles leaned against the house, left yesterday by Donnan and two of his friends. No bait bucket, but she knew where to find earthworms. She tossed her knife onto the table, and went straight to the wall, grabbing all three poles and marching back toward her young siblings.

"Let us go," she told Alan and Elizabeth.

"Where?" Elizabeth said, but Alan dropped the toy and leaped to his feet. "Fishing?" he yelled.

"Yes." She did not dare look at her mother, for Emily knew she would be sitting there, smugly grinning. "We are going fishing, Mum."

All her mother said was: "Have fun. But be back in time for supper."

They would never catch any fish, not the way Alan kept slapping the tip of his pole into Cane Creek, but Emily didn't care. She sat on the bank, keeping an eye on Elizabeth, who had about as much interest in fishing as Emily herself.

Of course, she had barely gotten half a mile from the settlement before she realized exactly where she was going. To Cane Creek. Which would carry her almost directly to the Robinson farm, but she was too stubborn to turn around and go somewhere else. Besides, she kept telling herself, it would turn out to be a great joke that while Joseph Robinson was drinking gin at Cormorant's Rock, wondering where Emily Stewart was, she would be sitting on the bank of Cane Creek barely a mile from his farm.

"Who is that?" said Elizabeth.

Quickly Emily reached underneath her apron, feeling for the ivory grips. Ever since that summer, she had carried the gold-finished pocket pistol whenever she left Ninety Six. She felt only some relief when she saw who it was. She stood, trying to swallow, but her throat had turned to sand. She let go of the pistol, and brushed the bangs off her forehead.

"It is he who saved you," Elizabeth said.

"Yes," Emily said as she watched Go-la-nv Pinetree paddle his canoe toward the bank.

She seemed rooted to the ground, just watching as the giant dugout canoe glided across the water until it brushed up against the bank. Elizabeth had dropped her pole and moved behind Emily, clutching the folds of her skirt. Alan stood unmoving, mouth open as Pinetree climbed out of the canoe.

"*Osiyo,*" he said, but no one responded to his greeting.

He cocked his head, and Emily tried to find her voice, but

couldn't. From behind her, Elizabeth whispered: "Hello."

Pinetree nodded. "Good. You can talk." He had switched to English.

"I can talk, too!" Alan snapped.

Emily just bowed.

Pinetree wore a cotton shirt, deerskin leggings, moccasins, a beaded belt, and a blanket over his shoulder. Earrings covered the rims of both ears, and two feathers were tied at the crown of his head. She smelled bear grease on him, probably coming from the canoe to keep the vessel watertight.

Pinetree turned to Alan. "Fish biting?"

"No. I think they're asleep."

Emily thought: *How can they sleep with as much noise as you've been making, Brother?*

"H-m-m. Sometimes, my people poison the water and scoop up the fish when they rise to the top."

Emily was surprised, never having heard Pinetree mutter much more than a few syllables fluently. In fact, he seemed far more capable of speech than she at this minute.

Alan made a face. "You eat poisoned fish?"

Go-la-nv Pinetree shrugged.

"I am hungry," whined Elizabeth, still hiding behind Emily's skirt.

Pinetree pointed to his canoe. "In that pouch you will find chestnuts and sunflower seeds." He looked back at Emily. "It is not much."

Alan was already climbing into the big canoe, grabbing the pouch, and filling his mouth with nuts before he was back on solid land. He walked right past Go-la-nv Pinetree and brought the leather pouch to his baby sister, holding it open for her.

"Have you forgotten your manners, Alan Stewart?" Emily said, proving that she could speak.

"No, ma'am," Alan said, spraying the remnants of seed and

chestnuts out of his mouth and on to Emily's skirt.

She cut loose with a string of profanity. Then she was on her knees, pulling her brother and sister close, telling them how sorry she was, that she hadn't meant what she said, and begging them to please stop crying.

"Alan," said Go-la-nv Pinetree.

Emily watched as her brother slipped away from her and turned toward the young Indian.

"Have you ever shot a Cherokee blowgun?"

Alan's head shook.

Pinetree smiled. "Would you like to?"

"Can I?" Alan asked, wiping away the tears and sniffing.

The Cherokee gestured toward Emily, who said: "Of course."

Then Elizabeth backed away from Emily, and said: "Can I shoot that gun, too?"

Later, Emily lay on the leaves, head cradled in her hands, staring at the trees, the blue sky, but mostly at Go-la-nv Pinetree, who leaned against an elm tree, carving what appeared to be a flute for Elizabeth and Alan. Her two siblings were back fishing, laughing, and this time Alan wasn't beating the water with his pole.

"You should return home," Pinetree said without looking up.

She sighed.

"You should not have come here alone. It is dangerous," he said.

Then he tested the flute. It made a pretty sound, Emily thought, though her brother and sister could not hear it because of their laughter.

"And I do not think you will catch any fish today."

Smiling, she pushed herself into a seated position. "What does Go-la-nv mean?" she asked.

He tested the flute again, then dropped it by his side.

"Raven." He pointed at the trees, probably to the nest she had seen.

"I know what a raven is," she said.

His head shook. "You have a temper."

"You do not want to see me angry. You. . . ." She turned away, remembering that summer day in the forest. Biting her lip, she tried to shake away that image of Blubber Cheeks with his head split open. She found herself starting to breathe hard, those memories coming back in a full assault. Running through the forest. Eye Patch and the Indian. Then that evening down on the Welsh Neck, and finding. . . .

I will not cry. Emily squeezed her eyes shut, and when she opened them again, Go-la-nv Pinetree was kneeling beside her.

His eyes looked like midnight, but she found a softness in them, concern. He was so close to her, it unnerved her, and she started shifting away from him, realizing almost at the same moment that he was inching away from her.

She stopped. He stopped. They stared at each other.

"What . . . ?" Emily wasn't sure where to begin, or even what she wanted to say. "That day . . . last summer . . . in the woods . . . when. . . ."

"You should not think of such things," he said.

Her head shook. "What were you doing?"

His head tilted, mouth slightly open. He muttered something in Cherokee, then said: "I do not know what you mean."

"What were you doing?" she repeated. "In the woods?"

"Hunting," he said.

"That close to Ninety Six?"

The softness drained from his eyes, replaced with an intensity that frightened her. "I was not with those men," he said.

"I never thought you were," she said. She looked past him, remembering to keep an eye on Alan and Elizabeth, but they were preoccupied, trying to splash all the water out of Cane

Creek into Go-la-nv Pinetree's canoe.

"I was . . . hunting," he repeated.

Hunting? She tried to hold his eyes, but she had to look away. *Hunting? That close to the settlements? Where most of the game had already been trapped out or run off? There are birds about, maybe a brave squirrel or rabbit, but . . . no, a Cherokee would not be hunting game. Not there.*

He stared at her.

"And what brings you here today?" Emily asked.

He looked up at the crow's nest in the tree, wet his lips, and seemed to shiver before he looked back at her. This time it was Go-la-nv Pinetree who looked away.

She felt weak, and did not like the feeling. She remembered, a year or two ago, when Rachel Rowe had told her: "You are the strongest girl I have ever known. Stronger than any woman in Keowee, I would allow."

Cherokee women were always strong.

"I . . . ," she began, but he held up his hand, and she stopped herself from saying anything else.

"You should go now," he said. "Before it gets too late."

He picked up the flute, tossed it to her, and moved toward his canoe. He got in without speaking to Alan and Elizabeth, who had stopped what they were doing to stare at him as he picked up a paddle.

"Damn," he said in English. "Hell. Son-of-a-bitch."

"Mother threatens to wash Emily's mouth out with soap when she says those words," Elizabeth told him.

"She says them all the time, too," Alan added.

Go-la-nv Pinetree crawled back out of the canoe, this time bringing his bow and quiver of arrows with him. "I cannot leave you alone. It grows late," he said. "I will make sure you get home safely."

Emily showed him the ivory-handled pistol. "I can look out for us."

"This I know."

"She's meaner than a witch," Alan said.

"No." Go-la-nv Pinetree ran his long fingers through the boy's hair. "You have a fine sister. Brave. Very brave. She takes care of you." He pointed to the trail. "We go."

The sun was sinking by the time they reached the settlement. Three horses were hobbled out front of the tavern. Emily could hear laughter and someone playing a Jew's harp inside. She found herself studying the horses, the saddles, trying to remember just what kind of horses Joseph Robinson owned. Several rods from the tavern, Go-la-nv Pinetree stopped.

"I go now," he said.

"Thanks for the flute," Elizabeth said.

"And for the nuts," Alan added.

His face was a mask now. He nodded at the kids, then turned to Emily. Neither said anything. He walked away.

"I'm hungry," Alan said.

"Those nuts didn't fill my tummy," Elizabeth said.

Emily didn't respond. She kept watching Go-la-nv Pinetree until he turned around the bend, and disappeared. Then a sigh escaped, and, full of dread, she turned around to steer her brother and sister toward Cormorant's Rock.

"Da' likes him," Emily said.

Donnan grunted, and said: "For the deerskins he brings. For the food. And the drink he taught Da' how to make."

She knew that drink, made up of cross vine, China brier, and sassafras roots boiled together for some Cherokee medicine. "Purifies the blood," her father would say, smacking his lips after drinking. When Emily had tasted it, she deemed it even worse than some of the beverages her father had concocted to sell to wayfarers.

Emily said: "You forget. . . ."

"You forget," Donnan interrupted, "that he's a Cherokee. And you are white. And you don't remember that damned war, because Da' sent you away. You weren't here. You didn't almost die in that damnable stockade."

His words silenced her, and she knew she never should have broached the subject of Go-la-nv Pinetree with her brother.

"I hate the sons-of-bitches," he said, sounding like James Middleton.

She didn't want to believe that, but she couldn't help thinking of Donnan at the old stockade near Robert Gouedy's post. Or the way Donnan looked at any Indian, Catawba or Cherokee, who came to the tavern or anywhere near Ninety Six. She remembered the day she had walked down the trail to the Cherokee Path with Donnan and Pinetree, the afternoon after the *incident* last summer. He had gone to protect her from Pinetree.

"He saved my life," she reminded Donnan now.

He nodded. "And, as you were so apt to remind me, you saved his."

Even in the darkness, Donnan's eyes frightened her. They were filled with hate and distrust. Donnan hated Indians, and did not trust his sister.

Having cleaned the hoofs of Ezekiel and Nutmeg, Emily came from the stables to find her mother, as usual, slaving over the winter kitchen. It had turned too cool to cook outside any more.

"Emily," Machara Stewart said, her voice hoarse. "Thank the Lord you are home. Quick, do me a kindness, please, and take those . . ."—she pointed to a tray—"to that fine English gentleman . . . at the table next to the main door." She continued to dish up more bowls, but not before shooting a glance at her youngest children coming in through the door. "Go wash. Now! Don't set foot in this kitchen until you have cleaned the mud off your hands and the leaves out of your hair."

No mention of Joseph Robinson. Emily had not heard of or seen the arrogant bastard in a week. Emily thought that a good sign. She hurried to the tray, picked it up, and backed out of the door to a cacophony of voices and raucous laughter coming from the tavern. She heard her father's voice, the clinking of pewter steins and clay mugs. She smelled tobacco and rum.

When she turned to find "the fine English gentleman", the tray slipped from her hands, crashing to the floor when she saw Reverend Douglas Monteith.

CHAPTER NINE

"I dare say that the floor was not as famished as am I." Leaning his head back, the Reverend Monteith laughed heartily.

The tavern had grown quiet right after the mishap, but now the dozen or more men inside echoed the laughter of the preacher. Emily found the rag her father rarely used to wipe the bar, and busied herself on hands and knees, mopping up the mess. At least the bowls had not broken.

"Well, Stewart," someone said, "looks like that girl of yours is a scullery maid, after all."

"She shall make someone a fine wife," another man commented.

"Not me. That girl scares the bitter hell out of me."

"Cease your raillery," the parson barked, no longer laughing. "We do not make vulgar comments about ladies in a tavern. Or anywhere, for that matter."

Emily stopped scrubbing long enough to look at Monteith, who had slid off the stool to challenge those who had spoken so rudely, at least according to the Anglican's delicate ears and sensibilities. She started to say something, but the door to the kitchen swung open, and Emily's mother muttered: "Oh, goodness." Quickly Emily returned to scrubbing the floor, and her mother joined her in a few minutes with a mop.

More men flocked into Cormorant's Rock that evening. Word must have spread quickly that the parson had arrived. As Emily busily served her father's alcoholic concoctions or just straight rum or gin, she wondered what Reverend Monteith, staunch Anglican, would think of Ninety Six.

Then Joseph Robinson arrived, but, to Emily's relief, he found a place at the bar, so it was her father who served him. But she noted that he scarcely chanced a glance in her direction as she moved from table to table, bringing stew and bread and libations.

Mostly the men listened and laughed at Monteith's stories of his travels and travails across the Back Country of the two Carolina colonies.

"Reveling and whoring. Drinking and fighting." The Reverend Monteith shook his head. "Throughout this wilderness, I have been shocked to learn that most of those who reside in this Back Country have abandoned their morals. They are rude and ignorant, and many mocked my sermons and service. They encourage vice and idleness. It is shocking, I say, just shocking. In some of these hamlets, I refused to even hold service for fear that they would embarrass the Lord as so many are void of good manners and Christianity."

"Aye," Donnan Stewart said with a chuckle. "I have heard tell that God fears to even show his face in North Carolina."

"Watch your blasphemy, young man," the preacher said, and Emily grinned. It was high time someone put her big brother in his place. "I do not speak solely of the colony to our north. South Carolina is full of men . . . white men no less . . . who act as though they have never heard the Common Prayer, not even an Episcopal prayer. Baptism is foreign to their thinking. I have traveled to settlements totally lacking any genteel person. No good breeding, and many children born out of wedlock."

Returning to the kitchen, Emily almost ran into a man just entering through the door.

Emily started to apologize, but the man, a stranger, swept off his wide-brimmed hat of black wool, and bowed. "My apologies, madam," he said. "I did not see you."

"Nor I you." But she saw him now. Thin, dark hair—no wig—and even darker eyes. Tall, full lips, a Roman nose. He was not attired in buckskins or homespun, but rather bleached trousers that came down to the ankles of his black boots, with a linen shirt, and a pleated white stock fit snugly around his neck. The shirt was topped by a sleeveless green waistcoat of fine silk, as well as a red silk coat with mother of pearl buttons, which hung to his knees. He carried a black walking stick in his left hand. Emily had not seen a man dressed in such resplendence since Charlestown. He returned the hat to his head, his black eyes beginning to twinkle.

"I seem to have found the most popular inn in town," he said above the myriad voices and laughs.

"It is the only inn in town. Will you be staying overnight, sir?"

"No. Alas, bound for the Cowpens am I, thus I have time only for ale and supper." He took her hand, brought it to his lips, and kissed it. She almost jerked the hand away, but couldn't, his eyes were that hypnotic. "Had I known I would find such loveliness here, I would not have made other arrangements." He glanced around, releasing Emily's hand, which she held there for the longest time before she realized she was acting like a damned fool. "But I dare say that procuring a seat might be next to impossible."

"We shall find you one, sir," she said, and spun around, guiding him to a small table with one chair in the distant corner.

"Is this place always bustling with such activity?" the stranger asked.

"Hardly." She pointed over cocked heads and animal-fur hats. "Do you see that gentleman at the bar?"

"Aye."

"He's a minister of the Word. An Anglican itinerant. Just got to Ninety Six today."

"A preacher?" The man chuckled. "Here?"

"Yes, sir. The Lord has come to Cane Creek."

He laughed, and then ordered rum and shepherd's pie.

Emily forgot about the other customers. Local people could wait, she figured, but a gentleman like that should get priority. Before she left the kitchen with his supper, however, she found herself wiping the sweat off her forehead and cheeks, combing her hair with her fingers, then running a corner of a napkin over her teeth.

"Goodness gracious, child!" she heard her mother call out. "Do not keep everyone waiting. Unless . . . is Joseph Robinson out there?"

She didn't answer, but hurried to bring the newcomer his food and drink.

"Your parson has a singular wit," the man said as she set down the bowl.

"He's not my parson," she said. "He's Anglican. We are Presbyterian."

"I am a backslider myself," he said, dropping a napkin to his lap.

She laughed. "You are one to talk about wit, sir."

"Not *sir*," he said. "My name is Finnian Kilduff."

Irish . . . but little left of a brogue, Emily thought. *In fact, he sounds like most of the men of the Back Country.* Aloud she said: "Well, sir, welcome to Ninety Six, Mister Kilduff."

He took her hand again, but did not kiss it. "I told you no *sir* . . . and certainly not *mister.* Call me Finnian."

"I do not think I ought to."

"And why not?"

"We have just met."

"But I hope this will not be our last encounter."

She blushed. Hated herself for it, but, by Jehovah, this man was certainly better-looking and more refined than Joseph Robinson. Or anyone else she had ever seen in Ninety Six. Better-looking than even Go-la-nv Pinetree.

"If you need anything . . ."—she didn't quite know how to address him—"you just yell for me. Even over all this ruction, I shall hear you."

"Thank you . . . ?" He drew out the question, waiting for her name.

"My name is Stewart," she said. "Emily Stewart. You can call me Emily, but I would not do that around my da'."

He lifted himself up, scanning the crowd in the tavern.

"And your father is?"

"That big man." She pointed behind the bar. "He owns the place. Breck Stewart is his name."

"I shall have to pay him my compliments."

"That and sterling would be fine," she said.

He laughed, which she enjoyed hearing. Then he said: "You have a fine wit yourself . . . Emily."

The tavern had cleared. Most of the customers had returned to their homes after grog and supper. She did not know where exactly Finnian Kilduff had gone, or even when he had left, though he had left far too much money for the liquor and meal, but the Cowpens was a long way from Ninety Six. Still, her father had always told her that in the Back Country, one did not ask a stranger's name, where he was from, or where he was going.

Machara Stewart was preparing the batter for the morrow's breakfast, and Alan and Elizabeth were upstairs, already asleep. Emily washed the dishes, listening through the open door at the conversation between the parson, her father, and Donnan.

"The people are not all bad, Reverend," Breck Stewart said.

"I hope that is the case. I have been riding the environs feeling that the Word of God has been lost."

"We lack two things in this district," Stewart said. "Law and a preacher. You have seen how lawless this region can be. The King and the governor ignore our requests."

When even her mother sighed, Emily could not stop a grin. Monteith was about to learn what a mistake he had made for yielding the floor to Breck Stewart.

"We have begged and pleaded for courts, for a militia, but to no avail. And as far as the Word of God is concerned, why, sir, it is just that we rarely have a preacher coming through. There are good citizens here, sir. Good, God-fearing men and women. It is not that they shun the Word, shun the Lord's Commandments. It is not that they desire to live in sin, but there is no one here to marry them, although I know of at least two who journeyed to North Carolina, where they were married by a magistrate."

"Which is contrary to the laws of Parliament and to the eyes of God," Monteith slipped in. "Marriage is a religious ceremony."

"Be that as it may, we welcome you, Reverend, to Ninety Six. How long shall you stay with us?"

Emily stiffened. *The parson is staying here? Upstairs?*

"If there are enough who would like to hear the Word, then I may stay through the winter. My legs and hindquarters are stiff from riding."

Until spring? Emily let out a heavy sigh, thinking she would have to watch her language for a long time.

"I wonder how many weddings the parson can officiate between now and spring," her mother said.

Emily began drying her hands as she looked at her mother. Machara Stewart grinned.

Beyond watching her language, Emily would have to watch

out for her scheming parents—and that poltroon, Joseph Robinson.

"Are there Anglicans in this settlement?" she heard Monteith ask, and held her breath for his answer.

"As you know, we are Presbyterians," her father said. "Most of the people here are likely Scots and Irish. I'd think. . . ."

When Stewart stopped to consider his answer, Donnan jumped in: "It is a medley of denominations and sects, Pastor." He didn't even sound sarcastic.

Monteith sniggered. "I have grown quite accustomed to preaching to such a diverse lot . . . when I have located those who would listen."

Something slammed against the table, causing both Emily and her mother to jump. "You shall find them here, Parson!" Her father must have slammed his fist on the table. "You shall preach your sermon here."

"Here? In . . . ?"

"Here, Parson. In Cormorant's Rock. Do not think of this tavern as a den of iniquity, sir. It is the meeting place of the white settlers of Ninety Six. I cannot speak for other settlements, but here in Ninety Six you will find a people who love the Lord and who desire a discourse."

And a people who desire grog, Emily thought, *their bumbo, and persico. And you will find a number of women who live in a state of concubinage. You will find. . . .*

"And what of the lawless element?" the reverend asked, breaking into her thoughts.

"They have slackened the raids with the changing of the season," Donnan answered.

"For the time being," Breck Stewart added. "Usually they cease such criminal activity till spring and summer, when there are crops to steal and when the horses are well-fed."

"Or perhaps they learned their lesson from what Da' and the

men of the Welsh Neck did this summer," Donnan said. "Perhaps the law has finally reached out from Charlestown to the Back Country."

"Then you have not heard?" Monteith's tone had changed. Emily ascertained a note of dread in his voice.

"Heard what?" Stewart asked.

She followed her mother out of the kitchen, through the door, into the dimly lit tavern. Donnan was lowering his stein of kill-devil, and Stewart had moved away from the rows of jugs he had been refilling. All eyes stared upon the minister, who sat at the bar, a cup of steaming tea in front of his limp hands.

Monteith's eyes looked over to Emily and Machara, then turned back to Donnan, and lastly to Breck Stewart.

"Heard what?" her father repeated.

Sighing heavily, the preacher drew his hands off the bar and wet his lips.

"What . . . did Devonald hang those curs?" Donnan said with a laugh.

"No." Monteith could barely be heard. He cleared his throat and said again: "No." Then: "The prisoners were taken to Charlestown and jailed. But I learned at Black Swamp that this new governor, Lord Charles Montagu, he pardoned five of the scoundrels."

"Pardoned?" Stewart's voice seemed to shake the thick timbered walls.

"This dealer of chattel had recently returned from Charlestown," Monteith continued, "and he said that Montagu pardoned five men."

"Pardoned?" Stewart repeated the word, his face masked with rage, his fingers tightened into fists, shaking, his knuckles turning white.

"Six were convicted. Five from the Welsh Neck and another from Lynches Creek."

"But the governor turned five loose?" Donnan said, sounding even angrier than his father, and he had not been along when they had gone to the Welsh Neck. He had not seen what those dirty dogs had done to the Jones family.

"Aye." The minister's head shook. "For good order and harmony of the colony. So said the governor."

"This trader must have been mistaken," Donnan said.

Monteith shook his head again. "No. He had returned with a newspaper, which he allowed me to read. The *South Carolina Gazette* reported the news and what the governor had said."

"For good order and harmony of the colony," Breck Stewart said, and let out a mirthless laugh.

CHAPTER TEN

The leaves turned gold and red, then brown, and it wasn't long before they left the limbs and blew away. Skies became gray and gloomy, and soon after the pigs were slaughtered and salted, the wind delivered a bitter bite.

Winter settled over the Ninety Six District. It came like most winters since the Cherokee War, slowly, dully, as monotonously as the sounds of the axes of Breck and Donnan Stewart splitting firewood, only it arrived early. Snow rarely fell in this part of Carolina, although ice storms did come, snapping branches off trees, and leaving many settlers nursing broken bones from slipping on the thick ice that coated the ground. Yet the winter of 1766-67 would not pass as routinely as past winters. An icy grip took hold of the wilderness in the Carolina Back Country as it did across the northern hemisphere.

When news finally arrived from Charlestown, the Stewarts would learn that the astoundingly high cost of bread had led to many riots across England—that when the River Annan's ice broke, floods swept away cattle, corn, and even homes in Scotland—that the Rhine River froze so hard that wagons crossed over it between Deutz and Cologne.

In a letter written on Christmas Day but not reaching Ninety Six until February 13th, Breck Stewart's father, William, noted that the yellow fever outbreak had passed, that the Stewarts were in fine health and spirits, but that the temperature had dropped to forty-five degrees in Georgetown, and that he and his wife just did not know when it would ever warm up.

In Charlestown, residents of the colonial capital warmed themselves by laughing to David Douglass's American Company of Comedians at the new theater on Queen Street.

In Ninety Six, they froze. Forty-five degrees would have felt like summer. Ice and snow fell. The wind rarely let up.

Every morning, while Stewart and Donnan split wood, gathered kindling, and kept the fires going, Emily and her mother would venture to the barn to break the ice so that the cow, mules, and horses could drink. Hauling water from the well left them shivering out of control.

Alan and Elizabeth were not allowed to play in the snow, or even leave the porch. The Reverend Douglas Monteith blessed the food, even as the portions grew smaller and smaller. Emily swept ice out from the tavern.

She did not see Go-la-nv Pinetree that winter, but often thought of him, worried over him, actually, even though Cherokees had lived in this country long before any Europeans had arrived. Go-la-nv would be all right. Indians rarely traveled or traded during the winter. Nor did white men in the Back Country. People did not move in this country during the cold months.

"It is a fine thing you did not journey to Charlestown or even to Pine Tree," Stewart told the preacher one morning. "To be caught in such weather as this could be fatal."

"So is staying in a cabin for such a damnable eternity of boredom," Donnan said. It was not yet noon, and already he had sweetened his porridge with rum.

Stewart and Monteith pretended not to hear.

Emily, however, stared at her smart-mouthed brother until he looked away, mumbling what might have been an apology.

She rarely saw James Robinson, either, for which she thanked God and the weather. Robinson's place on Cane Creek lay only seven miles from the tavern, which might as well have been seventy miles when the temperature fell to seventeen degrees and gray clouds, threatening snow or sleet, darkened the skies. When Robinson did venture into Cormorant's Rock, he usually found himself arguing with Stewart or Donnan about the Stamp Act protests, the King's wisdom, or even Monteith's sermon the previous Sunday. Eventually Machara stopped thinking of the fool as a worthy suitor for a daughter, even if she was doomed to spinsterhood.

Emily often thought of Finnian Kilduff and his fine clothes and hypnotic eyes. She even dreamed of him twice, and woke up feeling ashamed and thinking she might need to confess her sins to Douglas Monteith. Other times, she wondered if Finnian Kilduff actually existed. No one else seemed to recall him from his sole appearance in the tavern. No one had seen him. Mayhap he had been an apparition, but then she would recall the sterling he had left on the table or how he had pressed his lips to her hand, and she would still feel that gentlemanly kiss.

In early December, the man in buckskins, his wife, and their illegitimate son arrived at the tavern, requesting that the Reverend Monteith marry them. The man's name was Jonathan Conley. His wife was Betsy. Their son was George. They were dirt poor, dressed like the slaves Emily had seen at the Gouedy place with their woolen rags and moth-eaten, frayed coats, all much too thin for this kind of winter.

Stewart had to stand in as the best man, and Emily as maid of honor. The only other witnesses were the rest of the Stewart family. As soon as the bride had been kissed, and the groom given a free mug of bumbo, and the couple toasted by the preacher, the newlyweds left for their home on Cane Creek, not daring to stay longer and risk being caught in a winter storm. So Cormorant's Rock turned dull again—till Sunday.

Typically the coldest nights fell in January and February, but

December turned bitter that year. Six inches of snow coated a thick layer of ice on December 15th as Ninety Six prepared for Christmas.

"I miss the fox hunts," Monteith said on Christmas Eve.

"Fox hunts?" Emily asked.

"Yes, Emily." He sighed thoughtfully. "Balls and all sorts of wonderful entertainments. That is what I remember most about Hertfordshire when I was your age. Not that I was allowed to go dancing, or fox hunting, or to drink porter or ale, but I would stare with envy as my mum and father left. When I was finally old enough to go . . . oh, the wonders. The thrill of the hounds chasing the fox, and we riding after them."

"In Williamsburg," said James Middleton, who had dropped in the tavern for hot cider and stew, "I would walk past the shops to see what the storekeepers were saying one should buy for a gift."

"A gift?" Donnan swung around in his chair. "For Christmas?"

"Indeed." Middleton laughed. "I know, I know, we were a strange family, exchanging gifts on the day of our Savior's birth."

As there was no church in Ninety Six—although Robert Gouedy had suggested a meeting house be built come spring or summer—Cormorant's Rock had been decorated with winter berries and garlands of evergreens. The largest and best-looking pine cones, which had been decorated, adorned the bar.

Outside might be gloomy, but a brightness filled the tavern, even if the conversation that afternoon sounded, at least to Emily, like a dirge.

"My mother would hand me wonderfully illustrated Christmas paper with joyous borders," Monteith said, "and I would write to my grandparents, bidding them good tidings and wishing them a lovely Christmas."

"Twelfth Night," Middleton said. "From Christmas Eve to

the Sixth of January. That was my favorite time in Virginia. Everyone forgot their woes. . . ."

Emily looked at the parson, whose eyes seemed aglow from his fond memories of Hertfordshire, of civilization. He seemed more like one of them tonight. So did Middleton. Even Donnan seemed friendlier.

She blamed it on the winter.

Fox hunts and Christmas gifts. Twelfth Night and balls. These things sounded so foreign to Emily. Her father explained that these were customs in the Northern colonies such as Pennsylvania and Virginia, but not down south. In Ninety Six, Christmas Day came with prayer and food. She had never heard of a Twelfth Night celebration, and gifts were given—if at all—on New Year's, not Christmas.

She thought about suggesting that they try to put together a fox hunt—she recalled her grandfather participating in one or two in Georgetown—but quickly realized there were few foxes around Ninety Six, having been trapped out by the Cherokees and white hunters. But. . . .

"Perhaps," she blurted, "we could have a ball. . . ."

Christmas fell on a Thursday, and, bowing to Monteith's wishes, they fasted that day, eating only one meal—boiled turkey for breakfast—and prepared the tavern for church.

During Advent, the reverend read daily from his *Book of Common Prayer.* On Christmas, he read before more people than Emily had ever seen in the tavern. He read the heralds from Isaiah and John the Baptist, and then began his sermon.

"There is darkness," he said, "and there is light. There is heaven, and there is hell. There is good, and there is evil. We have seen that far too often in this wilderness. Ruffians and the havoc they have caused . . . the tears, the suffering, the hardships. But today we forget all of our travails. Today we think not of darkness, but of light, not of hell, but of heaven, not of evil, but of good. For today is the day that Mary gave birth to Jesus. She gave birth in a stable. I preach this morning in a tavern. There are similarities, I imagine. Outside, it is freezing. Inside, I feel the warmth. Of fellowship. Of joy. Of God. Let us bow our heads, and pray."

Then, it was over. The shortest, most direct, sermon Monteith had preached since his arrival in Ninety Six.

Immediately the men moved the tables and chairs over to the walls, and people moved back, ladies on one side, men on the other, and the children were sent upstairs.

Behind the bar, James Middleton rosined the bow of his fiddle, Breck Stewart hefted his bagpipes, and even dour-faced Alroy O'Fionnagáin stepped forward with a smile, withdrawing his pochette—a tiny violin—from his coat pocket.

"Nothing bawdy, gentlemen," the preacher warned, grinning.

Emily stood at the wall, smiling, her foot tapping as the band played "Highland Laddie" to the accompaniment of laughter. Her mother danced with Monteith. Rachel Rowe—now Rachel Zachary—danced with her husband Luke. The Gouedys danced. Emily found herself clapping her hands as Middleton, Stewart, and O'Fionnagáin finished the tune and then went straight into "The Fly."

Thirty minutes later, Emily was sweating. She had danced with Rachel Zachary's husband to "Fair Margaret and Sweet William", and with a man in buckskins with black teeth who said his name was Meacham to "Blow, Ye Winds, Blow," and even with Joseph Robinson to "A Fox May Steal Your Hens, Sir."

Even the Baptists danced.

"Grab your lady fair," Stewart announced, after the band had wet their lips and tongues and throats with grog, "for it is time for us to attempt 'Greensleeves'."

Emily took in a deep breath. Joseph Robinson was making his way across the floor, coming straight for her, but then, out of the corner of her eye, she caught a glimpse of something red. She lifted her head, and gasped, almost swooning against the wall.

"May I have the pleasure, Miss Stewart?" Finnian Kilduff asked, stepping up to her.

She must have answered, though she was unaware of saying anything. Then suddenly she was in Kilduff's arms, swaying to the music, catching sight of Joseph Robinson at the bar with a stein in his hand and a look of contempt on his face.

All as James Middleton's rich tenor voice sang:

> *Greensleeves was all my joy;*
> *Greensleeves was my delight;*
> *Greensleeves was my heart of gold;*
> *And who but my Lady Greensleeves.*

The song ended. Kilduff released her, smiling, then stood in front of her, clapping, nodding at the other couples, tilting his head in appreciation to the musicians.

The music resumed, this time with Rachel Zachary singing.

Kilduff said nothing, merely took Emily's hands into his own, and waltzed her around the floor.

> *Was in the merry month of May*
> *When flowers were a-bloomin',*
> *Sweet William on his deathbed lay*
> *For the love of Barbara Allen.*

" 'Tis a pleasing odor in the tavern today," Kilduff said.

Emily nodded, swallowing and stuttering: "Y-y-yes. Rose p-p-petals."

He cocked his head.

> *Slowly, slowly she got up,*
> *And slowly she went nigh him,*
> *And all she said when she got there,*
> *"Young man, I think you're dying."*

"Rose petals?" he asked.

She tried to nod. "My mother . . . and . . . M-m-issus Coch-rane . . . they sprinkled dried rose p-p-etals around the tavern." She looked at him, then away. "Oh, Rachel Zach-ary . . . helped."

They danced a while in silence.

> *He turned his pale face to the wall,*
> *And death was on him dwellin'.*
> *"Adieu, Adieu, my kind friends all,*
> *Be kind to Barbara Allen."*

" 'Tis not rose petals that I smell," he said finally.

"They put some bay leaves out, also," she said, pleased that she had completed one sentence without stuttering or pausing, although she had spoken so rapidly, she didn't know if Kilduff had understood.

> *"O Mother, Mother make my bed,*
> *O make it long and narrow,*
> *Sweet William died for me today,*
> *I'll die for him tomorrow."*

She felt she had to explain. "For Christmas." She breathed more easily now "Rose petals and bay leaves. So the tavern would not smell like spilled rum and smoke from pipes."

His head shook, and he grinned. "No, I am certain it is not bay or rose that I smell. But lavender. On you."

She had washed her hair in lavender shampoo that morning,

and had Joseph Robinson made such a comment, she might have laid him low.

> *They grew and grew in the old churchyard,*
> *Till they couldn't grow no higher,*
> *They lapped and tied in a true love's knot.*
> *The rose ran around the briar.*

The song ended. They parted, still looking at one another, clapping, waiting, she knew, for the next song.

Someone called out for "Ally Croaker", but the three members of the band paused to have a drink. So Kilduff led her off the floor. She tried to think of something to say, or ask, or do, but Kilduff, staring past her, spoke first: "I have hogged you all to myself, dear lass, and think this gentleman desires a dance with you." Then he bowed and kissed her hand, and as Emily watched him walk away, she felt a hand on her shoulder and then she was being led back to the dance floor.

"And who, pray tell, is that gallows and wheel customer?" Donnan asked. Instead of looking at Emily, he stared at the stranger as the band struck up again.

She glared at him as they began to dance. "He is not a criminal, but a gentleman . . . unlike you, Brother."

"He belongs in bolts."

"If anyone should be shackled and chained, Donnan, 'tis you."

"Who is he?" There was no joviality in her brother's voice, and his eyes glowed with hostility. She knew she had better answer, less Donnan start a row, or, even worse, bring up Kilduff to their father.

Emily answered her brother.

"Finnian Kilduff," Donnan said. "And?"

Emily suddenly realized that was practically all she knew of him. "He hails from the Cowpens." But maybe not. When she had met him in the tavern that fall, Kilduff had said he was heading to the Cowpens, roughly seventy or eighty miles from Ninety Six, just below the North Carolina border. Now that she thought of it, though, it struck her that he could not live in the Cowpens. The men she had met from that part of the country were rougher than cobs, an ornery lot of Scots and Irish who dressed in rags like Jonathan and Betsy Conley and looked more like the black-toothed man who had danced with her to "Blow, Ye Winds, Blow."

"The Cowpens? I think not," Donnan said, shaking his head and muttering an oath. "I have not seen him here before, Sister."

"I only met him once. He was here the evening the parson arrived. Remember?"

Donnan's eyes remained fixed on Kilduff. "I think that I would rather see you dance with a damned Cherokee than with that dandy prat."

"Well, Go-la-nv Pinetree is not here," she spit back. "Is he?"

"You meet a man once"—Donnan's voice was icy—"and you dance with him twice? I wonder if Da' knows he has sired such a bunter?"

The music ended just as Emily slapped her brother's cheek hard enough to sting her hand and turn Donnan's face. It left a fine red mark on his rough cheek. All laughter inside Cormorant's Rock stopped, but Emily was far from finished.

"I do not know what has soured you, Brother," she said. "But you will not speak to me like that. Never. You stink of kill-devil, and have let that rum pollute your thoughts." She waved a finger in his face, satisfied as he rubbed the spot where she had struck him. "No more. Do you understand me, Donnan? No more. Never again!"

Turning toward the wall lined with men, who stood with their mouths agape, she cursed, then lifted the hems of her dress, and headed for the door, where the cold air would stop her tears, cool her temper. Outside, she saw the torches fluttering in the wind, the snow on the ground, and the horses and mules tethered to the fence rail.

However, she did not see Finnian Kilduff.

* * * * *

1767

* * * * *

Chapter Eleven

Advent and Christmas passed, and winter continued, the chill staying inside the Stewarts' home and tavern, with neither Emily's nor Donnan's tempers thawing—even when the Stewarts exchanged gifts on New Year's.

December had been cold, but, true to form, January and early February proved more frigid. Rarely did neighbors visit the tavern, and even fewer travelers dared risk their limbs or lives in the cold and ice. The Stewarts passed their days doing chores. The reverend blessed the meals, worked on his Sunday sermon, and studied his Bible and prayer book the rest of the week, day and night. On the Sabbath, depending on the weather, neighbors came to the tavern in their finest clothes, even if their finest proved to be nothing more than colored linen stockings and freshly washed homespun shirts. They came from as far away as the district's upper reaches.

No one showed up from the Cowpens.

Reverend Monteith would pray that God spare them from endemic and epidemic disorders, which he had seen far too much in the dismal country to the southeast. He would talk of the evils of spirituous liquors—even though most of his congregation would imbibe after the women had retired to one of the homes for tea and bread. He warned the residents of Ninety Six not to turn into "a society of pedantic and impudent illiterates" or "a sect of covetous hypocrites." He would pray that a schoolmaster be sent in the summer, and that the freebooters would see the light and abandon their wretched ways. He would speak until his throat became hoarse. Then they would sing, pray, and the service would end, and the tavern would return to its original foundation.

"Sometimes you preach like a Baptist," James Middleton once said to Monteith, and, to show there were no hard feelings, he offered to buy the parson a mug of hot rum.

By the middle of February the temperatures rose to something more moderate, the skies turned blue, the sun melted the ice, and the roads and trails to Ninety Six, though often resembling a quagmire, began to see mules, carts, wagons, and men and women afoot.

"And a good thing that is," said Jonathan Conley on one of his Saturday visits to the tavern, "for the wife, child, and me was practically down to Indian meal and water."

"We are pretty much eating hog corn ourselves," the black-toothed Meacham said.

By the end of February, winter—the worst anyone could remember in the Back Country—had been declared over. No one had died in the district during the long cold spell. Nobody had even suffered frostbite. Injuries had been few, and none serious.

"A hard winter means a green spring," announced a farmer named Loudon.

"And the peltry I shall see from the Cherokees shall bring better prices in Charlestown," Gouedy declared.

Several people proclaimed that they had the Reverend Douglas Monteith to thank for that. His sermons and prayers had been heard by the Lord, who now smiled down upon the settlers.

When March swept in, the reverend announced that it was time he left the comforts of Ninety Six and took the gospel down the trail to Pine Tree. He preached his final sermon that Sunday, and, after partaking in the biggest meal since his arrival, he climbed aboard his mule, with Emily riding side-saddle on Ezekiel to the minister's right, and her brother Donnan on a gray gelding on Monteith's left.

"As God is my witness," Monteith announced, "I shall have these two warring siblings burying the hatchet by the time we reach Mister Gouedy's trading post. And I will return them to you with smiles on their faces."

"Just have them home by supper," Machara said with a smile.

With Stewart playing "Auld Lang Syne" on his bagpipes and Rachel Zachary and Mrs. Cochrane singing, the Reverend Douglas Monteith, Emily, and Donnan rode south down the Charlestown Road. The parson tipped his hat, smiling widely, and thanked the settlers for a fine send-off. Emily and Donnan did not smile.

The look on their faces had not changed by the time they passed the Cherokee Trail. When they reached the ruins of the old stockade, Donnan began to curse underneath his breath, just loud enough for Emily to hear. They had not made up by the time they had passed Gouedy's trading post. Although the preacher had said nothing up to this point, when they were passing Gouedy's muddy hemp fields, he reined in the mule.

"You may turn around now, children," he said without looking at either. "I can find my way from here."

Donnan cleared his throat. "Da' said for us to see you across the Saluda."

"If I promise I will not drown . . . ?"

"Suit yourself," Donnan replied, and, tugging his reins, he turned the gray, still not looking at his sister.

"Wait a minute, Brother," Emily said.

Donnan snapped: "He is a grown man."

"The river might be high," she said. "That is why Da' sent us along."

"That is why he sent me. You were sent as part of a scheme between Da' and . . ."—he jerked his thumb toward the preacher—"him."

"Not Da'." Emily shook her head. "Mum, mayhap. But it would be my guess that this was concocted by one man, and that man sits on a mule by us."

"Mum and Da' had to go along with it," Donnan said.

"There." Monteith clapped his hands, leaned back his head, and laughed. "See how easy it is?"

Emily blinked. "What do you mean?"

"How easy it is"—Monteith slapped his leg, and pointed at Emily, then Donnan—"to carry on a conversation."

She muttered an oath, but noticed that Donnan had reined in his horse. He no longer was looking at the preacher, but at Emily.

Monteith swung from the saddle, letting the mule graze as he walked toward the brother and sister. He frowned. "I do not know what happened at Christmas, and I have not pried into your disagreement." He stood between them now. "Yet this I do know." He looked at Donnan. "You are not Cain." Turning to Emily, he said: "And you are not Abel."

With a snort, Emily spat out: "I would be the one doing the slaying, Reverend."

"Yes, indeed." Donnan spit over the gray's withers. "You are good at that, Sister."

Blood rushed to her head, and she had to cut off the curse forming in her throat.

"Donnan," the preacher said, "you lash your sister with bitter words, but it is not she who makes you angry. You are like the criminals who roamed this country during the summer last. You find someone weaker than yourself, and you attack them. But when they strike back . . . as your sister did on Christmas. . . ." He shook his head. "I have prayed for you both, but you must not go on like this."

"Go to hell, Preacher," Donnan said, and kicked the gelding into a lope, heading back toward Gouedy's post and Ninety Six.

When he reached the woods and left their view, Monteith looked at Emily, his face heavy with sadness.

" 'Tis not your fault, Reverend," she said. "You tried."

"He is a lost soul."

"He has been like that since the Cherokee War," Emily said. "Growing worse. More bitter, I mean."

"Well, I will continue to pray for him." Monteith walked back to his mule. "But tell me, Emily, what happened at the dance? What did Donnan say to you?"

Feeling uncomfortable, she shrugged, then said: "He called me a name."

"Brothers and sisters have a tendency to do that," Monteith said as he climbed into the saddle. "I know my sister did. And so did I . . . when I was much younger."

"It was a dirty name."

"Once, my sister called me a niffy-naffy fellow, and I said she was something much worse."

"What Donnan called me was much worse."

"It is only a name, and names cannot hurt."

"It hurt," she said.

"Aye. I must correct myself. Names cannot hurt in the physical sense. But Donnan did not mean it, I am sure."

"That might be some Dutch comfort," she said, then, staring at Monteith, added, "but he meant it."

"Then I shall pray for you, too, child."

He kicked the mule. Emily watched him for a moment, then, sighing heavily, gave the dun a kick and caught up with the preacher.

"You do not have to follow me, Emily."

"Da' said to make sure you got across the river."

He chuckled, and said: "I forded many streams between the Welsh Neck and Ninety Six, Emily."

"That was in the summer. There has been much snow melt. And there is no ferry or bridge betwixt here and the Congaree."

"Which is something Mister Gouedy, your father, and many others lament about rather frequently. Mayhap I shall bring this up to the Assembly or governor when next I am in Charlestown."

They entered the woods, and fell silent. Emily appreciated the quiet.

Although winter had been long, spring came quickly in the Back Country. Already trees exploded with new leaves. Birds and squirrels bantered as the forest thickened, soon blocking out most of the sunlight. A carpet of sprouting green cushioned the hoofs of their mounts, and, after a few miles, Emily could hear the roaring of the Saluda River. *No*, she thought, *we will not be crossing the river today.*

Monteith must have heard the river, too, for he reined in his mule, and Emily pulled alongside him. Almost instantly she saw that the preacher had not stopped because of the sound of water. She reached inside her pocket and withdrew the ivory-handled pistol.

Three bearded men, brandishing lop-sided grins and long rifles, blocked the trail.

"Run, Preacher!" she yelled, and pulled back the little weapon's hammer.

A hand came around her wrist like a vise and she screamed, watching the pistol fall onto the ground, seeing the massive hand clamped on her arm. Angrily she turned, saw the green eyes and pockmarked face. She reached for the man's hair with her left hand, but that just made her lose her balance. The pockmarked man jerked, and Emily felt herself falling from the horse. But the man did not let go of her arm, and she felt as if it would break.

She landed hard, the breath whooshing out of her lungs—her head must have struck a root or rock—as the man, who still gripped her right arm, slammed onto her stomach.

This time, she knew, Go-la-nv Pinetree would not be here to rescue her. This time, she prayed that Donnan would return in time to help.

CHAPTER TWELVE

"Matthäus! Unhand her!"

"She is mine," the man atop her said.

Emily's eyes opened. Tears of pain, not fear, half blinded her, her head and right arm ached, and for a moment she thought she might vomit.

"If you do not release that girl, you damned little Hun, I shall be obliged to send you to hell."

Maybe a gun was cocked. She couldn't tell. She closed her eyes, trying to think clearly. She knew that wasn't Douglas Monteith talking. It wasn't Donnan. It was not Go-la-nv Pinetree . . . but she knew the voice.

The pressure left her wrist and her stomach as the man climbed off her.

"What kind of men are you?" That was Monteith.

"Blindfold them," the voice said.

She was trying to sit up, to regain her faculties, when a coarse sack was drawn over her head.

Squeezing her eyelids tight, she turned her head from the light as the sack dropped into the fire. Beyond the campfire, she smelled frying pork and baking bread, detected the sound of a Jew's harp and a fiddle, and, above all, loud voices that lacked tone and rhythm but not good cheer.

As I rose up one May morning,
One May morning so wurly,
I overtook a pretty fair maid,
Just as the sun was dawnin',
With me rue-rum-ray,
Fother-didle-ay,
Wok-fol-air-didle-i-do.
Her stockin's white, and her boots were bright,
And her buckling shone like silver;
She had a dark and a rolling eye,
And her hair hung round her shoulder,
With me rue-rum-ray,
Fother-didle-ay,
Wok-fol-air-didle-i-do.
"Where are you going, my pretty fair maid?
Where are you going my honey?"
She answered me right cheerfully:
"I'm on errand for me mummy."
With me rue-rum-ray,
Fother-didle-ay,
Wok-fol-air-didle-i-do.
"How old are you, my pretty fair maid,
How old are you, my honey?"
She answered me right cheerfully:
"I am seventeen come Sunday."
With me rue-rum-ray . . .

She felt hot tin being placed in her hands, and her eyes
opened. A man's face smiled at her, and she looked at the mug
of steaming tea she now held. The song continued.

"Will you take a man, my pretty fair maid?
Will you take a man, my honey?"

She answer'd me right cheerfully:
"I darst not for me mummy."

As the voices launched into the chorus, she lifted her eyes. Her face went tight, and she held her breath.

Finnian Kilduff was in front of her, smiling at her, and then he turned toward the singers and joined them.

"Will you come down to my mummy's house,
When the moon shone bright and clearly?
You'll come down, I'll let you in,
And me mummy shall not hear me."
With me rue-rum-ray,
Fother-didle-ay,
Wok-fol-air-didle-i-do.

Then all the men stopped singing, and a woman's voice began a solo. Emily looked at a freckle-faced redhead in breeches and a loose cotton smock belting out the words in a rich Welsh tenor.

Oh, it's now I'm with my soldier lad,
His ways they are so winnin'.
It's drum and fife is my delight,
And a pint o' rum in the mornin'.

Kilduff clapped his hands, and again joined in with the rest of the group as they sang:

With me rue-rum-ray,
Fother-didle-ay,
Wok-fol-air-didle-i-do.
With me rue-rum-ray,
Fother-didle-ay,
Wok-fol-air-didle-i-do!

Boisterous laughter filled the camp of tents and crude shelters, set in a clearing surrounded by a palisade of trees. Smoke, Emily noticed, rose into the blue sky not only from the campfire before her, but from others scattered across the camp. These men, and that red-headed woman, were not afraid of someone spotting the smoke.

Kilduff sat beside her, his legs crossed. Gone were the fine silk jacket and fancy duds, replaced now by deerskin pants, a plaid shirt, loose fitting neckerchief of blue and white polka dots, and a battered black hat. He still wore the high boots, only they were worn and scuffed, not shiny any more.

Doffing his hat, he bowed, and said: "Miss Emily. Please accept my apologies. Had I known you would be accompanying the parson, we would have waited to make the parson's acquaintance at a later date that would not have inconvenienced you."

The voice was the same. Just a hint of the Irish. The smiling eyes were the same.

"You had all fall and winter to make the Reverend Monteith's acquaintance," she said, dumping the tea between her shoes.

"As hard as the winter was?" Kilduff's tongue clucked. She said nothing, and he laughed again. "You are rubbing your wrist, Miss Emily. I have cast Matthäus out of our camp, but had I known he had hurt you, I would have had him flogged."

"You can flog yourself, you . . . highwayman."

"The name, you must recall, is Kilduff. Finnian Kilduff."

"That is the name you gave me."

"And the one my parents saddled upon me," he said, hooking a thumb at the redhead, now dancing with a scraggly bearded man to "The Escape of Old John Webb." "Tanwen? Now to her I might have called myself . . ."—he pursed his lips and knotted his brow before finally settling on a name—"Donnan Stewart."

She spit into the fire.

"But I could not lie to you, Miss Emily." He raised his right hand, snapped a finger, made a gesture.

She watched two men—one wearing the remnants of a British sailor's uniform and the other dressed like the Catawba Indian she had seen at the Welsh Neck—open the cowhide door to one of the huts, and bring out the Reverend Douglas Monteith. He shielded his eyes from the sunlight, as they crossed the camp, trying to pull away from the men who finally stopped in front of Emily.

He whispered as they pushed him onto his knees: "Are you all right, Emily?"

"Yes."

"And how are you, Reverend?" Kilduff asked.

The preacher turned. "By the Eternal, I shall see you in stocks, sir. And all of these ruffians. Have you no morals?"

"Not many," the Catawba answered.

Emily studied the man and determined that he wasn't Indian, just dressed like one.

Kilduff asked Emily: "What are your sentiments?"

She shrugged. "Stocks . . . forty lashes less one . . . or the cord."

"Maybe drawn and quartered," said the woman.

Emily turned toward the redhead, Tanwen, who laughed and tossed back her long hair. She was, Emily had to admit, an attractive woman with a beautiful voice. "Maybe," Emily said, and looked back at Kilduff.

"You waylay us on the road," Monteith said. "You almost break this poor, defenseless creature's wrist. You rob us of our livestock. And now you kidnap us, and sing lewd songs before a girl not. . . ."

"I am seventeen years old, Reverend," Emily snapped. Well, she would be. Come April.

"And I dare say she is not poor, and certainly not defenseless," Kilduff said, and reached underneath his smock, withdrawing Emily's small pistol and studying it a moment before tossing it back to her. "You will need powder for the pan, naturally, and the steel seems a trifle loose, Miss Emily. You also might wish to clean it now and again."

Tanwen laughed. "Preacher," she said, "we certainly do not want your poor mule and that tiny stallion."

The man wearing the sailor clothes slapped his thigh, spit out juice from the snuff between his cheek and gums, and said: "Even though poor mules is about all that's left in this part of the country."

"Thanks to us," added the white man dressed like a Catawba, then he laughed.

Silencing his companions with a mere look, Kilduff nodded at Monteith. "And you were not kidnapped, sir. We were saving you from certain drowning. Had you dared attempt to ford the Saluda, no one but the Almighty would have seen you again."

"We were not going to attempt to cross that river!" Monteith barked back.

"No?" Kilduff snorted.

"No," Emily asserted, waiting for the rogue to look at her. "I would not have let him."

He laughed, clapped his hand, and asked Tanwen if she would deliver him a jug of kill-devil.

Emily considered Kilduff for a moment, then studied the camp. The music had stopped, and men were gathering around Kilduff and his "guests" in a semicircle. Most looked like the bulk of her neighbors who lived on farms, or those who hunted in the Back Country and as far west as the Tennessee country. Two were men of color, and she thought she recognized the shorter man as one Mr. Gouedy's slaves. His clothes had worn so thin, she could not imagine how he had survived the winter.

He looked away from her once their eyes met, and she remembered hearing Mr. Gouedy complain that another one of his boys had run off. The man standing next to the runaway slave was the white man with the Roman nose who dressed like a Catawba, but next to him stood a real Indian, attired only in breechcloth and moccasins. A Santee, by the looks of him, Emily decided.

Tanwen slid between two of the Negroes, withdrew the cork from a brown clay jug, and took a long pull before tossing the container to Kilduff.

Twelve men and one woman, yet for some reason, Emily did not feel threatened. Maybe she would have had the German—Matthäus—still been in their midst, but Kilduff said he had kicked him out. For hurting Emily. She decided that these men were not the same as those marauders she had seen in the Welsh Neck.

"All right," Kilduff said. He did not drink from the jug, but instead passed it to Monteith. "Rum," he said. "To slake your thirst . . . before you deliver to us what we expect you to deliver."

"You will find our pockets empty of any stray shillings, sir," the preacher said, and Emily knew he had not recognized Kilduff.

Laughing, Kilduff tossed the jug to Gouedy's ex-slave. "You were not crazy enough to cross the Saluda, and we did not stop you for your own safety," Kilduff said. "Or to rob you. We brought you here for a glorious reason, Parson."

"Which is?" the preacher asked.

"Preach to us."

Breck Stewart rocked back in the chair, pushed up the brim of his hat, and lowered the chair's front legs onto the porch. After the words sunk in, he straightened, his head cocked at a curious angle, and said: "*Preach* to them?"

"Aye," Monteith said.

"Parson," Gouedy said, "what did you do?"

"Sir, I delivered a sermon full of fire and brimstone. I baptized two of the scoundrels. Then they fed us, blindfolded us, and led us through the depths of the forest until we were back on the Charlestown Road, just a mile or two from the intersection with the Cherokee Path."

"On that mule," Stewart said.

"Aye."

Emily ground her teeth. Finnian Kilduff had decided that the marsh tacky dun wasn't such a bad horse, after all.

"They stole my stallion?" Stewart said, staring at Emily.

"Yes, Da'," she whispered.

"A most brazen bunch of swine," James Middleton snapped. "For while they held you hostage, they sent more of their own devils to kill Alroy O'Fionnagáin and his family."

Sitting on the steps, Emily turned and gasped, the color draining from her face.

"Alroy O'Fionnagáin?" Douglas Monteith said as if numb. "Dead?"

"Yes," Stewart answered. "Meacham is out with some men, trying to find their trail, but. . . ." He sighed, and pushed his chair back, slowly rocking.

"Alroy's wife was . . . ," Gouedy began, than looked at Emily and let the words trail off.

"It was not those that held us."

Emily had not realized she had spoken loud enough for anyone to hear, but every head had turned toward her, and she cringed. Donnan hissed something she could not understand, and her father slammed his chair down so hard the porch seemed to shake.

"By the grace of God . . . ," Middleton began, but Monteith silenced him by raising his right hand.

"Emily is right," the minister said. "These men who abducted us were a hard lot, but murderers is something I would not call them."

"What would you call them?" Donnan's voice crackled with anger.

Monteith shrugged. "Horse thieves. Cattle thieves. Twelve men and a woman. . . ."

"A woman!" someone shouted.

Middleton's echoing oath was shouted down by Stewart's booming voice: "Let the parson finish, damn you all!"

After a moment, Monteith went on: "Yes, one woman. A loose strumpet, but a woman, nonetheless. I would not call this group a lot of mad killers. They were a pernicious lot who might propagate vice, theft, and beggary for certain." He paused. "But murder . . . and as foul of a crime as what you say happened to that poor but fine Irishman and his family . . . no, not these men."

"They are outlaws," Middleton insisted.

Monteith's head bobbed. "Aye. But thieves." He turned to Emily with a placating smile, speaking softly. "But, Emily, though those men treated us kindly . . . I guess that might be as good a description as any . . . they are outlaws. Their leader . . . he is not Robin Hood, and the thieves that he commands is not a group of merry men." He swung his head back to the men who had gathered at the tavern. "But horse thieves though they very well are, they did not have the look of killers."

"You take a man's horse, and," Gouedy inserted, "in this country, it can mean death. You take away a man's livelihood, and it can mean the same."

"And that marsh tacky cost me a small fortune in sterling." Stewart rammed a meaty fist into the palm of his other hand.

The preacher shrugged. "They let us keep the mule," he said.

"Mule." Stewart turned and spit into a cuspidor.

"And they tithed as well," Emily said.

"Hush, Emily!" her father barked. "Go help your mother. This is no conversation for a girl not fourteen."

Not fourteen? In a month, I will be seventeen. Girls my age . . . girls even as young as fourteen . . . are already married here in the district, some with one or more children. Emily would not argue with her father.

"So what shall we do?" Gouedy asked. "March is not half passed, and the marauders have already begun their treachery."

"Emily."

She stopped in the doorway, turned to see the Reverend Douglas Monteith standing, looking at her.

"They might not be killers," Monteith told her, "but they must be punished."

"I never said otherwise, Reverend," she said as she closed the door behind her. But she did not cross the tavern for the winter kitchen to help her mother. She thought of Alroy O'Fionnagáin and his wife. She felt dread at the thought of seeing their faces in nightmares she would have that evening.

"What shall we do, Stewart?" Middleton yelled.

"Hear me," the preacher said. "I will forgo preaching the Word of God this spring in the Back Country. I will travel to Charlestown and speak to Governor Montagu. I will make him understand what is happening here."

"When?" It was Donnan's voice. "As much snow as is melting, no one will be crossing the Saluda River without risking hide or hair for at least another week. And the Broad will be running even swifter and higher."

"Besides," said another almost too softly for Emily to hear, "we caught a gang of murdering rogues last summer on the Welsh Neck. These were sent to Charlestown for justice, and what justice did our new governor decide was appropriate? Five pardoned and sent back to torment us more."

Donnan added: " 'For good order and harmony of the colony.' "

CHAPTER THIRTEEN

They would call themselves the Cane Creek Regulators, but
only because, during a vote at Cormorant's Rock, James
Middleton had dismissed the suggestion of Long Canes Regulators as he thought people might think it meant a group led by
Birmingham Long, and Jonathan Conley believed that Breck
Stewart's pitch for the Saluda River Regulators could well apply
to another group of vigilantes as far south as the Congaree.

"Husband . . ."—Machara Stewart stood on her tiptoes to
kiss Breck's check—"proud of you, I am."

Blushing, Breck pulled on his cocked hat.

"You should call him captain," Donnan said with a laugh as
he jumped off the porch, and gathered the reins to his gray
horse.

"Captain." Machara nodded and smiled. "Aye. I like the
sound of that. Now be safe, Captain Stewart. And you, too,
Ensign."

Already in the saddle, Ensign Donnan Stewart snapped a
salute at his mother.

Emily stood near the door, one hand on Alan's shoulder, the
other gripping Elizabeth's hand. Alan sucked on a piece of
maple candy, but Elizabeth sniffed, tears streaming down her
cheeks. Stewart kissed his wife's cheek, and moved toward Emily, dropping to a knee, pulling out a handkerchief, and dabbing
Elizabeth's tears.

"No tears, Elizabeth," he said. "I shall return before you

know I am gone." He brushed the child's bangs off her forehead, then took Alan's free hand, sticky from the candy, and shook. "You must be the man of the house, Alan."

The boy's head shook. "No, Da'. That's Emily's job."

Chuckling, Stewart looked up at Emily. "Aye. Mayhap you are right, Son, but do your best and help her when you can. Can you do that for me?"

Alan's head nodded.

Stewart looked at his oldest daughter as he got to his feet. "We sha'n't be gone long, Emily," he said, then added softly: "You know where the blunderbuss is?"

"Yes, Da'."

"Keep an eye out," he whispered. "There are spies in this community. Spies who betray us and those around us to help the swine who would lay this country to waste."

Traitors in Ninety Six? Emily thought to herself, and then, as a chill ran down her spine, blurted out: "Who?"

"When we find out, they shall rue their deceit." He put his massive hand on Emily's shoulder, squeezing it tightly. "Do you know what, child?"

Emily shook her head. She had to breathe in deeply, then hold her breath, to dam the tears that threatened to cascade down her face.

"There is a side of me that wishes you could ride with us," he told her, then smiled before bending to kiss her forehead.

Damn, she thought as he turned away, how dashing he looked in the long red coat with its dark green stripes, pointed loops, and white lace. Even his cocked hat was trimmed with gold, and a brace of pistols had been stuck inside his green sash. The buckskin pants and buckle shoes might not look military, but he carried himself as a soldier.

She counted forty men in front of the tavern, most of them holding long rifles but some with lances, one gripping a pitchfork, and another with four hatchets hooked to some sort of canvas strap that stretched diagonally around his chest. A few brandished cutlasses, and at least two had bayonets affixed to their long guns. Others carried dirks, cut-down muskets, or fowling pieces. Fur-skin caps, blue bonnets, Holster caps, cocked hats, straw hats, broad-brimmed fur and felt hats, and several cockades of various colors. Tartan coats and Highland hose. Waistcoats, blue coats, and dirty smocks.

Every face showed stern fortitude. Any bandit would dread meeting up with the likes of this militia, and as her father led those two score men out of the settlement toward the Cherokee Path, she thought about Finnian Kilduff, and she wondered if it was really worry she felt about that outlaw.

"Let us carry justice to the vermin who have forgotten God's Commandments and the law of the King!" Stewart shouted above the sound of thundering hoofs. "Let us never forget Alroy O'Fionnagáin and his family."

Then they were gone, leaving behind churned-up dirt, horse apples, and a feeling of vengeance that lay heavy on the dew.

Virgil Hickox's wheelwright's shop was empty. So was the barn where cooper Thomas Taylor worked. Machara said to Emily: "Ninety Six has not looked so deserted since the Cherokee War."

The silence in the village left Emily feeling unnerved. Like a child, she dragged a tobacco stick in the dirt, before she finally heard a familiar sound. She headed straight to Benjamin Cooper's shed, stopping at the entrance, and clearing her throat.

Years ago, when she had first arrived in Ninety Six, she remembered asking her mother how come Benji was a carpenter and not the settlement's cooper. She grinned at the memory as she watched the big man work.

Already sweating, the freedman with a round face, close-cropped beard, and powerful arms, stood over a table, working a plane across a thick piece of wood. He wore linen breeches, sturdy shoes of black leather, and a heavy leather apron covered with sawdust. So intent was he on his job that Emily had to clear her throat again before he looked up.

"Why, Miss Emily." He set the plane on the table and wiped his brow with the sleeve of his cotton smock. "What may I do for you, ma'am?"

What could she say? That she was bored? That she wished she were riding through the woods and hills with the Cane Creek Regulators. "Sure is quiet around here," she said finally.

Smiling, he moved to a bucket, pulled out a ladle, and drank. "Yes, ma'am. How long has your father been gone?"

"Three days."

"No word from them yet, I expect?"

"No, sir."

Nodding, he dropped the ladle in the bucket, wiped his mouth, and returned to the table. "They shall be back soon. I would not fret."

She told herself she was not worried. "Why did not you go with the regulators?" she asked, immediately regretting the question. Her mother often warned her to watch her tongue, to remember that she was a lady.

Cooper did not appear to have taken offense, however, and pointed at the door. Emily turned, saw the long rifle leaning against a workbench, a powder horn, and leather sack lying on the edge of the bench, a Queen Anne's pistol nearby. "Your father asked me to stay . . . in case. For protection." Cooper grinned. "Not that a girl like you needs protection. Besides, I got a chore to do."

The plane glided across the wood, and Emily tentatively approached the table. "What are you building?" she asked.

The wood was huge, thick, curved. Pieces were also stacked

on the table, and she saw six wooden stands already built, lying on the floor on the far wall, with four-by-four square rods in the center of the stands, rising almost as tall as Emily.

"Stocks," Cooper said.

"Stocks," she repeated.

"Yes, Miss Emily. I suppose the regulators decided a ducking stool would not be a fitting punishment. You have seen stocks before, Miss Emily?"

Her mouth had turned dry, and she could only nod. She remembered the poor creatures in Charlestown, head and hands locked in the wooden structures. She recalled the young slave, so short, he was practically choking in the stocks.

"Yes," she finally answered, and spotted something else across the room—heavy wood that resembled an inverted L, a brace connecting the two bars, with long leather straps dangling from iron rings at the end of the top bar.

Cooper's eyes followed hers, and, without being asked, he said: "A whipping post, ma'am."

"Oh." Her voice sounded foreign.

"I like it no better than you, Miss Emily," he said. "I have seen too many of my own kind put in the pillory. On the other hand, miss, there has been too much lawlessness in this district for too long a time. The law must come to the frontier. Eventually it must come."

"I know," she said.

"You must get used to this, Miss Emily. For your father has paid me to place them betwixt the tavern and Mister Taylor's property. So everyone can see the culprits when they are brought to our community."

"Yes." She tried to think of something pleasant to say, but what came out of her mouth was: "At least you have not been hired to build a gallows."

"No, Miss Emily." His voice sounded raw, too. "We have the oak tree in Mister Hickox's yard for that."

On the fourth day, Emily helped her mother scrub the floors to keep her mind off the Cane Creek Regulators.

The fifth day was Sunday, which meant church at Cormorant's Rock, but only a few settlers showed up to hear Douglas Monteith's sermon and prayers. Afterward, they practiced their reading from the Bible, then spent the afternoon on the porch, looking down the empty trails, hoping to see the regulators return.

On the sixth day, the first morning after the full moon, they planted most of the garden. "Always plant your below-ground crops during the dark of the moon," Breck Stewart would say. Superstition or science—Emily wasn't certain which—she dug the holes with a hoe, Alan dropped in the bean seeds, then they covered the hole with dirt. On the row next to them, Machara dug the holes and Elizabeth dropped the pea seeds. Later, they sprinkled in the seeds for the carrots and radishes, and planted the onions, turnips, and potatoes. The corn, melons, cucumbers, and tomatoes would wait until the light of the moon.

The morning of the seventh day, Cooper began setting up the stocks and the whipping posts—he wound up building two—in the clearing behind the tavern and Thomas Taylor's cabin. Robert Gouedy brought two slaves to help the carpenter, and practically everyone in the settlement came to watch the installation.

"They come to see this," Monteith whispered angrily to Emily, "yet they miss church."

She pretended she had not heard, doubting the parson had meant for anyone to hear his remark. As she stood there, she wondered how Benjamin Cooper, a freedman, felt as he worked alongside two slaves. And what did Mr. Gouedy's slaves think of the carpenter? Then, when the first stock went up, she turned away, trying not to imagine Finnian Kilduff's head and hands sticking out of the holes.

"You young 'uns had best behave yourselves," Mrs. Cochrane told her small children. "Or else you shall find yourselves in those stocks."

Which made the children cry, and many of the adults to snigger. The comment made the blood rush to Emily's head, and she walked away, feeling angry.

On the eighth day, on her way to split kindling, as she opened the door, she saw a figure sitting, cross-legged, on the porch, head bent, back leaning against the railing. She let out a shriek, and raised the axe.

The head lifted, and Emily lowered the axe. "Damn you, Go-la-nv Pinetree!" she snapped. "You frightened me out of three years of my life."

"*Osda sunalei,*" he said, reaching up for the top rail, then pulling himself to his feet.

"Aye." Arms suddenly weak, she lowered the axe. "Good morning, I guess." Finally she managed a smile, and glanced around, making sure no one had heard her little yelp of terror, before looking back at the young Cherokee.

Her smile faded. He looked much thinner, his clothes were ragged, moccasins and leggings wet with water, and she noticed a crescent-shaped scar above his left eye. That was new. Beside him she spotted a bundle of pelts. The furs looked thick and rich, and would bring a fine price in Charlestown. It had been a hard winter.

"How have you been?" she asked.

Instead of answering, he stepped toward her and took the axe, then glanced around.

"Kindling," she said, "to make breakfast." She followed him to the woodpile, and stepped back as he split some pine into small strips to build a fire.

"Are the pelts for Mister Gouedy?" she asked, then felt like an idiot. Of course, they were for the trader, but then she thought again. Pinetree would have passed Gouedy's post on his way to the settlement, so why had not he done his trading first?

Pinetree split the last piece, leaned the axe against the pile of wood, and dropped to his knees, reaching for the iron-bladed hatchet to trim the wood he had split into smaller pieces.

He said: "Your father . . . he asked."

"When?" she asked, wanting to know everything. "When did you see him?"

He began trimming, shrugged, and finally replied: "Two days ago."

She wanted more information, but he seemed focused on the chore, and her father had taught her to be patient, not just with Indians, but everyone. Well, he had tried to teach her patience.

"Said to meet him here. I come." He had finished, and began picking up the kindling.

She dropped to her knees to help. "Carrying on a conversation with you, Go-la-nv Pinetree, is like pulling teeth."

He looked up at her, face devoid of any expression. She had to grin, then found herself laughing until the sound of hoofs caught her attention.

Pinetree stood, and Emily, feeling her heart jump, sprang to her feet.

"Mum!" she called in the direction of the tavern. The bits of wood fell to the ground as Emily lifted the hems of her skirt, and ran. "Mum! Elizabeth! Alan! It's Da'. He's home!" She felt the tears of relief rolling down her cheeks, and, for once, she was not ashamed.

Breck Stewart came out of the saddle before his horse had slid to a complete stop, and he scooped Emily into his arms, squeezing her, spinning her around. She wanted to kiss her father's bearded cheeks, but he wouldn't let her go, just kept spinning and spinning until they both collapsed into a heap.

"Daughter," he said, gasping for breath, "I have missed you so much."

She pulled herself to her knees, reached over, and hugged him around his neck, even tighter. She heard the door to the tavern open, and then the squeals of Elizabeth and Alan as they ran to greet their father. Blinking back the tears, she saw her mother standing in the doorway, wringing the towel in her hands.

Emily could not remember ever feeling so much relief. She pulled herself up from the ground as her father greeted his two youngest children.

Then, as only Donnan could, her brother spoiled the mood.

"What in hell's name is that damned Cherokee doing here?"

CHAPTER FOURTEEN

Sometimes her father's eyes frightened Emily more than her brother's looks of utter hatred. Breck Stewart certainly did not hate his son, but his face hardened even as he kissed the cheeks of Elizabeth and Alan, before rising slowly and turning around and taking three steps toward Donnan.

"Because I sent word for Go-la-nv to come," Stewart told his son. "And he came."

Spinning on his heel, Stewart walked over to Go-la-nv Pine-tree, and gripped the young Cherokee's hand with both of his, thanking him in both English and Cherokee.

When he was released from Stewart's hard grip, he pointed at the pelts on the porch.

Stewart saw them, and shook his head. "Go-la-nv," he said softly, the rage fading, "you misunderstand. I will pay you for your services, and pay you handsomely."

Stiffly Donnan dismounted, and dismissed the weary, bearded, red-eyed regulators, telling them that they would re-assemble in two days.

As the men rode off to their homes, Donnan grabbed the reins to his and his father's horses, and led them to the barn. There were no prisoners, for which Emily felt relief.

"A week in the woods, Machara," Stewart said, "and nothing to show for it but a chaffed backside and these infernal chigger bites." He began scratching his arm furiously.

He had bathed and shaved, and now Donnan sat outside in the washtub, scrubbing off a week's worth of horsehair and dirt. Sitting at the family table in the tavern, Stewart mopped up the remnants of the stew with corn pone, washing the food down with a healthy swallow of ale.

"The Cherokee will scout for us," he said after he wiped his mouth with the sleeve of the clean shirt. "And I have asked Doctor Bayard to keep an eye out for a peculiar individual we are beginning to suspicion."

"Who?" Machara asked.

Stewart's head shook. "I should not mention his name. We shall see what the doctor learns."

Emily didn't have to hear the name of the suspect. She knew. James Robinson, who lived close to the Huguenots. Her head shook at what she considered irony. Once Robinson had been considered a worthy suitor for Emily's hand. Now, she suspected, Robinson was bound for the stocks or the whipping post.

Machara sighed. "How long will you be gone this time?"

Emily studied her mother, and felt her heart break. Standing in the tavern, wringing her hands, she was not a woman to display her emotions, not in front of her children, and certainly not in a room crowded with men—neighbors though they might be.

"The Indian," Stewart said, "will make things quicker, I believe."

How did Emily feel? She wasn't certain. Go-la-nv Pinetree riding with the Cane Creek Regulators? With Donnan? Her brother had said few words since his arrival, not even to his mother, and he had brushed past Alan and Elizabeth without saying anything as he headed to the tavern's bar and found a jug of rum.

Before long, other members of the Cane Creek Regulators—

the bachelors, primarily, with no family to go home to, and those black-eyed men who had lost their families—joined Donnan. They drank with little conversation, and few bothered to even eat.

"With the Cherokee with us," her father said, "the renegades soon will pay for their misdeeds."

His words proved prophetic.

When she went to the well those summer mornings, filling the bucket with water, dreading the chore that awaited her, she recalled her father's prediction. Sometimes Ol' Benji Cooper would see her, and rush over to lend his giant hands, but usually Emily did it alone.

On this morning, she struggled with the bucket, sloshing the water over the rim, drenching her stockings and shoes. The sun had barely topped the tree line, yet she was sweating from the heat and humidity. From one of the distant cabins, she heard the door open, and knew Rachel Zachary stood there, staring, thinking of what stories she could tell her friends, what gossip she could spread.

Emily stopped at the first stock, tried to steady her nerves, then brought the ladle up in her trembling hands, and held it next to the sun-burned man's lips. She did not think a person could smell water—perhaps, maybe swamp water, but not the cool water from the Stewarts' well—but it seemed to arouse the man's heavy eyes. His lips parted as his eyes opened, rimmed red, swollen. His lips were cracked and bleeding, and when he opened his mouth, she saw the horrible condition of his teeth and gums, and his tongue was so swollen it must have hurt him even just to try to swallow.

"Can you drink, sir?"

He didn't answer, probably had no strength to speak, so she tilted the ladle, and saw the relief in his face from just the few sips he managed to get down. She bent, refilled the ladle, let him drink again.

Silently she looked down the path between Cormorant's Rock and the Taylor place. Every stock held a prisoner, three of them white, two men of color, and one about which she wasn't sure. Mrs. Taylor had said he must be a pirate—as if that was a nationality—but Reverend Monteith said he was a Turk. Likely a slave of some sort. Maybe a former prisoner who had escaped his sentence in Georgia. The man said nothing. Never, as if his tongue had been cut out.

Six men. Prisoners, caught by the Cane Creek Regulators, sentenced to four weeks in the stocks. Four weeks, and only one had passed.

This was July, and the six men blistering in the heat, drying up from the sun, had not been the first to be put in the stocks. Go-la-nv Pinetree had been a huge help to the Cane Creek Regulators. Three days after Breck Stewart had left with his band of vigilantes, they had returned to Cane Creek with four men. And Emily learned they had buried three others on the Georgia side of the Savannah.

In May, Dr. Bayard had brought word to Breck Stewart, and the following morning, Hickox, Middleton and Ferguson, under the command of Ensign Donnan Stewart, had brought a bare-footed Joseph Robinson, hands bound behind his back and his smock ripped and dangling behind his trousers to the front of the tavern.

She closed her eyes, trying to block out that memory, but, as always, failed.

"What is the meaning of this, Breck Stewart?" Robinson asked.

"Who paid you a visit three bells past midnight two days ago?"

"No one."

"Parson, bring out your Bible. Put the prisoner's hand on it. Aye.

Good. Yes, good indeed. Now, Robinson, tell us again, tell us before our Anglican minister and the Lord Jehovah himself . . . tell us that no one visited you."

"Are you spying on me, Breck Stewart?"

"Answer the question!"

"I live on Cane Creek. Hunters, white and red, pass by my house. Is it a crime to show Christian charity to a wayfarer heading north to the dark and bloody ground?"

"No. But it is a crime . . . it is high treason . . . to sell out your neighbors and friends for thirty pieces of silver."

Joseph Robinson had been the first man she had ever seen flogged. Whipped thirty-nine times. Then cut down and dragged into the wilderness, back to his home, he was told to leave while he still breathed.

Never had she cared much for the pompous Virginian, but even a man like Joseph Robinson deserved better treatment. Her father had called it justice, but Emily did not remember any trial. In Charlestown, in London, in Glasgow, men were allowed fair trials. But this . . . ?

No one had seen Joseph Robinson since. She had heard Mrs. Cochrane tell Mrs. Ferguson that the poor man had stolen a mule and retreated to Charlestown, and probably was back in Liverpool by now. Mrs. Cochrane believed anything she heard or imagined she had heard. But it was a better, more hopeful story, than others she had heard: that Robinson's stomach had been slit open, weighted down with stones before being thrown into Cane Creek to feed the gars and catfish—that Go-la-nv Pinetree had showed him just how cruel the Cherokees could be—that Donnan had shot the man in the back of his head while he prayed for mercy, while her father had watched with deaf ears.

Others had been whipped. Others had been put in the stocks.

How many? Emily had lost count.

At least, she did not have to clean up the prisoner's mess. For that task, Robert Gouedy sent some of his slaves each evening.

Her instructions were to give the prisoners water each morning, just two ladles, no more. They would be fed by Gouedy's slaves at noon, and only noon. The slaves would water the prisoners that night. A piece of stale bread, and four ladles of water. She did not know what these men's crimes were, but such a sentence seemed inhumane.

"Miss Emily!"

She moved to the next prisoner—a Negro with a full black beard—and was bringing the first ladle to his lips by the time Douglas Monteith caught up with her.

"Miss Emily." The parson took the ladle from her hand, and let the prisoner drink. "I do not know why you continue to do this. I said I would tend to these men. This is no place. . . ."

"For a lady?" She shook her head. "You forget, Reverend, that I live in Ninety Six."

"You are becoming as bitter as your brother."

That made her really mad, but she bit her tongue, and, even though she no longer held the ladle, moved on to the next prisoner, who had turned his head and was begging for water in a dry whisper.

"Do not feel sorry for this foul lot," the preacher said.

"An eye for an eye?" she said, and immediately regretted the words.

While the prisoner drank, Monteith stared at her. "You seem to forget, Emily, that I was at the Welsh Neck, too. I remember Dogmael Jones's family. I remember his daughters, especially the one whose body was never found, and I remember how his son was brutalized."

"These men were not there," she said. "This I remember. Because I was there, too. I saw the prisoners."

"Yes. You have seen too much."

She moved on to the next man, leaving the bucket on the ground for the preacher to carry.

"These men are lewd gamesters and thieves," he said. "And for all we know, they may have been among those swine that robbed the life from Alroy O'Fionnagáin and his wife."

"No," she said.

He turned to her. "And how do you know this?"

"Because Da' and Donnan did not hang them."

Although the flows of the rivers had fallen to normal levels, Monteith had postponed his return to Charlestown, saying his work remained in the Ninety Six District. Emily believed him. Here was the proof. They moved on to the next man.

There were other prisoners. The stockade constructed for protection during the Cherokee War had been rebuilt, turned into a jail of sorts. It, too, was full of men carrying heavy balls, or chained to pine logs. Dr. François Bayard and Pierre Maupin, the doctor's farmer neighbor, had been assigned as guards of the prisoners. She seldom saw them any more, not having the heart or the stomach to walk to the Gouedy place and see the stockade. The stocks here smelled foul enough.

She shot a quick glance at the two whipping posts, and found something for which to be thankful. At least no one had been flogged during the past week.

"I should take you to Charlestown." Monteith dipped the ladle in the bucket. "Our most merciful God has ended the smallpox outbreak in Georgetown, thus it will be safe for you to visit your grandparents' home. To be far, far removed from this lawless place."

To her surprise, the idea did not offend her. "Are you to return to Charlestown?" she asked.

"Yes." He let the next man drink. "There is much to be done in Charlestown, explanations are needed or I fear . . . well, yes,

I should leave here, and afterward I should continue bringing the Word to the residents of the Back Country."

"Explanations?" she said.

He paused, and she figured he would dismiss her, but instead he inhaled deeply, holding his breath while the prisoner drank, and then answered: "Governor Montagu, I fear, does not understand what we are doing here. Word has reached Charlestown of the actions of the Cane Creek Regulators . . . and other regulators."

"There are more?"

"Yes, indeed. In the Peedee. At the Congaree. Cheraw to Mars Bluff. And as far north and west as the Tyger and Enoree Rivers. Your father was not the first, nor will he be the last. But it is Lord Montagu's own fault. He could have done something. He could have listened."

Emily realized that, although Monteith had been in the Back Country for maybe a year, or even less than a year, his opinions had changed. He had hardened.

"The governor will not send troops here?" Emily asked as a sudden, palpable fear struck her. "Will he?"

"I do not know if Lord Montagu remains in Charlestown. It is late in the summer, and, as you well know, many men of wealth leave for the more temperate climes. But that trader that came through two days ago . . . the one bound for Fort Loudon . . . said that Lord Montagu has ordered all such forces of regulators to disperse." They moved on to the final prisoner. "He fears that these men are no more than . . . what was the word that trader used? . . . ah, yes, vigilantes. A nascent mob."

Maybe Lord Montagu was right. Perhaps the Cane Creek Regulators were nothing more than a wild mob, one that could indeed transform into something even more horrible. She looked at the bucket as the parson brought the ladle to the Turk, or whatever the dark-skinned man was. She could see her reflection in the water, and did not like how she looked. A year ago, she actually had considered herself pretty, but now she saw nothing but the bags under her eyes, a brow that seemed perpetually knotted, her hair filthy and uncombed, lips too thin, eyes too . . . unholy?

"Dearest God in heaven!" cried Monteith.

The ladle dropped at Emily's feet as the preacher backed away so quickly, he bumped into her and sent her sprawling on the grass.

"Miss Emily!" It was Benjamin Cooper's voice calling out. "Preacher!"

She sat up, saw Monteith still backing away, then looked toward the carpenter's shed. The big man ran toward them, but it wasn't Cooper that had startled the Anglican minister. She turned again, and looked at the Turk, saw his eyes, and then shut her own. Another face to haunt her dreams.

At the same time the prisoner next to the Turk rasped out: "God save us. God save us all. He is dead. They have killed him. They will kill us all."

CHAPTER FIFTEEN

Shortly after noon on July 25th, the Cane Creek Regulators hanged William Robert McIntosh at the gallows tree. Farmer Ferguson had caught him trying to steal a fat sow from one of his pens, and McIntosh had fought back, slicing Ferguson from wrist to elbow before the red-headed farmer had clubbed the would-be thief with the handle of his grub hoe. Even in Ninety Six, such crimes would not get a criminal hanged, but when Ferguson found a broach in the man's pocket, he and his sons had dragged McIntosh to the tavern, hands bound behind him.

"Do you recognize this?" Stewart asked as he held out the small piece of carved ivory in his massive hand.

Machara glanced at it, bit her lip, and nodded. Tears streamed down her face, and she pushed herself out of the chair, grabbed the hands of Alan and Elizabeth, and led them out of the tavern, saying something about needing to see how the corn was looking.

When the door closed, that giant hand swallowed the broach, and Stewart turned quickly, heading straight for McIntosh. With tears in his eyes, Stewart grabbed the man by his throat and lifted him off the floor.

Emily gasped. Behind the bar, Donnan laughed.

"Where did you get this?" Stewart asked.

The man gagged.

"He cannot answer you, Breck," the preacher said, pointing to Stewart's hand around McIntosh's throat.

Breck lowered McIntosh to the floor. "I shall ask you but once more."

"I . . . found it," McIntosh choked out.

"Aye. You found it. On the body of Kate O'Fionnagáin."

Stupidly McIntosh tried to bolt for the open door, but Ferguson's oldest son tripped him before he had gotten more than four steps, and the man fell to the floor, unable to break his fall with his hands. Ferguson's sons jerked McIntosh to his feet, blood oozing from his nose and lip, and slammed him against the wall.

"Where are the others?" Stewart asked him.

The prisoner sniffled.

"Then make your peace with God," Stewart declared.

"I do not know, but come September they shall convene at Jacob's Fork," said McIntosh.

Emily looked at Donnan, who shrugged and shook his head.

"Jacob's Fork?" Stewart repeated, and looked at the other men inside Cormorant's Rock.

"It is in North Carolina!" McIntosh cried out. "In the South Mountains."

"Draw us a map," Donnan said, and rifled underneath the bar until he had found a piece of parchment.

Unbound, William Robert McIntosh drew a map. He answered every question the regulators asked him. He said at least three bands of renegades met each September in the South Mountains, to get drunk on kill-devil, to bet on horse races, to brag, to fight, to mingle with whores. A procurer from the settlement called Charlotte Town along the Great Wagon Road brings in a wagonload of courtesans to entertain the outlaws. When the rum is gone, after they whore and gamble and fight themselves out, they disband.

"Fornication, gambling, drunkenness. You turn these colonies into Sodom and Gomorrah," Monteith said.

"Go help Mum," Donnan told Emily.

"I shall do no such," she whispered back at him, but then felt his grip on her arm, tight, hurting, and she whirled at him, but his eyes frightened her. They burned harder than those of her father. As Donnan's hand let go, Emily turned, not giving her brother the satisfaction of letting him see her rub her arm that she knew would be badly bruised, and moved toward the door.

"How many men?" she heard her father ask.

"Sixty," McIntosh said. "Maybe more."

They hanged him, anyway. They did give him a chance to pray with the Reverend Monteith, but did not allow him to wash the pig manure off his face, hands, and clothes.

By August, Monteith was gone, having joined up with the Gouedy clan as they hauled their pelts and other trade goods to Charlestown. Emily felt relief when the mules, carts, and wagons headed down the road, through the trees, and out of sight. She had feared her father would send her along, and this time she doubted there would be a smallpox outbreak in Georgetown to save her.

On a Sunday afternoon, after delivering a loaf of bread to Darlene Courtney and her toddling son—a handsome devil and quite the handful—Emily walked back home. In the cabin in the timbers, Rachel Zachary sat with her husband, laughing as he fumbled with his fiddle. Warblers and wood thrushes, meadowlarks and tanagers sang from their perches in their nests or on limbs. A bobwhite quail called out from the forest, and a pair of squirrels frolicked over her head, chattering, as they leaped from tree to tree. Emily realized she had been whistling as she walked, answering the bobwhite, and it struck her that she felt safe.

Safe. No fear. Her mother had not warned her to be careful, had not asked someone to accompany her to Darlene's home, and Emily had not even thought about carrying the small pistol with her.

She stopped, and looked at the path between the tavern and Mr. Taylor's property. The stocks were empty. No one had been strapped to the whipping posts recently. Emily could not even remember the last time she had been wakened in the middle of the night by nightmare of Blubber Cheeks, or the dead Turk, or William Robert McIntosh.

Her father still led patrols, but no hogs had been reported stolen. Horse theft had become a rarity. Certainly there had been no murders. She had to admit that the Cane Creek Regulators were doing their job.

A peace had settled over Ninety Six.

That would change, of course. Most nights, when they were home and not patrolling, her father and Donnan met with Dr. Bayard, Pierre Maupin, James Middleton, and the hog farmer Ferguson, studying the map. Sometimes, Go-la-nv Pinetree would be there.

September, Emily knew, was only two weeks away.

The aroma of shepherd's pie and Sally Lunn bread drifted out of the oven and cook fire her mother had going in the back yard—it was too hot to cook inside these days—and Emily stopped.

Bent over the pot, Emily's mother put her hand on her back, and straightened, then wiped sweat from her forehead. She beamed at her daughter, and Emily smiled back.

"Do you need help, Mum?" she asked.

"No, child, but thank you. Supper will be ready in half an hour or so."

"Thank you. Then I shall go upstairs and practice my reading."

"Hosea," her mother said. "Chapters One and Two."

"Yes, Mother."

She entered through the back door, stepped through the winter kitchen, and moved into the tavern, then up the stairs and into the loft, to the room where Alan and Elizabeth sat on the floor, drawing pictures. Emily found the Bible, sat on the stool, and opened the book to the Old Testament. She shot a glance at the children, who were preoccupied with their artwork, and she reached underneath the mattress, and pulled out the piece of paper, unfolded it as quietly as possible, and set the paper on the pages of the Bible.

Pretending to read, she studied the map. Cross the river and follow the train northeast, past Glenn Springs, to the Cowpens, a four-day journey. Then north, fording the Broad River at a place marked Boiling Springs, east of Kings Mountain. From there, the South Mountains were a hard day's ride, almost directly north. To the north and west rose the rugged Blue Ridge, and to the southeast stood Charlotte Town. Not many trails, and the country was hillier, apparently, certainly more rugged than around Ninety Six, but Emily thought she could make this journey. She knew she would regret leaving her mother alone with Elizabeth and Alan, worried sick, and she knew Donnan and her father would make her regret such disobedience.

Why? Emily had to think about that. Why did she want to go to Jacob's Fork and the South Mountains? She was a girl, no, a woman. She had no business chasing after the regulators, spying on them. Besides, following that map, vague as it appeared, would not be easy. Certainly she did not think she would find Finnian Kilduff at the South Mountains, and even if she did, she wouldn't be able to rescue him from the stocks or whipping post. As Reverend Monteith had reminded her, Kilduff was not Robin Hood. He was an outlaw, too lazy to earn an honest day's shilling.

She focused on the map. The hanged pig thief had made the

first copy, which Emily's father had shown to Go-la-nv Pine-tree, mentioning to him the South Mountains and Jacob's Fork and North Carolina. The Cherokee had borrowed that map, over Donnan's objections, and carried it with him back to the Cherokee village of Keowee. When he had returned, he had brought a new map, with more details, including a few symbols that Emily couldn't quite decipher. After talking with Go-la-nv for several hours, Dr. Bayard and her father had worked on the map themselves, until they felt confident it would lead them to the haven of the outlaws.

Emily had sneaked into the tavern after everyone had left or gone to sleep, found the map, and sketched her own copy.

"Catch the bandits in September," her father kept saying, "and we will crush their hold on the Back Country once and for all."

Hoofs sounded outside, and Alan and Elizabeth hurried to the window, staring down, pointing, whispering between themselves.

"Who is it?" Emily asked.

Her brother turned. "I do not know."

Elizabeth interrupted him. "But there is a lot of them."

Emily slipped the map out of the Bible, folded it, and stuck it inside her apron, before walking to the window.

She watched the men swing out of their saddles. A number of horses, their hides wet from sweat, already crowded the hitching post and rail, and she heard voices and footsteps on the porch.

"One . . . two . . . three . . . ," Elizabeth began.

Emily counted the horses herself. Four pack mules, and an ox-drawn cart loaded with . . . ? She couldn't tell.

". . . seven . . . eight . . . eleven," Alan said.

"Shut up!" her sister snapped. "You have made me lose my count, and nine comes after eight."

"Does not."

"Does too."

"Does not!"

"Emily!"

"Quiet," she said, shushing her siblings. "Da' is speaking."

". . . good tidings to you all," Stewart was saying from the porch. "You men look as if you have worked up a substantial thirst."

"And my father has just finished a new batch of persico," Donnan announced.

"Machara did not think you would be here so soon," Stewart said. "Nor did I. But we shall put more food in the pots, and bake more bread."

"Food," a voice said, "can wait, but mead would be welcome."

"We brought out own grub, Captain Stewart," someone else said.

"For the long journey to North Carolina."

One of the voices she thought she had heard before, but Emily could not place it with either face or name. She studied the men, some unsaddling their horses, a few drinking from gourds, one emptying his canteen over his long, sweat-soaked black head. Back Country men for certain, who, from the looks of their horses, had traveled far.

Now she could hear voices from inside the tavern, casks being moved to fill steins and mugs, chair legs scraping against the floor, voices mingling with laughter.

A figure rounded the corner of the tavern—a dark man who seemed to have little interest in joining the other men inside the building.

"Indian!" Alan sang out, pointing.

"That's not Pinetree," Elizabeth said. "Is it, Emily?"

"No," she said softly. "His name is Blue."

"Blue?" Elizabeth asked.

"How do you know his name?" Alan asked.

She didn't answer. She looked at the Indian with his long hair, no clothing except for the breechcloth, moccasins, and that strange cap. Ye Iswa. Now Emily knew where these men had come from. Now she remembered where she had heard that voice. The Welsh Neck. Owen Devonald and the others who had captured the killers of Dogmael Jones and his family. She watched the Catawba Indian sit silently in front of the well.

"Clarke!" came the voice that she had thought sounded familiar from inside the tavern. "Show Captain Stewart our uniform."

"Let me get it!"

She watched as a man came out of the building and headed for a ground-reined sorrel horse near the oak tree. He rubbed his hand on the horse's sleek hide, moved to the saddle, and opened a canvas sack fastened to one of the pommel holsters. Out came a cotton mask, dyed blue, holes cut out for the eyes. That went on his head, and the man returned inside.

"You hide your face like a night rider!" she heard Donnan shout.

"Not in shame," came the response, "but to strike fear in the raiders we will crush. Is not that right, Captain Devonald?"

Memories of Swift Creek and the Anderson place came back to Emily. The night attack, and the capture of the killers who then had been sent to Charlestown. Where the governor pardoned enough of them to reap a whirlwind across the South Carolina Back Country. She heard herself whisper: "For good order and harmony of the colony."

"What?" Alan asked.

Emily brought her finger to her lips, and the two children went quiet.

"We are the Peedee Regulators, Breck," Devonald was saying. "And I respectfully will follow your command as we ride to crush the vermin at the South Mountains. Have you heard from

Captain Pegues?"

"He will join us at Boiling Springs," Stewart answered.

Pegues. Emily had not met him, but she had heard her father speak of him often enough. A rich planter from Cheraw, Captain Claudius Pegues commanded Cheraw's vigilante group.

"And what of Henry Hunter and his boys?" Devonald asked.

Hunter. She knew of him, too, commanding the regulators at the settlement once known as Pine Tree but now being called Camden.

"I did not send word to Hunter," Stewart informed him. "Nor to Gideon Gibson at Mars Bluff. Nor the man . . . I disremember his name . . . leading the campaign on the Saluda."

"And what of William Wofford?" another man asked.

"I do not know him, and those who I know not, I do not trust," Stewart said. "Secrecy will mean the success of our mission, gentlemen. If word reaches the outlaws, then this campaign will be for naught."

"Well, Breck," Devonald said, "we are with you, and glad to be here, and glad that you know, and trust, the Peedee Regulators."

As Devonald broke out into some Welsh war ballad, Emily led Alan and Elizabeth away from the window.

"We need to do our Bible studies," Emily said, and opened the book to Hosea. Yet she wasn't thinking about the Scripture she read to her siblings. She was thinking about that mask, the uniform of the Peedee Regulators.

Now she knew how she could follow her father and his men to Jacob's Fork.

CHAPTER SIXTEEN

In the morning the two groups of regulators rode out of Ninety Six. Breck Stewart stood in the tavern, waiting for Emily to come down the stairs, hands behind his back.

She stopped as soon as she saw him, swallowed nervously, and continued down the steps. The tavern was empty, but through the open door she saw her mother hurrying out to the men as they saddled, handing them the biscuits she had spent all night preparing. A chorus, including Darlene Courtney and Rachel Zachary, serenaded the men with "The Flowers o' the Forest."

"Good morning, Daughter," Stewart said, smiling.

"Da'." She reached the main floor, holding her breath as he brought his hands out from behind him. Her eyes dropped to stare at her feet as soon as she saw the blue-dyed mask in his hands.

"Come here, Emily," he said, not harshly and without condemnation. She watched him drop the mask on a table, and when she could not make her legs move, she saw him approaching her, and then his massive arms were around her, hugging her with the strength of a black bear.

The tears broke free, and she sobbed. Squeezing her even tighter, he kissed her hair, and whispered: "You are a Stewart of Appin. Next to Machara, you are the love of my life. I know a father should not have favorites, but you are mine. You always have been. You always will be. Did you really think you could follow us to North Carolina?"

She cried even harder, and fought to get the words out. "I . . . thought . . . I could . . . try."

He pulled back, keeping his hands on her shoulders, smiling through the tears in his own eyes. "I have left Nutmeg with Ol' Benji Cooper," he said. "The saddle is in Cooper's barn. He has been told that you are not to have it, that you are not to leave this village, for three days. Now . . . I must trouble you for the map."

She felt regret when he released his hold. His hands, she feared, were the only things keeping her steady on her feet. Her left hand slid into the pocket of her apron, and came out with the folded piece of parchment.

He took it, shoved it inside the leather pouch hanging over his shoulder, and shook his head. "You are a wonder, child."

Emily wiped her nose. "How did you find out?"

His head tilted in the direction of the assembling men. "David Clarke discovered his mask was missing. Some of the boys said he must have lost it in a state of drunkenness, but I had another notion. You have been studying your Bible much more than usual, Emily, and your mother thought it odd that she found the quill and ink on the table in your bedroom."

Nodding, accepting defeat, she brushed the last of her tears from her cheek.

"Do you have a weapon?" he asked.

For just a moment, she thought he might just take her with them. After all, she had been with the men at the Welsh Neck just more than a year ago, but then she realized the foolishness of such a thought, shrugged, and said: "The pistol you gave me."

Stewart's head bobbed. "Keep it. Things have been peaceful here, but one cannot be certain the vermin who prey on others will not strike here whilst we are gone." He turned to go, but stopped, and came back to embrace her even harder, longer, before he finally pulled away.

"Wipe your eyes a final time, Daughter, and join Alan and Elizabeth to see the Cane Creek Regulators and the Peedee Regulators ride to glory. Remember . . ."—his voice lowered— "you are a Stewart of Appin. I love you. I have always been proud of you, and shall always be proud of you."

He whirled, and his long legs carried him out the door, but not before he snatched David Clarke's mask off the table.

Emily stood there, trying to gather her composure. Finally she managed a tentative step forward, then another, and, sucking in a deep breath, she found herself stepping through the doorway and onto the porch to the cacophony of shouts, songs, and curses mingling with the whinnying of horses and the stamping of nervous hoofs on the ground in front of the tavern.

Emily shivered. She remembered last year, how hard that winter had been, how early it had struck, and prayed it would not happen again. She realized that the chill she felt was not from the wind, which blew warm, but from somewhere inside her. Pulling up the collar of her dress, she moved down the porch where Alan and Elizabeth stood waving.

"I wish they'd let me go with them," Alan said.

"Me, too," Elizabeth said, and, looking up at Emily, she asked: "Do not you wish so, too?"

Emily smiled weakly and shook her head. "We must know our place," she said softly. "And we must be brave. We are Stewarts . . . Stewarts of Appin."

"I still wish I could go with them," Alan muttered.

Me, too, Emily thought as she watched Donnan bark orders at the tattooed Catawba Indian and Go-la-nv Pinetree before swinging into his saddle, and shouting at Ferguson, the pig farmer, whose mule kept kicking as two other men tried to slide a pack on its back.

Having dispensed the biscuits, Machara hurried to the porch. Underneath the giant oak, holding hands, Darlene Courtney and Rachel Zachary began singing an Irish ballad, "My Gallant Darling", in the old language. Emily felt a pang of jealousy. She hated Rachel's voice, and Darlene's as well, because she could never sing like those two women.

> *Sé mo laoch, mo Ghile Mear*
> *Sé mo Chaesar, Ghile Mear,*
> *Suan ná séan ní bhfuaireas féin*
> *Ó chuaigh i gcéin mo Ghile Mear.*

She sang softly with them, only in English.

> *He's my champion, my Gallant Darling,*
> *He's my Cæsar, a Gallant Darling,*
> *I've found neither rest nor fortune*
> *Since my Gallant Darling went far away.*

She watched her father as she sang, and felt the tears begin to flow again. When the girls had finished the song, her mother, now standing beside Emily, began a new song, her voice booming.

> *Hie upon Highlands,*
> *And lay upon tay.*
> *Bonnie George Campbell*
> *Rode out on a day.*
> *He saddled, and bridled,*
> *So gallant rode he.*
> *And hame cam his guid horse,*
> *But never cam he.*

Emily felt her mother's hand, and their fingers locked. She wanted to join her in song, but she was crying too hard now.

Several of the regulators had joined in the song with fifes, and then a drum began beating as the men rode out of Ninety Six, heading north.

Donnan spurred his horse past, grinning and tipping his cocked hat as he galloped across the yard, leaping his horse over a fence, shouting the savage Scottish battle cry—*"Creag an Sgairbh!"*—while riding to the point.

"Look at Donnan ride!" Alan screamed with delight.

Emily didn't. She just kept her eyes on her father, squeezed her mother's hand, and cried as the regulators rode out.

> *Out cam his mother dear,*
> *Greeting fu sair,*
> *And out cam his bonnie bryde,*
> *Riving her hair.*
> *The meadow lies green,*
> *The corn is unshorn,*
> *But bonnie George Campbell*
> *Will never return.*
> *Saddled and bridled*
> *And booted rode he,*
> *A plume in his helmet,*
> *A sword at his knee.*
> *But toom cam his saddle,*
> *All bloody to see,*
> *Oh, hame cam his guid horse,*
> *But never cam he.*

When the frost arrived the following week, she led Alan and Elizabeth to the garden to pull up the carrots. Alan naturally kept pretending the one he had gathered was a pistol, firing it at bandits, squirrels, and Indians. Emily had to keep her eye on Elizabeth to stop her from putting any of the vegetables in her mouth.

"Wait until we wash them, Elizabeth, and scrape the dirt off them!"

They had filled two baskets, and the third was growing heavy. It had been a good crop, not just for the carrots, but for the tomatoes and corn, practically everything. Even if winter proved to be hard, they would not likely go hungry.

"Where's Da'?" Elizabeth said.

"Killing bastards," Alan answered.

"Alan Stewart!" Emily said. "If Mum heard you say such a naughty word, your mouth would taste like soap and you would not feel comfortable sitting in a chair for a week."

"It's what Donnan says," Alan whined.

"Let him say it. You sha'n't."

He stuck out his tongue. "You say it, too."

She tossed a dirt clod at him, and the playful fight was on.

It stopped when Machara leaned her head out the back door. "Emily, can you help me?"

"Yes, Mum!" she called back, standing and brushing the mud and dirt off her dress. As she moved past the scarecrow and climbed over the fence, she said to her siblings: "Can you two concentrate on pulling carrots for a few minutes?"

Their heads bobbed.

"Dig deep. Do not just pull these up by the greenery. They will break off and you will leave a good portion of the carrot in the dirt."

"We sha'n't," Elizabeth said, but Emily had her doubts.

She met her mother inside the winter kitchen.

"We have a visitor," her mother whispered as she poured water into a pot.

"Aye? And who might it be?"

"I do not know, Emily, but he is hungry and he is thirsty."

"Oh." She shook her head at her stupidity, it having been so long since they had actually had a customer that Emily had practically forgotten that Cormorant's Rock did business as an inn.

"If you will fetch him a drink, I shall try to water down our leftovers enough that it might make a decent meal. Oh, my goodness," Machara said, pulling back at her hair. "What would Breck say? The stove is not hot, and the cornbread is at least two days' old!"

"Mum," Emily said, heading toward the tavern, "a bit of mead is likely all he wishes for supper." She pulled the door shut behind her, and saw the back of a man in a ribbon shirt, sitting alone, one leg stretched underneath the table, spur resting on the seat of the opposite chair.

"What is your pleasure for a drink?" she called out to the man's back as she moved toward the cask of mead.

"The persico is bragged about as far north as the Cowpens," came the answer, and Emily stopped, and quickly turned around.

Finnian Kilduff dragged his right leg off the chair, turned slowly, and grinned that devilish smirk of his.

"What are you doing here?" she whispered.

"Is this not a tavern? I am hungry. And thirsty. And have traveled far."

"We have no persico. My father is . . . visiting."

"Aye." He cocked his head at a rakish angle.

Since she had left her pistol upstairs, she reached with her hand for the bung starter her father kept underneath the bar.

"I have no sentiment when it comes to mead," Kilduff informed her. "I do not know how people drink that stuff, but a wee bit of rum with a splash of water would wash the grit off my tongue."

Finding a jug of the kill-devil, Emily filled a mug, and caught a glance of herself in the mirror. She groaned. Her dress was covered in filth, her hair looked a mess, and carrots and dirt had stained her hands a horrible brown-tinted orange.

I do not give a damn, she thought to herself, and rounded the bar, sliding the mug in front of Kilduff and putting both hands on her hips.

"I shall ask to see the color of your coin," she said.

Kilduff laughed. "Is that how you treat all of your neighbors?"

"Neighbor?" Her head shook. "We are a long way from your hide-out."

"I now reside on Cane Creek," he said.

She frowned, but said nothing. Instead, she walked to the door, pulled it open, and stared outside.

"Looking for something?" he asked. "I came alone."

"I am looking at your horse."

"Indeed. That dun is a beaut'. Won me a hogshead of rum in a race at Wilmington."

She slammed the door, and glared.

"Are you angry?" He scratched his chin. "Well, the man who sold me his home did say that the people of Ninety Six are not friendly."

She made a guess, saying: "Joseph Robinson."

He laughed. "Indeed."

"And where, by chance, did you see that lout?"

"In Charlestown."

"Did you rob him on a dark street?" she asked.

He picked up his mug, toasted in her direction, and took a sip. "I bought him several drinks in Dillon's Tavern. Then I bought his home. Before he met with Lieutenant Governor Bull to complain about . . . your Cane Creek Regulators."

"Aye," she said, feeling a need to fill the silence between them. "I thought your home was a hut in the forest . . . with . . ."—she had to think back to remember the name—". . . Tasmin."

He was sipping the rum when she spoke the name, and he

almost choked. He set the mug on the table and produced a handkerchief to wipe his mouth. "By Jehovah, Miss Stewart, you have a memory, but her name was Tanwen."

"Was?" Emily asked.

Kilduff's eyes dropped, and he fingered the cup absently. "Aye," he said after a long moment. "Was. The bloody flux laid her low."

"I am sorry."

"As am I. As were we all . . . those of us who were left afterward." He tried to smile when he looked up at her. "Those days are behind me now, Miss Stewart, for I have found a new vocation."

She looked back at the kitchen, saw the door closed, and leaned closer, lowering her voice: "If the Reverend Monteith returns, he will remember you. And my brother will remember you, as well. And that marsh tacky that you ride will carry you underneath our gallows tree."

"Indeed. Where is your brother, Miss Stewart? And your father? And . . . where are most of the men in Ninety Six? This place feels like a cemetery."

"You better leave, sir. After your supper."

"Yes, where is my supper?"

"I will see if it is ready."

She turned, her heart pounding against her ribs and sweating hard despite the chill. The door opened with a crash before she had even gotten close, and her mother came in, looking nervous. She wet her lips as she served the platter containing a bowl of lukewarm soup and stale bread.

Kilduff sprang to his feet, removing his cocked hat, bowing and saying: "Please, please, Missus Stewart, there is no rush."

"It is not very filling, I fear," Machara said.

"Have a seat," Kilduff said, and eased Machara into the chair that recently had housed his right boot and spur. "I wanted to come by and make your acquaintance, as I am newly settled in the district. I wanted to introduce myself to your husband."

Machara tried to catch her breath as Kilduff motioned Emily toward another chair, but Emily shook her head.

"You are new here?" Machara asked.

"Yes. I have acquired the home of Mister Joseph Robinson."

"Oh, yes." Machara's head bobbed. "He was. . . ." She looked at Emily, blushing, and shook her head. "You bought his property?"

Kilduff sat back down, shaking his head. "Not personally. In a sense, it belongs to Lord Montagu. In another sense, I suppose my landlord is Richard Cumberland."

Machara blinked. "Richard . . . Cumberland?"

"Yes," Kilduff said.

Having moved closer to the table to protect her mother, Emily was so stunned, she blurted: "The provost marshal?"

"Aye." Kilduff beamed as he nodded at Emily. "You know much for a young woman so far from Charlestown. Richard Cumberland, provost marshal for the colony of South Carolina. Lord Montagu has appointed me his deputy. I am Kilduff." He bowed at Machara. "Finnian Kilduff. Deputy Provost Marshal Finnian Kilduff."

CHAPTER SEVENTEEN

"Why did they send you to Ninety Six, Deputy Kilduff?" Robert Gouedy asked. He tested the tea Machara had poured him, found that it was too hot, so blew on it, all the while never taking his eyes off the deputy provost marshal.

"There is grave concern in the colony about what is going on in the Back Country," Kilduff said.

"Would you do otherwise?"

Kilduff's eyes caught Emily's and held for a moment before he fumbled in his pocket for his pipe and container of tobacco. He shrugged, and said: "The governor feels strongly about these regulators. Lord Montagu has heard rumors that they will march on Charlestown in the spring. Revolution . . . it strikes fear in the gentry, and in those holding office in the Assembly. And Parliament, as well."

"We are loyal to King George," Gouedy said.

"But not to Lord Montagu. You have ignored his order to have your militia disperse."

"If Breck Stewart disbanded his army. . . ."

"Then you admit it is an armed force."

Gouedy shook his head in disgust. "If you go unarmed against bandits, you would not accomplish much, would you, sir?"

"And if you marched on Charlestown?"

"We have no intention of marching against the Crown, sir. But as I said, if the Cane Creek Regulators marched against the criminals in this country without weapons, they would be slaughtered, and those fiends would be free to wreak even more havoc on farmers, traders, and travelers."

Kilduff's head shook. "Charlestown. . . ."

"Charlestown is too far from the Back Country," Gouedy said. "Charlestown does not know what is happening to the King's people. In Charlestown, you revolt against Parliament's Stamp Act, and that is fine for your wealthy merchants. You celebrate your cause. You turn away the King's ships. But when those of us revolt against outlaws who commit robbery, rapine and murder, you call us criminals. You, sir, seem to forget that the majority of this colony's settlers reside not along the tidewater, but out here in the frontier."

"Once, I resided here, too, sir."

"I remember you." Gouedy picked up his mug, and sipped the tea. Emily decided that was a good excuse to bring the kettle from the kitchen and refill their cups, though Gouedy's was practically full, and Kilduff's still steaming.

"You remember me, sir?" asked Kilduff.

"Certainly. You traded with the Cherokees. You were a barrister in Dublin, London, and later in Charlestown."

Emily arrived at that moment, and filled Kilduff's mug, then motioned toward Gouedy's, but he waved her away with irritation.

"May I bring you some bread, sirs?" she asked.

"No," Gouedy snapped, but Kilduff smiled and said: "Please. If it is no trouble."

She curtsied and raced back to the kitchen, found the bread and a bit of butter, and sprinted back to the tavern.

"I would not expect to see you here as a provost," Gouedy was saying, "but rather as one the provost's prisoners bound for Charlestown."

Kilduff had the audacity to wink at Emily as she set the plate on the table. "There are many in agreement with you, sir. But be that as it may, I am the deputy, and I can produce the documentation from Lieutenant Governor Bull if you so desire."

"You have always been a man of your word, Finnian."

Finnian? They were on a first-name basis, Emily thought to herself. Then she heard herself saying: "If you do not mind, I would like to see such proof."

Gouedy stared at her in horror, or maybe he felt rage at the audacity of a seventeen-year-old girl, but Kilduff chuckled, and reached for the leather valise at his feet. The grip came onto the table, almost knocking over his mug of tea, and he opened it, still laughing, and reached inside. She expected him to come out with a pistol, and for his face to become savage, but his expression never changed, and out came a parchment, which he unrolled, and slid toward, not Emily, but Robert Gouedy.

"You are familiar with the governor's royal stamp, are you not, Squire Gouedy?" Speaking now with strict formality.

Gouedy sighed, nodded, and produced the spectacles he carried in his pocket. At least, he didn't take Kilduff at his word. He leaned forward, holding the glasses on the bridge of his nose, and his mouth moved as he read. Finally he lifted his head, dropped the eyewear inside his pocket, and frowned at Emily, who backed away from the table.

Damned if she would apologize. Not to the likes of Finnian Kilduff, and certainly not to Robert Gouedy.

"I have work to do," she said, and returned to the bar, keeping herself busy, or at least pretending to work as she polished mugs and steins, and wiped the counter—something her father rarely did, except when there had been a fight.

"The Cherokee War ruined me, Gouedy," Kilduff said. "But made you richer than God."

" 'Twas your own doing, Finnian. You were branded a rebel."

"In more ways than one, Gouedy. Would you care to see my back?"

"A distasteful punishment, but I had no hand in it."

They paused to drink their tea and partake of bread and butter. Emily grew impatient, hoping the conversation would resume, but when it did, they had moved away from Kilduff's past.

"So you are to turn Mister Robinson's house into an office?" Gouedy said, finishing his tea. "And a jail?"

Kilduff shook his head. "That was the plan, but Robinson said his place was close to Ninety Six. I fear it is too far from the tavern and other buildings to do much good as a jail. It is, after all, quite a walk from your stocks and pillory." Gouedy remained silent. "Robinson's sense of location was somewhat lacking, so we will have to find a more fitting location for a jail."

"Robinson's sense of duty was also lacking. But Lord Montagu thought of building a jail?" Gouedy's voice rose in anticipation.

"I do not know how much of this is the governor's idea and how much credit should go solely to William Bull," Kilduff said. "That Anglican minister who spent the fall and winter with you, he spoke to the Assembly recently and cited many requests . . . dare I call them pleas . . . to help you, as well as those in the Peedee, on the Saluda, the Broad, the Catawba."

"And what did that itinerant ask for?" Gouedy asked, shaking his head. "Churches?"

"Churches? Aye. But he also asked for courts. He said there is a need for courthouses, schools, and, as you see by my presence, jails."

"That foolish preacher did that?"

"He did not sound foolish to me, sir. And I think he preaches fine Old Testament brimstone."

Emily's head jerked up, and she had to stop herself from calling out: *And when, sir, did you have the privilege of hearing the Reverend Monteith preach?* What stopped her was Finnian

Kilduff, who turned away from the trader to look at Emily as if he expected her question. Immediately she looked away, hating his smirk.

"The governor listened to him?" Gouedy asked.

"Your parson is one to be heard, but . . ."—Kilduff laughed— ". . . well, I am not sure calling our Assemblymen 'aristocratic poltroons' and 'overgrown planters who wallow in opulence and prosperity' and other such verbiage is a good idea. But we shall see what action the Assembly proposes come spring."

"What about . . . a militia?" Gouedy asked. "You are but one man, and I do not believe you understand just how many outlaws roam these forests."

Emily choked down her laugh. *Oh, well he knows, sir,* she thought to herself. *How well he knows.*

"Keep your regulators under control, Gouedy. Hold on till spring, and let us see what happens in the Assembly. I shall return to Charlestown to speak to the governor. Just know this . . . the tide is changing, sir."

They were just putting the last of the potatoes in the cellar when metallic clangs cut through the morning air. Emily grabbed Alan and Elizabeth by their hands and hurried out of the darkness, sprinting around the back of the house. She could see Mrs. Taylor, banging the rod against the iron triangle that hung from a rafter. Standing outside his shed, Benjamin Cooper was pointing his massive hand, and yelling: "They come! They come! It be the regulators!"

Emily let go of Elizabeth's hand to shield her eyes, and immediately Elizabeth sprang down the road. Emily harshly called out for her to stop. By then, she could see the shadows moving through the trees, hear the creaking of leather, the clopping of hoofs. She held her breath, and prayed.

Machara stepped out onto the porch, sweat beading on her

forehead, as she furiously wiped the flour off her hands. "Do you see him, Emily?" she called.

"No, Mum."

The door to the Zachary cabin opened, and Rachel stepped out. Mrs. Taylor had stopped ringing the bell, and now she sprinted toward the path for a clearer view.

"What day is it?" Emily asked.

Alan looked up at her, and muttered: "I don't know."

She had not even realized she had asked the question aloud. Wetting her lips, she tried to do some quick arithmetic. Her father had left on September 7th. A Monday, she seemed to recall. How long ago? Green leaves had covered the trees on that morning, but now they had turned gold and red. She recalled Rachel Zachary and Darlene Courtney singing ballads of war and waiting women, the beat of drums, the whistles of the fife, how proud those men who called themselves the Cane Creek Regulators and the Peedee Regulators had looked. She could picture Donnan leaping his gray gelding over the fence while shouting that ancient battle cry: *Creag an Sgairbh!* She could almost feel her father's embrace.

Then the regulators from the Ninety Six District and the Welsh Neck rode into the settlement in silence. Bearded faces. Eyes unblinking. Emily gasped. More than a few mounts carried empty saddles. Some of the men wore bandages.

"Mum?" Alan whirled around. "Where's Da'?"

"He's coming," Emily heard her mother's faint whisper. "See. There is Owen Devonald."

Yes, Emily saw the innkeeper from the Peedee. Walking. In mud-covered clothes. Leading the horse, and behind the horse was a litter. On the litter was a body.

"I do not see Donnan!" Elizabeth wailed as she ran back to the tavern. Emily reached for her, but she spun from her hands, and hurried up the steps, wrapping her arms around her

169

mother's legs.

"It is all right, Elizabeth," Machara said hoarsely. "Donnan is fine. Fine and strong he is."

"He told me he was invincible," Alan sobbed, and then also ran to his mother.

"Aye. And he is. That he is. Invincible," Machara assured her two youngest.

It was the quietness that unnerved Emily. She realized she stood alone in the yard now, and how desperately she wanted to feel her mother's arms around her shoulders, comforting her as well. To feel the way she had felt when her father had hugged her. To hear the words he had spoken of his pride for her. She struggled to recall how he sounded.

"Da'." She felt the tears roll down her cheeks. "Oh, Da'."

The regulators rode in a long, dreary line. More litters appeared. Silently the riders stopped at the well. Benjamin Cooper was already there, bringing up the bucket, passing the ladle to the first of the men.

Luke Zachary, Rebecca's husband, stood there, taking the reins to the horse Owen Devonald led, then moved to the man in the litter behind the horse. Devonald wet his lips, and slowly approached the porch of the tavern. Maybe he didn't see Emily, because he walked right past her, and Emily just stood there, noticing the dirty bandage wrapped tightly around his left hand and the way the innkeeper favored his left leg.

Devonald stopped at the foot of the stairs, cleared his throat, and turned around. "Donnan!" he called out. "Donnan Stewart!" Then Devonald faced Machara again. "We whipped the curs, Missus Stewart. Savage it was, a morning ablaze in butchery, but those fiends will torment good citizens nay again."

He might have said more, but Emily didn't hear. She saw a dun horse trot past the pack mules and the regulators afoot, and recognized the rider, but not the horse—Donnan had left on a gray he considered the best racing mount between the Tyger and the Edisto. Now Donnan's face was bearded, his eyes bloodshot, but she saw no injuries, no blood on his clothes, just mud and dust.

He pulled the salt-caked horse to a stop and swung out of the saddle, not bothering with the reins. He stopped by Emily, and studied her briefly. His Adam's apple bobbed, but he did not speak. No one said anything, until Machara Stewart's voice wailed, causing the dun horse to shy away, and men to look up from the well, forgetting their thirsts.

"Where is your father?" Machara asked.

Donnan's mouth opened, but the only sound to come through was a croak. He cleared his throat, and gestured at the line of horses and mules, the litters behind them. "He's back there," he finally managed to utter.

"He . . . he . . . is alive!" she cried out.

"Yes," Donnan said. "But. . . ."

"Show me," Machara ordered. "Take me to him. Emily . . . stay with Alan and Elizabeth." She ran down the steps, through the throng of horses and soldiers—living, wounded, and some dead. She did not wait for her son, just kept running, holding up the hems of her skirt, stopping to examine each body in the litters behind the horses.

Donnan started after his mother, but realized the hopeless-ness of it, so he turned to give orders to some of the regulators before walking toward the tavern's door. He said to Emily: "I must heat up water." Then he disappeared inside the log cabin, closing the door behind him.

Emily knew that he was not moving toward the kitchen to put water on the stove, but to the bar, to find the nearest jug of rum.

"Emily?" Alan whined. "Where is Da'?"

"Mum has gone to fetch him," she said stiffly. "Just. . . ." But she couldn't think of anything else to say.

Owen Devonald turned to Emily, whispering: "Your father always said you were strong, Miss Emily. Now you must show your strength. For your mother. For those young children. Can you do this? For Breck Stewart?"

Maybe her head bobbed. She wasn't sure. She just kept watching the men, many of them wounded, being helped from their horses and moved to the shade. A few began to call out for water, for their mothers. Emily felt the bile rise in her throat. She felt dead herself, as if she were an apparition.

Ferguson walked past her, his head shaking from side to side, muttering something Emily could not understand. She really didn't comprehend what Owen Devonald had said, either. Although he had told her the fight at the South Mountains had been a victory for the regulators, from the sight she was witnessing, she found that hard to believe.

CHAPTER EIGHTEEN

Almost paralyzed, Emily watched the Catawba, the Peedee man named David Clarke, and two other regulators carry the litter up the steps and inside the tavern. She couldn't look at her father, lying helplessly, but rather focused on her mother, holding Alan and Elizabeth by their hands, tears pouring down their faces as they silently followed Captain Breck Stewart inside.

Like a funeral procession, Emily thought. *Only Da' still lives.* She felt helpless. She couldn't even comfort the other wounded men, twenty or more, lying or sitting in the yard, a few leaning against the giant oak. But Benjamin Cooper kept working the well's bucket.

Dr. François Bayard came running down the path, black bag bouncing against his leg. The Huguenot did not even notice Emily as he bolted up the steps. The door slammed behind him. It sounded like a gunshot, and Emily cringed.

How long she stood there, she did not know. It was still daylight. Still morning. She felt someone standing beside her, caught the scent of rum, and knew it was her brother.

"How did it happen?" Emily heard herself ask.

"I did not see it happen."

"What happened?"

William Robert McIntosh had not lied. Scores of bandits had converged near Jacob's Fork. The gradually rolling hills were ablaze in colors—red, yellow, gold, and orange—and wood smoke rose like early morning fog. The outlaws had camped in a clearing, and were sleeping when the regulators struck.

Emily jutted her jaw toward the wounded. "They were asleep . . . and this is what you reaped?"

Donnan cursed underneath his breath. "There were more than we anticipated. We expected sixty. There must have been a hundred. And when they hid in the thick woods . . . do you remember Da' taking about the Seven Years War?"

She ignored the question. She knew her father had not been with General Braddock or George Washington. He had merely been telling them the stories he had heard from wayfarers who had passed through Ninety Six. Emily wasn't even sure where the Monongahela River was or why the British were fighting the French and Indians.

"We crushed them, Emily. Twenty-six men wounded, and seven dead. Gloriously dead. All but one of their wounds came in their front, Sister. No *white* regulator turned and ran." She squeezed her eyes shut. "More than fifty of those swine are dead, hacked to pieces. Twenty more now wear a giant T branded on their cheeks, so everyone in America shall know they are thieves. Aye, a few scattered into the woods and thickets, and escaped near the waterfall, but they sha'n't trouble God-fearing citizens of the Carolinas any more. And another sixteen . . . we hanged."

The nausea passed, and Emily bit her lip, leaning against the railing to keep from falling. She heard Donnan drink from the jug he had found in the tavern. When the door opened, she held her breath, opened her eyes to see the Catawba Indian walking to the well. Only then did she come to understand the true meaning of her brother's words, why he had emphasized the word *white*. She spun to face him.

"Where is Go-la-nv?"

As he lowered the jug, she saw his grin, the delight in his eyes.

"Dead," he assured her.

She did not remember falling. One second Donnan was staring at her with a devilish glint, and then the whole world began spinning, and she lay on her back while her brother lifted the jug to his mouth.

Ferguson had appeared from somewhere. So had Jonathan Conley. They helped her up, the red-headed hog farmer putting a damp cloth on her forehead before she brushed it aside, freed herself from the two well-meaning men, and reached for the railing.

"The Cherokee caught a ball through his back," Donnan said. "Is not that how it happened, Conley?"

The dizziness hadn't passed. She had to lean against the column, but she looked to Jonathan Conley, who shuffled his feet and stared at the porch floor.

"Yes, Miss Emily. I found his body after the fight was all done."

"We buried him with the rogues we killed at Jacob's Fork," Donnan said. "I would not let a damned Cherokee with a ball in his back spend eternity with the brave regulators who fell in battle with honor."

Emily flew into her brother, knocking the rum from his hands, catapulting him over the rails of the steps, landing in the grass and manure. She pounded his chest, tried to claw out his eyes. She spit into his face. "You son-of-a-bitch! You bastard! You killed him. You murdered Go-la-nv! I hate your guts. I hate. . . ."

All Donnan did was laugh.

What she could recall, would never forget, was Dr. Bayard's face. He must have pulled her off her brother, with help from Conley and Ferguson, and then slapped her. The hard shock produced its desired effect, because she blinked, realization coming slowly to her. The doctor, white sleeves rolled up to his elbows, his hands stained with blood, came into focus. Emily broke down, buried her head against Bayard's shoulder, and cried harder than she had ever cried.

The doctor—too much a gentleman to hug her, lest he stain her clothes with her father's blood—whispered something in French, before speaking gently in English. "It is all right, Miss Emily. Cry now, but cry it all out. Your father wishes to see you, and you must be strong for him. Strong for your mother and those two children." He turned toward Donnan, who was sniggering as he tried to stand, and when he could not get his legs to work and fell, he laughed even harder.

"*Vous êtes un âne,*" Bayard said harshly. "I do not know what caused this *bagarre,* but you will not do so any more. *Jamais!*" His right arm swept toward the wounded men in the front yard. "Not before such brave men as these. And not while your own father lies on a table in that cabin with mortal wounds." He pulled away from Emily. "He desires to see the both of you."

On the ground, Donnan was like an insect on its back, trying to right itself. Finally he stopped trying, and pressed his palms against the grass. "Captain Stewart will have to wait, Doctor," he said. "You see . . . I cannot get up."

"*Buveur.*" The doctor spit toward Donnan, and motioned for Emily to follow him into Cormorant's Rock.

How small he looked, how weak, how feeble.

Machara sat in a chair on her husband's left, holding one hand, stroking the back of it with her worn fingers. She did not look up as Emily sat in the chair across from her. Elizabeth and Alan stood at the foot of the table.

Stewart was conscious, and his eyes moved from Emily to Dr. Bayard. His mouth formed words, but Emily did not hear what he said.

"Donnan," Dr. Bayard said, "is outside, tending to the wounded. He will be here momentarily."

He gave a slight nod, and grimaced as though the movement had sent pain rifling through his body.

Emily reached over and took her father's other hand. It felt so cold, she feared if she squeezed it, it would shatter like ice.

"*Monsieur* Alan, *Mademoiselle* Elizabeth," Bayard said softly, "would you be so kind as to take me to your kitchen, so that I might wash up?"

"Go . . . with . . . him . . . children." Machara's voice sounded mechanical.

When the kitchen door closed, Breck Stewart said: "Peace has come to Ninety Six." His voice was as ragged as his breathing. "The bandits have been crushed."

Neither Emily nor her mother spoke.

"What happened whilst I was away?" He turned his head and coughed slightly. "I missed Alan's birthday. Meant to bring him . . . something."

Then they just sat there, holding hands, looking at one another, until the front door opened, and Donnan came inside. He swept off his hat, and moved—steadily, to Emily's surprise—to the long table.

"Ensign Stewart, you will assume command of the Cane Creek Regulators during my absence."

"Aye, aye, sir," Donnan said.

"How does it feel to be a captain?" Stewart asked his son.

"Fine, sir."

"Rely on your men. That is what my father . . . your grandfather . . . told me. Rely on your men. The Cherokee . . . Gola-nv Pinetree. He is a man to trust."

Emily gasped, but she did not let go of her father's hand, and would not look at her brother.

"A good Indian," Donnan said. "Yes, sir."

"Led us straight to that camp, did he not?"

"Yes, sir."

"I do not think . . . ," Stewart began to say. Then: "My God," he said softly, "feel that breeze. The tide comes in. God must have made Eden at Pawley's Island." Delirious he must have been, thinking he was back at Georgetown. "Mum, cannot I stay here for just another hour? The fish will surely bite by then."

To everyone's surprise, two days later, Breck Stewart seemed to rally. He was lucid, though weak, and had little appetite. When Robert Gouedy came by to check on him, Stewart insisted that he stay and talk. He even made Machara drape his regulator coat over his shoulders, the one he had worn as a volunteer during the Cherokee War.

"Where is that preacher?" he asked Gouedy.

"Stirring up trouble in Charlestown," Gouedy replied. "Making things hot for Lord Montagu."

Stewart laughed one of his famous belly laughs. "Good for him. By God, if only Monteith had the wisdom to become a Presbyterian. Have there been any troubles here?"

"No. Peaceful for once. Thanks to you."

Stewart waved his hand in dismissal, saying: "Balderdash. But we shall keep the regulators active. Winter comes, but we know what can return with the warmth of spring."

Gouedy took a deep breath, held it, then exhaled. "Breck, mayhap I should tell you. . . ." He shot a glance at Emily.

"Aye, Gouedy. Tell me what?"

"Governor Montagu . . . or maybe it was the provost marshal . . . anyway, a deputy provost marshal has been appointed. Finnian Kilduff. Do you remember him?"

"Kilduff," Stewart muttered.

Emily edged closer so she could hear her father. He was sweating, so she took the damp towel, and placed it on his forehead, which he grabbed, rolled into a ball, and flung toward the bar. "Kilduff. The Irishman?"

"Aye."

"The one branded a traitor for dealing with the Cherokees?"

"The same."

Stewart tried to lift himself up, but sank onto the pillow. "Well, I always thought him to be an honorable man. He came here?"

"Whilst you were gone."

"Where is he now?"

"He returned to Charlestown."

Stewart snorted, shook his head. "He sha'n't return. They never do. It remains up to the settlers of the Back Country to make their own law."

"And you have made it, Breck Stewart."

Before Owen Devonald left with the Peedee Regulators two days later, he sat by Stewart's bedside, swapping jokes and insults, and telling lies.

"When shall you be going to Charlestown this year, Breck?"

"I do not think I shall make it this year, you old Welshman. I have no need. But next fall, I shall come for sure, to trade with you for some Cheraw bacon."

"Fine. And perhaps you can bring that wayfaring Anglican preacher with you."

"Aye. He preaches a fine sermon for a traitor to Scottish Presbyterians. I hope he will preach at my funeral."

Which ended the conversation and left Owen Devonald at a loss for words.

★ ★ ★ ★ ★

On the sixth day since the return of the regulators, he called Emily to his bedside.

"Daughter," he said in a faint whisper, "I must ask you to bring someone to me."

"Who?"

"Go-la-nv Pinetree."

Emily's response was to bury her face in her father's chest. As the tears came, she cried: "Da', he cannot come. He is. . . ." She sniffed as the Cherokee's face flashed through her mind, and she remembered asking him what he was doing on that awful summer day. Hunting, he had said, but she had known he was lying. He had been following her, protecting her. Slowly she pulled herself up, and wiped away the tears. She had to be strong. For her father. For her ancestors. She was a Stewart of Appin. "Da', Go-la-nv is in Keowee. I cannot fetch him."

"Damnation," he said. "Then fetch me one of Gouedy's slaves." Tears now filled his eyes. "Daughter . . . oh, God . . . I have wet myself. I have pissed my pants like a damned baby."

She leaned over and hugged him, no longer afraid of hurting his bones as she realized that it was his spirit that was broken.

"Please . . . please . . . Emily!" he cried. "Do not let your mother. . . . Do not let anyone . . . especially Donnan . . . see me like this."

That dreadful morning when the Cane Creek Regulators had returned to Ninety Six from the South Mountains, Dr. Bayard had told Machara, Donnan, and Emily that Breck Stewart would live no more than five days.

The tenth day came, and he was sitting up, Alan on his knee, telling him lies about fighting pirates and alligators on Winyah Bay as a boy. It was that afternoon that the Reverend Douglas Monteith returned to Ninety Six.

He looked older now, Emily thought as she pulled back the curtain they had hung in the downstairs to give her father some privacy, Stewart having lacked the strength to go up the steps, nor his pride allowing him to be carried up.

"Besides, I sha'n't have Virgil Hickox whining about carrying my fat carcass down when I am dead." He had laughed, but no one else had. He had lost much weight since coming home.

With the ease of a young man, Stewart swung Alan off the table and onto the floor, lifted himself into a semi-sitting position, and bellowed at the Anglican. "Parson Monteith, it is grand to see you, sir! Come for the death watch, I warrant?"

Monteith cleared his throat. "Breck Stewart," he said as he strode across the room, "you shall bury us all."

" 'Tis my wish, Parson. 'Tis truly my wish."

Emily pulled up a chair for the preacher.

"And what rude, ignorant, and amoral scoundrels with a propensity for vice and idleness have you found mocking your sermons in hamlets across the Back Country, sir?" Stewart asked as he leaned forward, fluffed his pillow, and leaned back, his hands clasped behind his head.

"I married three couples on Lynches Creek," Monteith replied, "and baptized several on the Waccamaw."

"And has any marsh tacky kicked you in the balls?"

Emily smiled, and returned to the kitchen to fetch the preacher tea and bread. Yesterday her father in an hour of delirium had babbled on about mad dogs, screamed for his mother, and asked to see his brother, dead these last fifteen years. And now look at him. When she returned, the conversation had changed.

"A pardon?" Her father's voice was raspy. "What nonsense."

"It is from your friend, William Bull," the preacher said. "In Governor Montagu's absence, he has issued two proclamations. One is an order that all regulators must be suppressed, of their

181

own volition, of course, but the other grants a general pardon for all regulators, providing they keep the peace."

Stewart leaned forward, grimaced, then swore. "By Jehovah, keeping the peace is what we have done, sir. Tell that to that ape-faced baboon." He dropped back against the pillow, then sat up again, grabbed the pillow, and flung it at the curtain.

"I did not mean to cause him such distress," Monteith whispered to Emily as she led him out of the area, pulling the curtain closed behind her.

" 'Tis all right, Preacher," she said. "He gets this way. I think it is good." She smiled. "It is the Breck Stewart that I remember."

Two days later, Breck Stewart was swearing that his tavern felt hotter than Charlestown in August. Donnan kept applying a cold towel to his forehead, and his father kept cursing.

That is when Emily knew that Dr. Bayard was right, and that her father would not recover. She pulled on her coat, and went outside, her breath white as she crossed the frost-covered ground to gather more wood.

On that Sunday, Reverend Monteith held service in Cormorant's Rock, the curtain drawn back so Stewart could participate. Emily had not seen the place so crowded since that day the residents had gathered after those three butchers had tried to kill her in the woods, all of which seemed a lifetime ago. Tears ran down her cheeks as the sermon was preached, even though she really didn't hear anything the reverend said.

She was remembering Go-la-nv Pinetree sitting there that afternoon, playing with one of Alan's marbles, and the way his eyes had caught hers. She could see his smile. She wished that he had been as comfortable around her as he had seemed around men or children, like Alan and Elizabeth.

Her mind came back to the present when her father tried to

play the bagpipes, even though he lacked the breath and stamina. Those present applauded, despite the fact that this was supposed to be church, and the music spiritual, not secular.

After the service, ignoring Reverend Monteith, the men and women of the district—even Birmingham Long—walked past to shake hands with Captain Breck Stewart, tavern owner, captain of the Cane Creek Regulators.

That day Stewart was lucid, coherent, jovial, happy, snapping jokes, kissing the ladies' hands, telling lies, and sipping his own bumbo.

Two days later, on Tuesday, October 4, 1767, William Breck Stewart died. He was forty-six years old. No fanfare, no last words. He had gone to sleep that evening never to awaken.

She found it strange that of all the members of her family, Donnan took it the hardest. At first, he wouldn't even believe it, and kept pulling at his father, screaming at him to wake up, wake up, until Machara, stone-faced, her hair now more gray than auburn, pulled him away, and led him, bawling like a newborn, into the cold outside.

Emily lifted Alan and Elizabeth up to kiss their father farewell, then handed them over to Mrs. Cochrane, who had come by as any good neighbor would do under the circumstances. Emily sat at her father's bedside. She felt no tears. No pain. No regrets. Not even relief now that it was all over.

She put her hand on Breck Stewart's shoulder, squeezed it, and whispered: "I sha'n't forget you, Father. Ever. No one in Ninety Six shall ever forget you, sir."

Emily even smiled. Her father appeared to be smiling as well.

★ ★ ★ ★ ★

1768

★ ★ ★ ★ ★

CHAPTER NINETEEN

Emily slid the healthy pour of rum in front of Jonathan Conley, and, not wanting to see the poor man drink alone, splashed a couple of fingers into her own mug of tea.

"Would you like something to eat, Jonathan?" she asked.

It was awkward, speaking with such formality to a married man with one son and an infant daughter back on his farm, but Emily felt that she was getting better at it. Running a tavern, her father's tavern, kept proving to be a much harder job than she had ever imagined, but if the ladies of Charlestown could pay the price of a license and operate an "ordinary" in that city, then she most certainly could do it in Ninety Six. She was, after all, Breck Stewart's elder daughter, and she did not have an artisan handy—only an uncouth brother willing to drink all her profits.

Conley did not touch the rum, just stood with the bar rag he had asked for, wiping his hands so roughly, Emily feared he'd rub his skin raw.

In the five months since her father's death, Emily had learned how to deal with the infrequent arguments that broke out among patrons, and how to handle the more frequent drunkards. She learned not to tear off a drunken man's head when he pinched her hindquarters, and how to laugh at their foolish jokes, and how to bash one upside his head with the bung starter when he deserved it. Yet something troubled Jonathan Conley, and that something she had not yet learned how to manage.

Two weeks earlier, Machara Stewart had departed for Georgetown, taking Alan and Elizabeth with her to see Breck's parents. Unable to write a letter during the fall and winter to send word of their son's death, Machara had determined that bringing the news in person would be easier and kinder, and taking their two youngest grandchildren with her might help ease the pain of loss. They would return before the summer and the threats of the myriad summer diseases so prevalent along the coast.

Donnan still commanded the regulators, of which Jonathan Conley was one, but the number had decreased to no more than twenty, sometimes as few as five or six. Someone had made off with eggs from Pierre Maupin's chicken coop, and a filly had been stolen during a horse race on the Long Canes, but such petty crimes seemed trivial compared with the lawlessness of the past two or three years.

Breck Stewart, she thought, could be proud. He had brought law and order to at least this part of the Back Country, for which he had paid the ultimate price.

As had Go-la-nv Pinetree.

She sipped the rum and tea, and cleared her throat, leaning against the bar, trying to find words, something to comfort Jonathan Conley, something to make him stop scrubbing his hands with that rag.

"You have not touched your drink," she said.

Without looking up, Conley said: "I cannot seem to get the soot off my hands."

Like Pontius Pilate, Emily thought. Reverend Douglas Monteith had preached a good sermon about the Roman prefect and Jesus Christ before he had left in early February to bring the gospel to the Cowpens and then Charlotte Town and down to Cheraw and Lynches Creek and the Welsh Neck and over to the newly christened Camden, formerly Pine Tree, with plans maybe to return to Ninety Six before fall.

"I give up." Conley brought up his hands, red and raw, and tossed the towel beside his stein. "They shall never be clean."

Emily picked up the rag, and dropped it behind the bar. She clinked her mug against Conley's pewter stein, and painted that bartender's smile on her face. She saw not a trace of dirt or soot or anything on Conley's hands.

When the stein reached the farmer's lips, Emily smiled with relief. Conley's Adam's apple bobbed as he drank. He shook his head when he put down the stein, wiping his mouth with a sleeve. The muslin cloth, Emily noticed, did appear to be stained with charcoal and ash.

"It is early in the day," Emily said, "and early in the week for you to be at Cormorant's Rock, Jonathan Conley."

With a shrug, he drank again.

"And how are Betsy and the children?"

Another shrug. Another drink.

"I baked a Sally Lunn yesterday, and tried my hand at scones. Might I interest you in trying them?"

"Betsy makes a good Sally Lunn," he said. "It's the brown sugar."

"Aye. I thank you for sharing her secret. I shall remember that." Releasing his grip on the stein, he turned his hands over, and stared at the palms. "All that soot," he said softly.

Emily gently put her hands on his, and waited for him to look up. When he did, she could see the tears welling in his eyes, and she whispered: "There is no soot, Jon Conley. Your hands are as clean as a baby's bottom. Now what ails you so?"

"You . . . you'd make a man a good . . . wife," he said.

Suddenly uncertain, she withdrew her hands, put them behind her back, even stepped back from the bar. Emily would turn eighteen in April, and since she had taken over running the tavern, despite Donnan's and her mother's strong objections, she figured she had condemned herself to being a spinster, which was all right with her. Even had Go-la-nv Pinetree not been shot dead at Jacob's Fork, she had always figured she would never marry.

"You should go home to Betsy," she told him. "And tend to your children."

"We burned down the Robinson place," he said.

She blinked, then moved forward, and picked up her mug. "Joseph Robinson's place?" He did not respond. "On Cane Creek?"

He drank down the last of the rum, which did not seem to affect him in the least, and slammed the heavy stein on the table, then, elbows on the bar, he put out his hands and buried his head in them.

"Aye. Burned it to the ground," he confirmed after several moments.

"Who?"

"The . . . Cane . . . Creek . . . Regulators."

A chill raced up her spine. She shook her head in disbelief. "And what on earth for?"

He did not reply, just stood there, head in his hands, snuffling.

"Joseph Robinson has not been in the district since the regulators ran him off to Charlestown," she said hotly. "And good riddance to a man like him, I say. But to burn down his home. Did you know that he sold his home? It did not belong to him any more. It belonged to the deputy provost marshal."

"We knew."

"Then why burn it? Even Finnian . . . even the deputy provost marshal has not been here since late last year."

Conley lowered his hands and bit his lip, before he answered. "Travelers were using it. Sleeping in it."

"I would think so. Along with rats and mice and raccoons

and snakes and anything in need of shelter in that country." When Conley said nothing, Emily continued: "And what of it? If a man traveling through this district finds an empty house, he is free to use it. That has always been our way. If he does not wish to pay the rent I charge for a bed upstairs, I do not begrudge him. Besides, the Robinson place is miles from Ninety Six."

"The captain said it might be used by bandits."

Emily swore, and splashed more rum into her mug. "My brother ordered you to burn that home?"

"Yes. And the barn. And the coop. And we tore down the pigpen."

"And did you salt his well while you were at it?"

She had meant it as a joke, but when Conley looked up and began to answer, she flung the mug against the wall.

He said: "James Middleton had killed three wild dogs, and those we dropped into the well."

As Emily stood there, heat and anger rushed to her head with such force she felt dizzy. Her heart was pounding hard as the tavern's front door opened. Donnan Stewart and James Middleton blocked the entry, standing there, faces blank. When the door to the kitchen opened, and two other men stepped inside, Emily tried to collect her wits. The two men at the kitchen door she had seen before, but did not know their names. The one with the barrel chest and bulging arms she thought owned a farm on Ninety Six Creek just east of the settlement. The other, a lean man with a mauled left ear, she had heard made his living as a long hunter and was usually gone from the cabin he had built on the Long Canes for months on end. Both had ridden with the Cane Creek Regulators when her father was alive.

"Jonathan Conley," Donnan said, stepping forward and putting his right hand on the butt of a pistol in his sash. "Turn around."

Slowly Conley did as ordered, keeping his hands far from his sides, even though he was unarmed. He had left his long rifle leaning against the wall by the door.

"In the name of the Cane Creek Regulators, I arrest you, sir."

The poor farmer merely nodded his head, as Emily cried out: "And why do you arrest this man?" She felt her brother's icy stare, but did not back down. "A poor farmer who rode with my father. A regulator himself, who was at the South Mountains."

"And a poor provider for his wife and children," Donnan said, as James Middleton moved toward the bar, pulling a thick leather thong from his possibles bag.

"Since when is that a crime, Donnan?" she asked.

He didn't answer, and Emily felt her mouth turn dry as the two brutes who had entered through the back roughly shoved Jonathan Conley against the bar and held his hands behind his back, allowing James Middleton to lash them securely.

Only then did Donnan step forward, putting his hands behind his back, staring into Conley's tear-stained face. "Your breath reeks of kill-devil, Conley."

"Aye," Conley whispered.

"Whilst your young son lies in bed with the croup, and your wife, poor Betsy, is left to care for him and a seven-month-old daughter."

"Aye."

Shaking his head, Donnan stepped back. "Take him to the whipping post," he ordered, and Middleton marched outside, while the two other men escorted the prisoner toward the front door.

"Wait a minute!" Emily called out, hurrying from behind the

bar to wave a finger under her brother's nose. "Since when is it a crime to be a poor husband? If you start arresting every man jack of those who. . . ."

Donnan brushed her hand aside. "Then you would surely be out of business, Sister."

"What will drive me to the poor house, Brother, is your propensity for drinking kill-devil for free."

Conley and his escorts had already left the tavern, and Donnan was practically to the door before Emily blocked his path.

"He rode with you," she said. "Jonathan Conley helped you burn down the Robinson barn."

Her brother just stared.

"Is this why you order him to the pillory, Donnan? Because he regrets what you ordered him to do . . . to burn . . . ?"

"To burn down a blight on this community!" Donnan yelled as he straightened his back. "A haven for outlaws."

"A haven for men like that vagabond you call a regulator who has a cabin on the Long Canes but is more often to be found in the Blue Ridge Mountains or as far north and west as Kentucky."

Donnan said nothing.

"You know who owned the Robinson place, did you not?" Emily said. "It belonged not to that pompous Virginian, but to the deputy provost marshal."

"Who has not dared show his face in months, Sister. Who for all I know is back with his boss in London, writing for the boards, trying to become the newest Shakespeare."

"That was an office for a Royal official," Emily corrected him.

"Balderdash. What has your deputy provost marshal done for Ninety Six? That damnable stockade by Goudey's place remains our jail."

"Which is likewise empty," she said. "Thanks to Da'." She

193

made herself add: "And you."

"It sha'n't be empty for long."

His voice made her cringe. "Do not do this, Donnan," she whispered.

His hand moved, and she flinched, fearing he would strike her, and hating herself for showing such cowardice. Yet Donnan merely pulled his cocked hat tighter.

"I take no pleasure in whipping a man like Jonathan Conley," he said. "He was always kind to Da'. He could make Da' laugh. And he showed much bravery at Jacob's Fork last fall."

"Then why . . . ?" Emily asked. "Why flog a man like Conley?"

"Did you not hear what I said, Sister? He has not been at his home in more than a week. His son is sick. His daughter is not yet a year old. He has not lifted a hand to help his wife. He would become a vagabond, a derelict. For all I know, it was he who stole Pierre Maupin's eggs."

"You do not whip a man for being a poor husband. Or for stealing eggs," she told him, and put her finger in her brother's face again. "And you have no proof that he stole any egg."

"He is not charged with theft," Donnan said as he grabbed her wrist, tightly, and shoved it to her side, leaned forward, and said in an icy tone: "If you want to stop a flogging, run to his farm. See his wife Betsy! It was Betsy who came to me. In tears. It was Betsy who asked the Cane Creek Regulators to do something about her husband."

Later, Emily would remember how it all felt like a dream. She followed Donnan outside, but stopped on the porch, watching him as he crossed the yard, moving to the path lined with the stocks, long empty, and toward the nearest whipping post. Middleton and the two others had already lashed Conley's arms to the bindings, and ripped off his shirt. Red-headed Ferguson slowly walked from a pack mule, from which he had retrieved the blacksnake whip, and handed it to Donnan.

"Benji Cooper!" Donnan shouted.

The black carpenter stood in front of his work shed, face covered in sawdust and sweat. He took a deep breath, and slowly removed the stout leather apron, tossed it atop a barrel, and slowly, silently made his way toward the whipping post.

After handing the freedman the whip, Donnan stepped aside, turning toward the settlers who had gathered. Cooper uncoiled the whip, and took a few steps back. He knew why he had been summoned, and his face told how much he dreaded the task.

"Jonathan Conley has abandoned his wife and children," Donnan said. "He is idle. He is drunk. One of his children is sick with the croup. The punishment assessed is forty lashes less one." Donnan turned, went back to Cooper, and for a moment, Emily thought her brother might take over the duty as executioner, but he merely whispered into the freedman's ear, and stepped back.

Emily looked away, refusing to watch that poor farmer be whipped like a dog. She cringed at every lash, and watched the faces of the settlers she knew, many of them friends of hers, all of them friends of her father. Underneath an elm, Darlene Courtney held her baby, patting the infant's back as if she were burping it, watching as Cooper laid the stripes on Conley's back.

What amazed her was how stoic Jonathan Conley took the punishment. He did not cry out, did not beg, just let out stifled grunts, until the last strike. Middleton and the long hunter released him, and dragged his limp body into the tavern.

There, Emily rubbed bear grease onto the welts and cuts, before the Cane Creek Regulators escorted the farmer back home to his wife.

Only that part did not feel like a dream.

CHAPTER TWENTY

The slaves moved back and forth, sweating, silently transporting casks, hogsheads, and bottles into the storeroom. One stopped, and Emily muttered both an apology and thanks as she squeezed past him, and headed toward Robert Gouedy, who sat at a window table, fanning himself with his cocked hat. But then she stopped and turned and, after clearing her throat, said to the men: "You will find a plate of scones in the kitchen. I cannot cook like my mum, but the food is yours when you are done. And there are two buckets of water, cool and fresh, there, too. Please take all you want, with the thanks and blessings of Cormorant's Rock."

The slaves just kept right on hauling the liquor into the storeroom, and Emily went over to Robert Gouedy's table, sank in the chair opposite him, and smiled.

"I hope you do not mind, Mister Gouedy," she said.

He did. He treated his slaves like dirt.

Emily hefted the leather pouch and slapped it on the table; the clinking of the coins halted any more complaining from the man.

"Of course not, Miss Emily."

Laying his hat on the table, Gouedy reached inside his waistcoat and pulled out a small ledger, which he placed on the table and slid toward Emily. She studied the numbers as he fished for his spectacles.

"A bountiful trip to Charlestown," she said as she tugged on the pouch's drawstring.

"Indeed. And business has been good whilst I was gone?"

She shrugged, faked a smile, and said: "Despite my brother, who thinks he deserves free grog. . . ."

"Aye, yes, Donnan. . . ."

Once Emily had counted out the coins, she slid two piles toward the trader. He left them there and reached for the mug of tea.

"I brought you some newspapers," he said.

"Thank you, sir. There is not much to read in Ninety Six."

"You may not like all that you read."

She nodded, knowing what was coming next, and said: "Donnan."

The Cane Creek Regulators had not stopped with the burning of the Robinson place and the whipping of Jonathan Conley. Although there were no outlaw gangs to bring to justice, the regulators found criminals anyway. Men were flogged for crimes such as being shiftless, being lazy. Others were exposed to dunking stools on the suspicion that they had abetted horse thieves. At least two had been tarred and feathered for protesting the actions of the regulators.

It was not limited just to Ninety Six. Emily served many travelers bound for Keowee, Fort Loudon, Charlotte Town, and bid farewell to those who had given up making a life in South Carolina, some moving as far away as Delaware or New Jersey. Mars Bluff appeared almost to be in a state of civil war, and the cause seemed to be their regulators. Word had spread of similar complaints against the vigilance committees on the lower Saluda, along Lynches Creek, and up to Cheraw.

Emily sucked in a breath, and shook her head. Although no one was lashed to either pillory, and the stocks were empty, she knew that at least five were imprisoned in the old stockade by Gouedy's post. She brought them bread and water every night, and each morning.

"Donnan," she whispered again. Then not even knowing why, she said: "He murdered Go-la-nv."

The trader sighed, looking older, wearier. "You do not know that."

She knew it in her heart. Could see it in her brother's eyes. She expected Gouedy, who had married a Cherokee woman and who had half-breed children, to be irate, but he was calm, as always.

"From what I heard," he said, "that young brave was found dead on the field. Do not believe what your brother says, that the young Indian was yellow. A bullet in the back is not always the result of cowardice. I have seen enough violence on this frontier to know of such things. It could have been an accident, shot by our own men. He could have simply turned, and caught a ball from some scamp. Your brother says many things. Donnan is not . . . prone to . . . kindness."

Emily regretted the fact that she had brought up Go-la-nv Pinetree and all those awful memories. "He had Jonathan Conley whipped," she said.

"Aye, but his wife, young Betsy, indeed complained of his sloth and intemperance. And you must admit that Conley, since his punishment, has been acting much better, as a husband should. And do you know what your brother told Ol' Benji Cooper before he executed that sentence? Cooper himself told me that you brother told him . . . 'Be soft with the blacksnake.' "

"He is not always soft . . . Donnan, I mean," Emily said, and turned to watch the slaves, hoping to find some way to regain her composure.

Gouedy said: "But Donnan has caused much trouble and could, I fear, bring more misfortune to this district."

She faced Gouedy again. "You spoke of Charlestown newspapers."

Gouedy looked around, but other than his own slaves, the tavern was empty. "Has not your mother returned from Georgetown?"

Shaking her head, Emily said: "I expected her and Alan and Elizabeth last month, but the summer has been mild, so mayhap they extended their stay."

"Aye, the Carolina coast is lovely."

"Not as lovely as Ninety Six," she said. "At least not to me."

Gouedy smiled. "I have not been to Georgetown in some time. Perhaps I should go. Breck . . . your father often told wild tales about fishing in Winyah Bay, looking for pirates' treasure on Waccamaw Neck and Pawley's Island, and even fighting alligators on Mingo Creek."

She made herself grin. "Aye. He told us the same stories. Sometimes I think he believed them himself." His hearty laugh almost made her join him.

He shook his head at some long dormant memory, saying: "I remember once, he was telling me about. . . ."

When Emily lifted her hand slightly, the old trader stopped. "Mister Gouedy," she said mildly, "my father never was one to beat around the bush, as they say." He nodded. "Should I read the *Gazette*?" she asked.

"There is much talk about the regulators in Charlestown." His tone sounded ominous.

"There is talk in Ninety Six, as well," she said, thinking that is was in whispers and never in front of anyone who rode with the Cane Creek Regulators.

"It is one thing to brand thieves, even to lynch murderers. William Bull and Justice Shinner supported our cause as much as they could, but I fear Donnan and his men have gone too far, and Shinner has been removed as chief justice."

"For supporting my father's cause?" Emily said.

"No." He sighed, and shook his head, then suggested: "Mayhap we should test your wares, Miss Emily? You never know how those Charlestown thieves might cheat you, and 'tis best you know before you give it to your customers."

When they each held a noggin of rum, Gouedy leaned forward. "The colonies are astir," he said. "And not just in the Back Country. Even in Charlestown, I saw fear, anger, and resentment. Your father said that Parliament's Stamp Act had nothing to do with the Back Country, but I think Breck was wrong."

She knew little about the Stamp Act. It had arrived in Charlestown in the autumn of 1765. Donnan had laughingly recalled that effigies of the stamp collector had been hanged from the gallows on Broad and Church Streets, *Stamp Act* printed on one and *Liberty* on another. After the effigies were removed and as the bells of several churches rang, a crowd had carried the dummies to the home of the stamp inspector, burned them in his yard, and the one that had been named Liberty was buried in a mock funeral.

"Aye," Emily said, "but did not I read that Parliament repealed that act?"

"Indeed, that is what happened," said Gouedy, "because in London the Crown realized it could not be enforced. Lieutenant Governor Bull made that obvious when he said stamp paper was not available and opened the port. Justice Shinner agreed. Eventually, because of that, and other affairs, including the justice's support even if somewhat lukewarm of the regulators' actions, Lord Montagu had him removed."

She thought about that as she sipped her rum, and shook her head. "The Stamp Act and its protest, that all happened years ago, even before our troubles started. I still cannot see how this affects us in the Back Country."

"Not just the Back Country," Gouedy said. "Not just South Carolina. It is unrest among all of us in all of the King's colonies. . . . It is the need to govern . . . ourselves." He smiled. "We in the Back Country pride ourselves as a most independent lot, do we not?" Emily couldn't help but grin at that as Gouedy continued. "We do not think much of those in Charlestown, but many are not much different than we. Had your father lived in Charlestown and not Ninety Six, I could picture him marching toward Tradd Street and burning the effigies to frighten a poor Royal tax inspector. In Ninety Six, we have the Cane Creek Regulators. In Charlestown, an organization has been formed that calls itself the Sons of Liberty." He repeated the word. "Liberty." Then took a hefty swig of rum.

Emily studied the innkeeper's face before saying: "I would not liken our regulators . . . at least those riding today . . . as anything worthy of the name Liberty."

"War is coming, Emily," Gouedy said. "I feel it in my bones."

"Are you suggesting, Mister Gouedy, that we in the Back Country would revolt against Lord Montagu?"

His head shook. "Not Charlestown, Miss Emily. But the Crown. And not just the frontier, and, mayhap, not just South Carolina."

She fell back as if she had been kicked. The mere thought caused her to take in a deep breath. Exhaling, she shook her head. "King George? England?"

"Indeed." His answer had been barely audible.

Now she laughed. "Mister Gouedy, my father would never commit such treason. He was loyal. . . ." The words died in her throat.

A heavy silence descended on them, and they sat staring at one another as the slaves finished bringing in the last of the rum and supplies that would have to last Cormorant's Rock for another year.

"It will be an ugly, most horrible kind of war," Gouedy whispered, "for it will not just be colonists against the King's bayonets. We will be fighting one another. Already we have seen that, and I even more now . . . with the Cane Creek Regulators."

"I do not believe . . . ," Emily began. But she did believe, and she knew that Robert Gouedy was right.

He drained the last of his rum, and pushed back his chair. "I am an old man, Emily." He dropped the "miss." "I doubt that I shall live to see my neighbors fighting His Majesty's redcoats." He leaned forward, pointing a long finger at her. "But your children, and possibly even you, shall see this. All its tragedy. And what your brother is doing with his regulators is just a portent of the coming storm."

"It cannot happen," she said, hoping she could convince herself by saying it out loud. But she didn't.

"There is something else you should know," Gouedy said. "You shall read about it in the *Gazette*." He gestured at the satchel he had laid atop the bar when he first arrived. She waited. "Complaints have been filed in Charlestown." He pressed his lips together, dreading what he had to tell her. "Written and filed by those abused by our regulators. There is nothing even Justice Shinner could do, even were he not in a state of disgrace thanks to that idiot made governor by King George. Even William Bull knows that the regulators have gone too far." He paused to pour a little more rum, then said: "They will be sending someone with authority here, with writs, mayhap with sheriff's bracelets, or even a sheriff's picture frame."

Handcuffs and a gallows. For the regulators. The words passed in disbelief through Emily's mind. She said: "Someone . . . such as . . . a provost marshal?"

"Such would be my guess. And if the provost cannot quiet the disturbances here, then, by my guess, Lord Montagu will send either a Charlestown militia . . . or the His Majesty's army."

Gouedy stood, gathered his coins, put them in his vest pocket along with his ledger, and reached for his cane. "Were I a praying man, and not the heathen I am, I would drop to my knees, Emily, and pray my damnedest that such not be the case, such not be the will of God." His knees popped as he straightened. "But if there be a God, he would surely not listen to me." He winked. "But you . . . ?"

With a smile, he gathered his slaves, leaving Emily alone in the tavern with her thoughts, and her fears.

CHAPTER TWENTY-ONE

Emily missed having her mother and siblings around—even Donnan, or, at least, the Donnan of old. Mostly she missed her father, wondering how he had managed to keep the tavern running as smoothly as it had always seemed. She filled the empty jugs and bottles in the storeroom, estimated what would be needed to slake the thirsts of visitors over the next week, and then moved the containers underneath and behind the bar, all before going out to the summer kitchen to check on the stew and cornbread.

Outside, she surveyed the garden, seeing only the weeds that would need hoeing. When the bell rang above the tavern's front door, she sighed heavily, and hurried up the back steps and into the winter kitchen, removing her bonnet and wiping the sweat off her forehead, then drying her hands on her apron before stepping through the door into the tavern, with that beaming Breck Stewart smile on her face. But it quickly turned into a frown.

"And since when did I hire you, James Middleton, to pour rum from behind my bar?" she asked.

Without turning around, the regulator laughed as he continued filling the mugs of seven other men who leaned against the bar. Middleton seemed to be splashing more liquor on the wood than into the stoneware.

"Get out!" Emily demanded, moving toward Middleton, who turned and tossed her the jug before grabbing the stein he had filled for himself.

She had to take a few hurried steps to catch the jug. Her face flushed, and not just from the heat outside.

The bung starter lay on a shelf beneath the bar, and beside that her Queen Anne pistol, but she knew better. Eight men. Eight regulators, ready to fill their bellies with kill-devil, and all arrogant as an Edisto planter. She let her temper ease, and moved toward Middleton.

"And would it be a trouble to you if I asked just how you plan to pay for those drinks?"

Middleton swallowed, and slammed his stein against the bar, wiped his mouth with his sleeve, and laughed.

At the opposite end of the bar, the big man from the farm on Ninety Six Creek snorted, spit, missing the cuspidor, and then said: "Regulators lush for free, and we are here to liquor our boots."

"Before we ride to the Long Canes to pay a visit to Birmingham Long."

"We eat, too," said another, "and I spied smoke from the chimney in your summer kitchen."

"*Gratis*," a wiry man in a straw hat added.

"The bread I bake," she said, heat flushing her face again, her voice trembling with anger, "is for the prisoners in Mister Gouedy's stockade." She moved to the center of the bar, never looking away from the hard stares the regulators gave her.

"Would you give them rum as well?" said the man from Ninety Six.

"Just water."

Her right hand disappeared behind the bar, landing on the bung starter. Eight rough men or not, she would not be abused in her father's own tavern. Still trying to keep the peace, she attempted to change the subject. "And why should the Cane Creek Regulators ride to see Birmingham Long?"

"He is a fogey . . . ," one man began.

Middleton whirled, ordering the man: "Shut your trap!"

But the man finished: ". . . with a gift for gab."

So the old man who worshiped the Church of England and King George himself had written a few complaints to Charlestown.

A fat-cheeked man slammed his mug on the bar, and shouted: "Bring us something to eat! You damned hedge whore."

To hell with keeping the peace. Emily moved her hand from the bung starter, and picked up the pistol, brought it up, and was thumbing back the hammer when Middleton's hand clamped down on her wrist. His grip held like a vise, and Emily screamed. Through the tears forming in her eyes, she watched as the man who had insulted her grabbed the pistol with a laugh.

The vise-like grip eased, but another man, who had rushed behind the bar, shoved her against the backbar. A few bottles clattered and one fell, breaking on the floor. Her left hand went to her throbbing right wrist, and she looked at the one with the pistol, now aimed at her.

"Your brother raved about your mother's shepherd's pie. I doubt if you are much of a cook and. . . ."

"Shut up, O'Keeffe."

Emily's eyes found the man who had spoken. To her surprise, it was the long hunter from Cane Creek.

"And put the damned gun down," he added.

"Put it up," Middleton echoed. The man lowered the hammer, and laid the pistol on the bar.

Blinking away tears, Emily watched the long hunter reach into a pocket and pull out a few coins, which he laid on the bar. Two others did the same, and quickly finished their drinks in silence.

She thought it might end there, peacefully, with no real loss except for a busted bottle of gin, and some bruising to her wrist and ego. Indeed, it might have, but the door opened and in walked Finnian Kilduff. She whispered his name.

"And what have we here," he said, cocking the blunderbuss he held at his hip, "but a fine group of rapparees and priggers? Are they being a pest to you, m'lady?"

The men turned, and Emily took advantage of the moment and swiped her pistol off the bar, cocking it again, while moving to the side, out of range, she hoped, of any stray ball from that massive weapon in Kilduff's hands.

"Just some boys who shall be taking their leave," she said, keeping the muzzle of her weapon on O'Keeffe's back.

"I don't like hoggish men or draw latchers," Kilduff declared, and stepped toward them, both hands on the massive weapon. Once again he was dressed the part of a gentleman, although his clothes were ruffled from several miles in the saddle, and his face sported a few days' growth of dark whiskers.

"I know you," Middleton said.

"As I remember you," Kilduff responded.

It was then that a shadow crept through the door, and Emily sucked in a deep breath, shouting: "Finnian!" But by then, Donnan Stewart stood in the open doorway, and behind him Emily saw at least three other regulators.

"Before you lay your blunderbuss on that table," Donnan said softly, "could you answer a question for me?"

Kilduff's face revealed his frustration with himself for having been an idiot. Shaking his head, Kilduff slowly eased down the hammer on the blunderbuss, and butted the weapon against the floor. He did not turn around.

"Let me inform you all that I am the deputy provost marshal for the colony of South Carolina," Kilduff said easily. "My papers are in my waistcoat." Then he lifted the rifle by the barrel with his right hand, and gently laid it on the table.

"Indeed?" Donnan stepped inside, followed by Ferguson. The other two remained outside.

"With several warrants as well." Kilduff turned to face Donnan. "By the authority of the governor, Lord Charles Montagu. One such warrant has your name on it, Donnan Stewart."

"Indeed?" Donnan repeated, and smiled, keeping his pistol aimed at Kilduff. Raising his left hand, he hooked his thumb toward the open door. "And would you happen to have a bill of sale in your waistcoat as well, Mister Deputy Provost Marshal? For that marsh tacky horse you are riding, bold as brass?"

The regulators at the bar moved. Two now aimed their pistols at Kilduff's head. Another picked up his blunderbuss. Middleton turned toward Emily, holding out his big right palm, eyes glaring. Muttering an oath, she handed him her pistol.

"You have not answered my question, Mister Deputy Provost Marshal," Donnan said, as he edged closer to Kilduff. "Ask my sister if she remembers that horse. My da' bought it at the New Market racecourse in Charlestown. My sister was there. I would gather that she remembers the stallion. She rode it often enough, especially after it kicked a preacher in his manhood."

A few of the men sniggered.

"Da' had a mind to breed those small horses with a mare we have in the stables outside. Now, I still have his bill of sale. But we have not seen that dun since my sister here was riding it one day, a year or so back, mayhap longer, and some freebooters took her and the preacher prisoner and into their camp for a wee bit of time. However, I will give those rogues their due. They harmed neither that cod's head of a parson nor my sister, but they kept the marsh tacky dun. So I shall be asking you again. Have you a bill of sale or any proof of ownership for that stallion?"

"What I have," Kilduff said stiffly, "are my credentials and warrants."

The Cane Creek Regulators

Grinning with pleasure, Donnan shook his head.

"Now I remember the cur!" Middleton cried, and stormed over, raising Emily's pistol and slamming the barrel against Kilduff's head. He dropped to his knees, and Emily ran from behind the bar, cursing, but the long hunter from Cane Creek grabbed her arms and pulled her back, his grip firm but his voice surprisingly calm and kind. "Easy, miss. Any row you start will make things worser for that gent."

She had lifted her leg, aiming to slam her sandal against the hunter's toes, but his words made her stop. Blood ran down Kilduff's forehead and over the bridge of his nose.

Middleton grabbed a handful of Kilduff's dark mane, and lifted his head. "This knight of the road aided the Cherokees during the uprising a lustrum or more ago." Releasing his grip on Kilduff's hair, he grabbed his waistcoat and pulled it off. He tore off Kilduff's vest, and then his silk shirt, revealing scars from a previous whipping and something else.

"There!" Middleton cried as he jammed his fingers into the scar between Kilduff's shoulder blades. "That is where we branded him. A damned renegade and rebel."

"And a horse thief!" someone shouted. "To the morning drop with him!"

"No!" Emily pulled away from the hunter's grasp, tripped over a chair leg, and went sprawling to the floor. She watched as the men shoved Kilduff outside, heard their shouts and laughter. She came to her feet, and ran to her brother who hadn't left the tavern. "He is not lying, Donnan!" she cried. "He is a deputy provost marshal."

Donnan's head shook in pity.

"I saw his papers," she insisted. "I saw the governor's stamp. So did Mister Gouedy." Donnan's face hardened. *My God,* Emily thought, *how much he looks like Da'.*

"I saw that dun horse!" he shouted.

Emily dropped beside Kilduff's waistcoat. Papers slipped through her trembling fingers, but she found the leather wallet, opened it, and withdrew the paper, unfolding it as quickly as she could. "Here! Here," she said to Donnan. "The Royal seal. Read it. He is a deputy provost marshal."

"I do not give a tinker's damn." He turned on his heels, and strode for the door. "To me he is a horse thief and a scoundrel."

She was up and past him, blocking the door, rattling the paper in his face. "You cannot do this. Even you, Donnan, cannot do this. You hang him, and His Majesty will send an army to scorch the entire district and they will not cease until this land is in ruins and you are dead."

He laughed.

"You are not Breck Stewart's son . . . ," she said. Then the breath left her. Her lungs would not work, and she realized slowly that Donnan had hit her in the stomach with that rock-hard fist of his. Drool ran down her chin, she gagged, and vomited. Even before she had finished retching, Donnan jerked her up by her hair. Tears blinded her. She was about to pass out.

She smelled the mead on his breath as he whispered: "You are not Breck Stewart's daughter. You are a crack. And you sure can pick your cuckolds. A red Cherokee, and an Indian-loving horse thief." He let her go, but, before she fell, he swung his fist again. This one caught her in the face, and she felt the cartilage give way in her nose, tasting the blood. She landed heavily on the floor as Donnan and the long hunter dragged Kilduff from the tavern to the gleeful shouts of the men outside.

CHAPTER TWENTY-TWO

Finnian Kilduff flinched when Emily eased the yarrow poultice onto his back. He lay on his stomach, sweating, breathing heavily, and his eyes fluttered, opened, and after a long moment focused on Emily, whose face was now looking calmly at his.

His voice was faint, when he finally managed to speak: "Have I any skin left on my back?" But then as his eyes focused, he said: "By God," he said, "what did they do to you?"

Instinctively she covered her nose, then moved away, so he could not see her. She picked up another poultice from a bowl, and placed it over the wounds on his back. "They could have hanged you, I suppose." Her voice sounded so nasal, she swore underneath her breath, and tenderly touched the swollen, crooked nose, wishing she had remained mute. When she looked up, she happened to catch her reflection in the Chippendale mirror across the room. It took all of her control not to throw the bowl and shatter the glass. "I warned you about that marsh tacky," she said.

"Why didn't they hang me?" Kilduff asked.

She answered with a shrug, then, realizing Kilduff could not see her, made herself speak again, the sound of her voice angering her. "Donnan said a blacksnake would last longer than the cord."

He laughed. "Your brother is smarter than he looks. I sha'n't leave this bed for a week, if ever."

"The cord," she said, "would have left you in a coffin . . . forever."

When the last poultice was in place, she made herself move back to the chair, where Kilduff could move his head on the pillow and look at her.

Donnan had spared Kilduff's life for his own reasons. At least, that's how Emily figured things. He had known she was right. Harassing a provost marshal's deputy is one thing. Killing him would bring His Majesty's army out in force. So they had flogged him, but, drunk as the lot had been, there had been no mercy. Sixty lashes laid well on. It was a wonder Finnian Kilduff still breathed.

"Doctor Bayard has been here," she said. "He gave you some hemlock to stop the bleeding, and something he bought from an apothecary in Charlestown for the pain. I have some chamomile. It can help you sleep."

"I do not wish to sleep." He sounded stronger now.

"The doctor said he would return on the morrow," Emily continued. "Left me the poultices to put on your back until then. Can I bring you something to eat?" His head shook weakly. "Drink?"

He lifted his eyes. "Not tea. Not chamomile. But rum?"

"If there is any left." She sighed. "The Cane Creek Regulators had quite the thirst after your flogging."

Of course, plenty of rum remained. Even regulators could not drink a year's worth in one day of revelry. She went downstairs and got a jug, stepping over the broken glass, the shards of pottery, and the débris, and climbed back up the steps. She would have to clean up, salvage what she could.

Back in the guest room, she watched as Finnian Kilduff, groaning, managed to roll onto his side and take the mug she held out. He was barely able to lift his head and take a sip, so Emily grabbed the mug before he collapsed back on the pillow.

"Damn you, Finnian Kilduff!" she said, feeling the tears well. "Why did you bring Ezekiel back to Ninety Six?"

He motioned toward the mug she held. This time, she lifted his head, and let him drink, then gently lowered his head onto the pillow, already damp with sweat.

"If you would believe in a bully ruffian such as I, then, honestly, I was returning that horse to you."

Folding her hands across her chest, Emily shook her head.

" 'Tis the truth. Your brother neglected to mention that there was another horse tethered outside. A fine blue roan. More becoming for a man of my size than that dwarf you call a horse."

She had seen the roan, and, thinking it had been forgotten by one of the drunken regulators, she had asked Benjamin Cooper to take it to the stables with Ezekiel.

"You did not mention that to Donnan."

He twisted his head in some sort of shrug. "I surmised that Donnan and his boys had already made up their minds."

She helped him drink again, pushed the wet bangs off her forehead, and asked: "Now . . . tell me true, Finnian Kilduff, how did you get to be a deputy provost marshal?"

"I repented."

Emily cursed.

" 'Tis true. That devil-driver Monteith had me see the light."

"Liar."

His laughter caused him much agony, but when she came toward him with the rum, he shook his head. "No more for me, Emily." His eyes misted over, and his voice lost the humor, the roughness. "If you must know the truth, after the damned bloody flux did its business, snuffing out the lives of lovely Tanwen and the others, I rode alone to Charlestown. I don't know . . . I thought I might sail somewhere, Jamaica or London, Greece or Ireland. And by chance . . . or fate, if such is your belief . . . I met a man who remembered me from my days at the bar. Before you know it, I am dining with Lady and Lord Montagu as the new deputy provost marshal." He smiled, and his voice returned to normal. "I am not without qualifications, I'd have you know."

"I remember your qualifications. Does Lord Montagu know of them all?"

He started to laugh, but it died in his throat, and his voice turned cold, serious. "The regulators must be stopped."

Knees weakening, she drank the rest of Kilduff's rum.

"You," he said, "must stop them."

She laughed. "I cannot. . . ."

"Not you, personally. The men of Ninety Six. Those who are not cowards, who bow to such snafflers as Donnan Stewart."

"We are not cowards, Kilduff." She was angry again, not caring how bruised her face was, how much her stomach hurt when she breathed or bent, or how much pain Finnian Kilduff must be in at that very moment. "We are. . . ."

Downstairs, she heard the bell above the tavern door ring. She was up, the clay mug falling to the floor, rolling over toward the bedpost. Finnian Kilduff said something to her, but Emily was already at the door. She had the blunderbuss as she moved out of the room, to the stairs and down.

Seeing the door flung open, she raised the weapon, but quickly lowered it when she saw Benjamin Cooper standing inside, holding a valise in each hand.

"Miss Emily?" he called out before spying her on the stairs. He lowered the luggage, saying softly: "Miss Emily . . . ?"

That's when her mother stepped out from behind the massive carpenter's body, her brother and sister right behind her.

The blunderbuss fell against the wall, slid down, and tumbled down the steps, but Emily reached the floor long before the weapon landed. She could barely see as tears blinded her, but she felt no shame. Let Cooper, let the whole world see her cry.

Let everyone in Ninety Six know that, although she had turned eighteen years old, no matter how tough she acted, how she swore, and drank, and worked in a tavern often full of drunkards, she remained in some ways a frightened little girl.

"Mum!" Emily fell to her knees, feeling Machara Stewart's arm embrace her, feeling her kiss her sweaty hair. "Mum! Mum. Mum. . . ."

"Emily," Machara whispered. "Oh, sweet daughter of mine."

She felt Elizabeth and Alan hugging her.

"Mum. . . ." Emily basked in her mother's warmth.

The door to the tavern closed, but she did not hear Benjamin Cooper walking away.

"Emily," Alan blurted, "what happened to your face?"

Chapter Twenty-Three

Most of the men sat around the long table—the table that had served as Breck Stewart's bed until he died—sipping coffee, not touching the bread Machara Stewart had baked. They looked at one another, waiting for someone to speak.

It was Emily who broke the silence. She came around the bar, and said: "The deputy provost marshal lying upstairs with the hide flayed off his back said you were cowards. He said you bowed to a bunch of snafflers." She planted her hands on her hips. "I told him that he was mistaken. Do you dare make a liar out of Breck Stewart's daughter?"

The cooper, Thomas Taylor, shifted uncomfortably, and said: "It is a delicate situation, Miss Emily."

"No," Benjamin Cooper said. "Miss Emily's right." But that was all the carpenter said.

After a period of thoughtfulness, Robert Gouedy lifted his mug, sipped, and said: "It is a question we must answer. Do we wait for Lord Montagu to send King George's redcoats, and risk a revolt? Or do we finish ourselves what we started?"

"They hanged Birmingham Long," Jonathan Conley said. "Left him swinging in the breeze."

Virgil Hickox, who had once ridden with the regulators commanded by Breck Stewart as well as those under Donnan's reign, said: "We should call ourselves the Moderators."

"Moderators." Pierre Maupin cursed in French, slammed his fist on the table, and swore again, this time in English. "Regulators. Moderators. We formed the regulators to crush the scoundrels stealing our pigs and horses. And when the regulators become the criminals, we talk of forming a group of moderators. So two years from now, when the moderators begin flogging children and beheading chickens, who will rise up against the moderators. When will this stop?"

"It will not stop," Robert Gouedy said, staring at the coffee mug in his hand. "It shall never stop. At least, not for a long, long, long, long time."

Another long silence. Finally Dr. Bayard stood and said: "But the Cane Creek Regulators must be stopped. Yes, moderators. We have always governed ourselves in this district, more or less. We must police ourselves as well."

Hickox stood, and, shaking his head, moved away from the others, fishing a pipe from his pocket, lighting it by the window with a candle. When he had the pipe smoking to his satisfaction, he looked back at the others. "Are we certain?"

No one responded, until Cooper announced: "I sure miss Breck Stewart."

Which brought a smile to the faces of a number of the men, as well as Emily's, then Thomas Taylor cried out: "Breck Stewart! Breck Stewart. It was Breck who got us into this damnable mess." He stopped abruptly, sucked in a deep breath, and turned, shame-faced, and muttered: "I mean no offense, Miss Emily. Your father was. . . ." His words died and the silence resumed.

Hickox returned to the table, groaning as he sat down, then asking: "Who leads us?"

"Mister Gouedy?" Dr. Bayard asked.

The old trader gestured at his nearby cane. "I am way too old to be galloping across this country."

"How about that marshal upstairs?" Pierre Maupin said.

"He cannot ride," Emily assured him. "He can barely stand."

"It's why we need sheriffs across the colony," Dr. Bayard said.

"Save that argument for the Assembly next time you are in Charlestown, Doctor," Taylor said.

"How many regulators are left among them?" Cooper asked.

Everyone shrugged. The number had always risen and fallen depending on the mood, the weather, the men, and the amount of rum consumed.

"What you must understand," Gouedy said, "is that there are other regulators, in other regions, in Cheraw, the Peedee, Mars Bluff, the Tyger River. And I dare say that in every one of those regions, men like us, are sitting in some 'ordinary' talking about this very same thing."

Taylor laughed. "I cannot believe. . . ." But then he paused, perhaps realizing that he did believe.

"And if these outlaws, these former regulators, band together . . . ," Dr. Bayard said, shaking his head.

"Then the moderators must join forces," Maupin said.

"What we speak of . . . ," Taylor began.

". . . is civil war," Gouedy finished for him in the lull.

Emily was relieved that she had sent her mother, Alan, and Elizabeth to the quilting bee at Mrs. Cochrane's cabin near Spring Branch. Especially when the doors, front and back, slammed open and Donnan, coming in the front, led a group of men inside. James Middleton came through the back. Long rifles and pistols were cocked.

Donnan crooked his finger at Virgil Hickox, and said: "Outside."

As Hickox left his pipe in the tray and made a beeline for the door, Taylor leaped to his feet, yelling: "You son-of-a-bitch! You damned traitor. You were my neighbor. You were my friend!"

The door closed behind Hickox, and the silence become ominous. Donnan Stewart looked at the men of Ninety Six, then he turned his gaze on Emily. His face held no emotion.

"Do not worry," Donnan said finally when he looked at the men sitting around the table. "You sha'n't swing. But you will pay." He hooked his thumb. "Outside . . . all of you. Do as we say, or you will die."

Middleton's men came forward, prodding the moderators through the front door. They went hesitantly. Thanks to Virgil Hickox, they had no choice. Emily did not move. Donnan approached her, studied her swollen and bruised face, and laughed.

She wanted to spit in his face, but, instead, asked: "What do you plan to do?"

"I plan, dear Sister, to burn this den of sedition."

It felt as though her throat was filled with sand. "Donnan, please. Da' built this place. With his own hands." She hated herself for begging.

"And you are responsible for burning it to the ground," Donnan said. "For you betrayed your own blood."

She knew she would pay, but she had always found it hard to rein in her anger. Leaning closer to him, she said: "How can I betray my own blood? The only brother I have . . . is Alan."

That was the last thing she remembered until she woke up outside, in the cool air, a wet rag on her forehead, blood seeping again from her nose and lips, her head pounding like the hoofs of a thousand cattle were inside it. Then she smelled the smoke.

"Easy," Dr. Bayard whispered. "Lie still."

She tried to sit up, but dizziness sent her back onto the grass. When she opened her eyes, she had to lift her hand to shield them from the flames.

Emily almost broke down completely at the terrible sight, but then fear enveloped her, and she sat up, throwing off the cloth Dr. Bayard was using to wipe her face, and turned her head to vomit. Coughing, she grabbed the lapels of the doctor's coat

219

and cried out: "Finnian! Finnian! He is upstairs." Then releasing her grip, she spun away from the doctor, tried to stand but couldn't. She was blinded by both the blaze and tears, as she willed herself to stand. She stumbled a few steps, then collapsed as Dr. Bayard's arms wrapped around her waist and pulled her back.

"Let me go! He'll die! He'll die!"

"Emily," Dr. Bayard said.

"Damn you, he'll die. He'll. . . ."

"He is all right, Emily. Listen. Benji Cooper got him out of there as soon as the regulators left."

"Thank God," Emily whispered as she slipped into the deep void.

Chapter Twenty-Four

She led the marsh tacky dun out of the stable, already saddled, grained and watered well, and ready to ride. She walked the horse past the smoldering ruins of Cormorant's Rock, and toward the men tightening the cinches on their saddles, saying good bye to their wives, their children, and checking their weapons. She glanced at the blackened timbers, the ashes, and then beyond to the little knoll where a crooked wooden cross marked her father's grave.

Emily Stewart did not cry.

"Miss Stewart . . . ," Dr. Bayard said, speaking formally as the duly elected captain of the moderators.

She swung into the saddle, hefting a rifle she had stolen from Virgil Hickox's cabin, and said: "Let any man among you say that I have no right to ride with you . . ."—she waved the rifle at the smoking remains of Comorant's Rock—"after that." The rifle came down, and she laid it across her pommel. "Say it," she said, softer this time. "Say it good and loud. Say it loud enough for my father lying yon to hear."

Leather creaked as Benjamin Cooper climbed onto his big gray. "She rides with us," the carpenter said.

This time there were no cheers, no songs. On the morning of July 25, 1768, the fourteen Moderators of Ninety Six loped out of the settlement toward the Cherokee Path.

★　★　★　★　★

Shortly after noon on the 30th, they found the long hunter from the Long Canes. He sat by a smoldering campfire at a clearing, staring at the smoke, his horse ground-reined near him, his long rifle leaning in the crook of an oak.

"Teague Braden," Thomas Taylor said, "are you ready to die?"

Up until that moment, Emily had not known the hunter's name.

Braden looked up, shrugged, and stared back into the smoke.

Dr. Bayard made a gesture, and Cooper and Maupin swung from their saddles, moving toward the hunter, who seemed oblivious to what was happening. Emily wet her lips, as Luke Zachary, behind her, cocked his long rifle.

Braden lifted his head, found the eyes of Dr. Bayard, and said: "Do you want to know where you will find them?"

"Why would you tell us?" the doctor asked.

The hunter shrugged, and looked back at the smoke.

"He would sell out his friends," Taylor said, "the same as Virgil Hickox, for thirty pieces of silver. Hang the damned Judas and let us be gone."

"No," Emily said. "That is not why he would tell us."

Braden looked over at Emily.

"He is a good man," Emily heard herself murmuring. "Deep down."

"Hell"—Maupin spit—"I suppose they were all good men at one time or another. Suppose I was once, too."

"Where are they?" the doctor asked after a pause.

Looking back at the fire, Braden answered without any emotion: "The High Hills of the Santee."

Jonathan Conley snorted. "That is a right far piece."

"Not from hell," Braden said, still staring at the smoke.

"It is a trap," Taylor said. "This rogue sends us to our deaths."

Emily kept looking at the hunter, and for a moment she felt

an urge to turn Ezekiel around, ride back to Ninety Six, take her mother, Elizabeth, and Alan into her arms and forget about Donnan, forget about everything.

"No," Dr. Bayard said. "I do not think it is a trap." He turned to one of Gouedy's trappers, Rory MacCance. "Can you get us there?"

"To the Santee?" MacCance shrugged. "Aye. With pleasure."

"Doctor?" Luke Zachary called out, and indicated Braden. "What about him?"

Emily looked back at the tired hunter, and heard Dr. Bayard ask: "Do you wish to ride with us?"

"I think not, Doctor," Braden replied.

"It is a trap!" Taylor bellowed, but the doctor's head shook.

"Leave him be, Thomas. We ride for the High Hills."

When MacCance eased his bay horse alongside Dr. Bayard's mount, Emily kicked Ezekiel and moved closer, just behind the doctor.

MacCance was saying: "The High Hills be a mighty big place."

"*Oui*," the doctor responded.

Emily was familiar with that region. Perhaps even slightly better than Rory MacCance. Long, narrow, hilly—not really that high, not compared to the mountains north and west of Ninety Six, but substantial if you never got out of the swampy country north of the Santee River.

"Well," MacCance said, "it could take a lot of looking to find anyone with a mind to hide out there."

"I know where we will find him," Emily said, feeling like Judas Iscariot as she wondered what her father would think of her now. She blinked away the image of Breck Stewart, and found Dr. Bayard and Rory MacCance turned in their saddles, looking at her as they trotted through the pine-lined trail.

Bayard tugged on his reins, and MacCance swung his horse around, then reined up.

Pulling Ezekiel to a stop, Emily stopped. "Our grandfather from Georgetown has a summer home there," Emily said, taking a deep breath and letting it out. "On an ox-box, twelve, fourteen miles up the Wateree before it joins the Congaree."

Dr. Bayard and MacCance said nothing, just turned around, and kicked their horses into a walk, heading through the forest.

In Camden, they rested themselves and the horses for six hours, had something to drink and stew to eat at the inn—Emily not daring to ask from what animal the meat had been taken. Before they rode south toward the High Hills, Luke Zachary and Jonathan Conley turned back. They gave no reason. No one asked.

Now they numbered twelve.

Stewart's Rest on the Wateree lay roughly thirty miles, almost exactly due south, from Camden.

On the morning of the second day, the moderators ran into a group of twenty-six riders from the Welsh Neck. The riders stopped their mounts several rods ahead, then a lean man rode forward, a dirty piece of homespun muslin tied to the top of his musket. When he reined up, Emily whispered to Dr. Bayard: "That is Owen Devonald."

"I remember him. Captain of the Peedee Regulators."

Dr. Bayard and MacCance rode out to parley with the innkeeper. They spoke for several minutes before loping back.

When the doctor began talking, Emily's stomach started to see-saw. She had not really believed what Robert Gouedy had said back in the tavern in Ninety Six, the rumors she had heard from other travelers. What was happening along Cane Creek could not be happening elsewhere, but it was. Owen Devonald and his bunch, who called themselves liberators, joined the moderators in riding against the fifteen scavengers who had once rid the Peedee area of ruffians and killers.

Joining up, they rode south. Now they were thirty-eight.

Compared to the Georgetown plantation, it was a small place. A one-story house, whitewashed, standing out among the pines, a privy and cistern out back, barn to the left, and, on the right, a cabin for the slaves her grandparents always had accompany them.

As Emily looked across the yard, she tried, but failed, to block out the memories of herself and Donnan playing hopscotch with some of the slave children in the yard in what seemed like a lifetime ago.

"How many?" Dr. Bayard asked.

"Ten," MacCance replied. "Just ten."

"Your boys, then," Owen Devonald said. "Not our'n."

MacCance's head bobbed.

Dr. Bayard asked: "Are you saying you want to sit this one out, Devonald?"

The man spat. "Hell, no. My boys be itching to fight, and there be no guarantee that we'll ever catch those scum who once called themselves Peedee Regulators."

"We can burn them out," MacCance said.

"You are not burning my grandparents' summer home," Emily said sharply.

"What the hell?" Devonald spit again. He leaned forward, pushed back his hat, and swore again. "You got a damned snot-nosed girl . . . ?" He paused as recognition came to him. "Oh, hell, no, you got Breck Stewart's daughter!"

It was Benjamin Cooper who came up with the idea.

One of the Peedee boys, a good Baptist named Oliver, spurred his buckskin out of the woods and straight for the house, firing one pistol into the air, sliding it into the pommel holster, and drawing the other.

"Moderators!" he cried out, reining in the horse to a sliding stop in front of the main house. "Moderators are coming!"

The door opened. Emily couldn't identify the man on the porch who aimed his pistol at Oliver.

"Moderators!" Oliver yelled again, and shot into the air before wheeling his horse around.

A man came out of the slave's cabin, and Emily recognized James Middleton.

Oliver saw him, and cried out: "Mister, I ride with David Clarke's bunch from the Peedee. I reckon we are about the same as you boys. Well, there's a bunch of citizens aiming to hang us all . . . and you boys, too. They call themselves moderators and . . . hell's fire, they's no more than ten minutes behind me. Best light out whilst you can." Then he spurred his horse, and thundered past the privy, through the empty fields, and into the woods that ran along the river.

Middleton shot a glance south, then sprinted toward the barn. "Let's ride, boys! Everyone mount up!"

Emily watched, her throat dry as men flew out of the main house and the slaves' quarters, running, some of them barefooted, others shirtless, toward the barn. She rubbed her palm against the stock of the rifle. Behind her, to the south, ten of Owen Devonald's boys and Rory MacCance waited with their weapons ready, long guns and muskets, knives and hatchets.

Donnan came out of the cabin last, pulling on his waistcoat, glancing back down the trail, shoving a pistol into his sash before he disappeared inside the barn.

Whipping the horse with his hat, a rider galloped out of the barn. Another followed. The stopgap broke, and riders thundered down the trail, following the path Oliver had taken. No one headed in the direction of Emily and Devonald's men; they had been stationed there as merely a precaution. Just in case some of the outlaws did not take the bait. Still, they did not move but stared at the house, waiting to see if anyone else would come out.

"I counted ten riders, sir," one of the men—a boy actually— told MacCance. "That should be all of them."

"Aye," MacCance said, "but we shall wait just the same."

Two minutes later, she heard the first muzzle blast from the north.

They led their horses up the trail. When they found the first regulator, they stopped. He was pinned underneath his dead roan, shirtless, his eyes staring at the towering pine trees, but seeing nothing.

"You know him?" Rory MacCance asked.

"Virgil Hickox," Emily answered. Someone had branded his face, carving a **T** in the center of his forehead with a knife.

"Thief, I reckon," MacCance said.

"Traitor," Emily corrected, and pulled Ezekiel, skittish from the blood and the scent of gunpowder hanging in the forest, behind her.

Another regulator had ridden his horse over the edge of the bluff, landing on the banks of the Wateree. Neither horse nor rider moved.

Nobody even bothered to stop and look at the third body. Minutes later, they found the rest of the men. Here the stench grew so great, the horses would not move ahead, so they led them a ways back, tethering them to trees and shrubs. Those that had hobbles used them. One horse pulled away from its rider and galloped off back toward the Stewarts' summer retreat.

Emily whispered in Ezekiel's ear, rubbed his neck, and left him with the other horses. She walked past James Middleton's dead body, hacked badly, and found moderators and liberators surrounding three men, the last of the Cane Creek Regulators.

Her eyes landed on Donnan, who was kneeling, hands tied behind his back, face pale, his left ear reduced to a bloody pulp. If he felt pain, he did not show it, just stared at the bloody leaves and grass before him.

One of the men, face pale, tears streaming down his bloodstained face, saw Emily. He sang out: "This is the one!" He pointed at Donnan. "Miss Emily . . . he killed that Cherokee. At Jacob's Fork. I saw him. He done it. I swear. I. . . ."

He was the man from the tavern, O'Keeffe. The man beside him, one of the Peedee bandits, said to him: "Shut your mouth, you yellow-livered swine." The other man Emily did not know, but came from the Peedee, which meant the bands of regulators and liberators had joined together.

Donnan said nothing. He did not even look at Emily.

"Take them to Charlestown?" someone said.

Devonald tilted his head back and bellowed: "Do you know what happened the last time we turned over cut-throats such as these to the law in Charlestown?"

"We are here for justice," Dr. Bayard tried to remind them.

"Aye, and justice we can deliver here," Devonald declared.

Dr. Bayard's head shook.

Devonald said: "This fellow yon just told you how this . . . bastard . . . shot down that Cherokee, did he not? I was at Jacob's Fork. Where Breck Stewart was called to glory. That Cherokee was a damned fine boy."

Emily felt as if her heart was breaking all over again, but this time no tears came.

"He was just a red savage," one of the liberators said.

"Shut your trap, Bill. You've been on the Peedee for eighteen months. I have been there twenty-three years. You don't know the Indians the way I do."

"They hanged Birmingham Long," Thomas Taylor reminded them. "For no damned reason."

"Did not you say that there is a provost marshal in Ninety Six?" It was the young boy, Oliver, who had performed so magnificently at the Stewarts' summer place.

"A deputy provost marshal," black-toothed Meacham said.

"Then deliver them to him," Oliver said. "In Ninety Six."

"You do what you want," Devonald said, "but we still have that bastard David Clarke to bring to justice. And he shall not ever see Charlestown to be pardoned . . . or a deputy provost marshal." He pointed to the Peedee prisoner. "Nor shall that son-of-a-bitch. He goes nowhere . . . but to hell."

"Do we take Donnan and O'Keeffe to Ninety Six?" Dr. Bayard asked, looking at Benjamin Cooper and Pierre Maupin. "Deliver them to Kilduff? He did say he had a warrant for Donnan's arrest."

"No," Emily said without even thinking. She stepped away from MacCance, moved beside Dr. Bayard, and butted her rifle on the ground. "No," Emily repeated. "You cannot take him back to Ninety Six."

"Emily . . . ," Dr. Bayard began, but she raised her hand.

"You would do that, Doctor? You would shame my mother? You would let my baby sister and baby brother see what their brother has become?" Her head shook. She could feel Donnan's eyes on her, but would not, could not, look at him. "You would have him buried alongside my brave father. To rest there . . . together . . . for eternity?"

"Emily . . . ," the doctor tried again.

"Your mother already knows what Donnan has become," Cooper whispered. "She must know."

"But Alan and Elizabeth sha'n't know." Emily's heart felt heavy, but she refused to quit. "He killed Go-la-nv Pinetree in cold blood, my brother did. He killed Birmingham Long. He

almost murdered a deputy provost marshal. He is as reckless a rogue, as heartless a thief and killer, as any bandit my father ever pursued. He hangs. Here. Today. Right now." She caught her breath, and lowered her voice as she said: "We will swear ourselves to secrecy. For all anyone here knows, Donnan Stewart rode to Fort Loudon. That is the last we ever saw of him."

"And what of these two scum?" Thomas Taylor asked, and slammed the stock of his pistol against O'Keeffe's skull.

"Brand them as thieves and send them on their way!" one of Devonald's crew cried out.

"I'd like to see our bastard hang, too," Devonald said.

"Haven't you killed enough, Devonald?" Meacham said.

"Not until Clarke's head sits atop a pike in front of my inn."

Maupin's head bobbed slightly. He looked at Dr. Bayard before saying: "Hang Stewart. Brand the others. Miss Emily is right."

"As long as we hang somebody," one of the liberators from Peedee said. He laughed, but no one joined him.

"If the Reverend Monteith was here . . . ," Benjamin Cooper started to say after a hard silence.

Maupin silenced him with a stare, then said: "He is not here. God is not here."

"God is here," Dr. Bayard assured him. "And He will curse us all if we do this."

"So be it," Emily said. "I will not shame my mother. Or my brother and sister. I will not destroy my father's legacy."

"Hang the bastard," Devonald said. "He is no son of the Breck Stewart I knew and loved."

Emily moved closer to Dr. Bayard. "Do you remember Finnian Kilduff?" she asked. "Do you remember the scars on his back? Or how Birmingham Long was left to rot from an oak limb? Do you remember . . ."—it was difficult to say—". . . Go-la-nv Pinetree?"

Maupin came closer, and whispered in Dr. Bayard's ear. "She is right, François. It is better this way."

Bayard said nothing, gave no order. He just stood there, eyes closed, letting Devonald's men haul the two outlaws away, to brand them as thieves, and do whatever they needed to do to ease their bloodlust until they found Clarke and his gang. A noose was thrown over Donnan's head and tightened around his neck. It was Cooper and Taylor who led him to a tree where they sailed the rope end over a stout branch.

Someone shoved Donnan up onto a horse as Taylor secured the rope around the tree trunk. It was only then that Emily managed to look up at Donnan Stewart.

His eyes showed no fear, but his voice betrayed him. "Why do you do this, Emily?" he asked.

She wanted to look away. She wanted to be far away from here. She also wanted Go-la-nv Pinetree to be alive. And her father. And Finnian Kilduff not to be lying, suffering on a bed inside Darlene Courtney's cabin. She made herself hold Donnan's gaze. Her mouth opened. Her voice sounded hollow.

"For good order and harmony of the colony."

CHAPTER TWENTY-FIVE

After thanking Rachel and Luke Zachary for her kindness, Emily turned away from their cabin, and headed down the path to Ninety Six.

Robert Gouedy's two wagons had stopped in front of the ruins of the tavern, where his slaves loaded on the last of Machara's luggage. Machara stood talking to Mrs. Cochrane, while, behind her, Alan and Elizabeth were busy trying to pinch one another.

Emily took a deep breath, but kept walking. In the second wagon, she saw the back of Finnian Kilduff's thin, dark head where it was resting on a pile of pillows, in preparation for the grueling journey to Charlestown.

By the time Emily reached her mother's side, Mrs. Cochrane was walking away, dabbing her eyes with the tie of her apron, and Alan and Elizabeth had stopped tormenting one another.

Machara sighed, looked at the blackened remnants of Cormorant's Rock Tavern, and turned back. Her eyes found Emily, and she smiled. "Emily," she said, "are you ready?"

Now came the biggest test of Emily's life thus far. She had buried her father. She had hanged her brother. Looking up at her mother, she said: "I am staying, Mum."

Machara must have expected it, but still she said: "Emily . . . you cannot."

"I can," she said, finding her resolve as somehow she always managed to do. "Da' told me a woman can own the license to operate a tavern. And that I shall do. This I have been doing. Even before . . ."—she nodded at the remains—"that. So I shall pay for the license, and continue to follow Da's dream."

"What tavern?" her mother's raised voice caused Emily to step back. Machara pointed angrily behind her. "That? Ashes? Blackened timber not fit for kindling?"

Emily licked her lips. "A tavern," she said, "can be rebuilt." *But can a family?* she wondered. *A settlement? A colony? A life?*

Her mother appeared about to cry, so Emily stepped closer, put her hands on her mother's shoulders, pulled her close, hugged her tightly, and whispered into her ear: "Someone has to look after Da', Mum. Someone has to follow his dream. And I can do it."

"It is not . . . ," Machara sobbed, "not fitting for a lady."

"Mum," she said softly, "I am no lady. Everyone in Ninety Six has been saying that for years."

"You are precious to me," she said.

"And you are precious to me," Emily said. "But do you know who I am?"

She felt her mother's head nod, and heard her say in a resigned voice: "Aye. You are a Stewart of Appin."

Smiling somehow, Emily gently pushed her mother away from her shoulder, and gave her time to compose herself before saying: "No, Mum. I am the daughter of Machara and Breck Stewart."

Machara smiled back, shook her head sadly, but proudly, and pulled Emily into an embrace that was as strong as any of her father's had been. Then Machara stepped back from her daughter, and said to Benji Cooper: "Mister Cooper, would you mind unloading our luggage?" Machara turned back to Emily, saying: "We shall stay here as well."

Which is when the tears exploded, and Emily fell into her mother's embrace, sobbing without shame, without control as she felt Elizabeth wrap her arms around her right leg, and Alan grab hold of her left. She would need her mother's strength. She would need her brother and sister. She would need everyone in the district. And when the Reverend Douglas Monteith returned that fall, she would need him, too. She had a tavern, a home, and a life to rebuild, and a terrible secret, a sin, for which she must repent. She would need God. God . . . her mother . . . and Ninety Six.

It was then Emily heard the voice that came from the second wagon. A weak voice, but one that still managed to carry power with it. And promise.

"I am staying, too," Finnian Kilduff said.

AUTHOR'S NOTE

Although most of the characters in *The Cane Creek Regulators* are fictitious—Mr. and Mrs. William Bull, Robert Gouedy, Lord and Lady Charles Montagu, and Charles Shinner being the primary exceptions—the events detailed here are based on fact. While it did not all happen exactly as written on these pages, some of the depicted violence did not come from my imagination. The Carolina Back Country could be inhumanely brutal, and it would get even worse in the years following where this novel ends.

James Mayson, not Breck Stewart, was the actual captain of the vigilante band from Ninety Six, and Douglas Monteith is loosely based on Anglican minister Charles Woodmason.

Still, history records that in the decade before the American Revolution, with pleas for help falling on deaf ears among most colony officials in Charlestown (which became Charleston around 1783), vigilante groups called "regulators" did form to fight outlaw bands running rampant across the South Carolina Back Country. And when the regulators began taking extreme measures against what would be considered petty crimes, if crimes at all, citizens had to rise up against them.

All of which helped fuel the bloody revenge and retaliation—as Gouedy predicts in this novel—that erupted when colonists revolted against the British Crown in 1775. During the American Revolution, that anger and animosity turned South Carolina's Back Country into scenes of some of the worst atrocities—on both sides—between colonial patriots and their neighbors who remained loyal to the British Crown. As Light Horse Harry Lee recalled in his memoirs, the Revolutionary War in the Back Country of the Carolinas "often sank into barbarity."

For research, I am indebted to the park rangers at Ninety Six National Historic Site in Ninety Six, South Carolina. They not only answered my questions for this novel, they helped my son on a research project he was doing on Colonial America for school.

For language, I often opened the pages of *Colonial American English* (Verbatim, 1985) by Richard M. Lederer Jr. and *1811 Dictionary of the Vulgar Tongue: A Dictionary of Buckish Slang, University Wit, and Pickpocket Eloquence* (Follett, 1971).

For Charlestown, I turned often to "Revolutionary Charleston, 1765-1800", a 1997 dissertation by Stanley Kenneth Deaton, courtesy of the George A. Smathers Libraries at the University of Florida; *A Short History of Charleston* (University of South Carolina Press, 1997) by Robert N. Rosen; and email blasts to Leigh Jones Handal, director of communications, tours and fundraising at The Preservation Society of Charleston and a beer-drinking buddy during our days at the University of South Carolina.

For Ninety Six and Back Country history, I frequented the pages of *Ninety Six: The Struggle for the South Carolina Back Country* (Sandlapper, 1978) by Robert D. Bass; *The Carolina Backcountry on the Eve of the Revolution: The Journal and Other Writings of Charles Woodmason, Anglican Itinerant* (University of North Carolina Press, 1953) edited by Robert J. Hooker; *South Carolina: A History* (University of South Carolina Press, 1992) by Walter Edgar; *Old Ninety Six: A History and Guide* (History Press, 2006) by Robert M. Dunkerly and Eric K. Williams; and *Ninety Six: Landmarks of South Carolina's Last Frontier Region*

Author's Note

(University of South Carolina Press, 1950) by author Carl Julien and photographer H.L. Watson.

Other sources include *Colonial South Carolina: A History* (University of South Carolina Press, 1997) by Robert M. Weir; *The Oligarchs in Colonial and Revolutionary Charleston: Lieutenant Governor William Bull II and His Family* (University of South Carolina Press, 1991) by Kinloch Bull, Jr.; *The History of Georgetown County, South Carolina* (University of South Carolina Press, 1970) by George C. Rogers; *Rise Up So Early: A History of Florence County, South Carolina* (The Reprint Company, 1981) by G. Wayne King; *Peace and War on the Anglo-Cherokee Frontier, 1756-63* (Louisiana State University Press, 2001) by John Oliphant; *The Dividing Paths: Cherokees and South Carolinians through the Era of Revolution* (Oxford University Press, 1993) by Tom Hatley; *John Stuart and the Southern Colonial Frontier: A Study of Indian Relations, War, Trade, and Land Problems in the Southern Wilderness, 1754-1775* (University of Michigan Press, 1944) by John Richard Alden; and *The History of South Carolina: Revised Edition* (The State Co., 1922) by William Gilmore Simms.

Thanks also to the staffs at the Preservation Society of Charleston; Fort Loudoun (Tennessee) State Historic Area; Colonial Williamsburg (Virginia); Jamestown (Virginia) Settlement & Yorktown Victory Center; the South Carolina Historical Society; and, for helping me track down some of these books, the Vista Grande Public Library in Santa Fe.

Finally I must also thank my late friend, Robert J. Conley, Sequoyah Distinguished Professor of Cherokee Studies at Western Carolina University in Cullowhee, North Carolina, for his insight regarding the Cherokee Indians.

Johnny D. Boggs
Santa Fe, New Mexico

ABOUT THE AUTHOR

Johnny D. Boggs has worked cattle, shot rapids in a canoe, hiked across mountains and deserts, traipsed around ghost towns, and spent hours poring over microfilm in library archives—all in the name of finding a good story. He's also one of the few Western writers to have won six Spur Awards from Western Writers of America (for his novels, *Camp Ford,* in 2006, *Doubtful Cañon,* in 2008, and *Hard Winter* in 2010, *Legacy of a Lawman, West Texas Kill,* both in 2012, and his short story, "A Piano at Dead Man's Crossing", in 2002) as well as the Western Heritage Wrangler Award from the National Cowboy and Western Heritage Museum (for his novel, *Spark on the Prairie: The Trial of the Kiowa Chiefs,* in 2004). A native of South Carolina, Boggs spent almost fifteen years in Texas as a journalist at the *Dallas Times Herald* and *Fort Worth Star-Telegram* before moving to New Mexico in 1998 to concentrate full time on his novels. Author of dozens of published short stories, he has also written for more than fifty newspapers and magazines, and is a frequent contributor to *Boys' Life* and *True West.* His Western novels cover a wide range. *The Lonesome Chisholm Trail* (Five Star Westerns, 2000) is an authentic cattle-drive story, while *Lonely Trumpet* (Five Star Westerns, 2002) is an historical novel about the first black graduate of West Point. *The Despoilers* (Five Star Westerns, 2002) and *Ghost Legion* (Five Star Westerns, 2005) are set in the Carolina backcountry during the Revolutionary War. *The Big Fifty* (Five Star Westerns, 2003) chronicles

239

the slaughter of buffalo on the southern plains in the 1870s, while *East of the Border* (Five Star Westerns, 2004) is a comedy about the theatrical offerings of Buffalo Bill Cody, Wild Bill Hickok, and Texas Jack Omohundro, and *Camp Ford* (Five Star Westerns, 2005) tells about a Civil War baseball game between Union prisoners of war and Confederate guards. "Boggs's narrative voice captures the old-fashioned style of the past," *Publishers Weekly* said, and *Booklist* called him "among the best Western writers at work today." Boggs lives with his wife Lisa and son Jack in Santa Fe. His website is www.johnnydboggs.com.